Over and Under

Other Five Star Titles
by Mat Coward:

In and Out
Up and Down
Do the World a Favour and Other Stories

Over and Under

A
Don Packham and Frank Mitchell
Mystery

MAT COWARD

Five Star • Waterville, Maine

First Edition
First Printing: July 2004

Published in 2004 in conjunction with Tekno Books and Ed Gorman.

Set in 11 pt. Plantin by Liana M. Walker.

Printed in the United States on permanent paper.

Library of Congress Cataloging-in-Publication Data

Coward, Mat.
    Over and under : a Don Packham and Frank Mitchell
    mystery / Mat Coward.—1st ed.
      p. cm.
    ISBN 1-4104-0186-3 (hc : alk. paper)
    1. Cricket players—Crimes against—Fiction. 2. Police—
England—London—Fiction. 3. London (England)—Fiction.
I. Title.
PR6053.O955O94 2004
  823'.914—dc22   2004046987

Over and Under

CHAPTER ONE

"That's his coffin, over there."

"That's his *what?*" said Frank Mitchell, the first detective on the scene.

The short, round WPC pointed at a three-foot-long, red holdall, possessed of both wheels and handles, which sat on a bench in a corner of the pavilion. "That flash kit bag," she said. "Cricketers call them coffins. I've told no-one to touch it. I'm keeping an eye, while my mate fetches the crime tape from the car."

"So if you know which is his coffin," said Frank, "you've identified the deceased."

"Yup." She checked her notebook. "Name of Bruce Lester, aged forty-one, an accountant. Lives in Bristol." Her partner arrived, waving a roll of crime scene tape. "I'll show you the body, Frank."

It was a hot evening in late July, still as light as day. As the WPC led him out through a back door, Frank checked his watch: fourteen minutes past nine. Behind the pavilion, amid some shrubbery, two more uniformed officers stood guard over a dead man. A dead accountant, apparently.

"If he's from Bristol, do we know what he's doing here?"

"Here for the game."

"Long way to come," said Frank, "for a game of cricket."

The WPC said, "You're not a cricketer, I take it?"

"Not really."

"Geordie, are you?"

"I am."

She nodded, as if that explained all. "Ah, well."

Frank belatedly registered, given that hint, that her accent was Yorkshire. "He must have been a keen player, the deceased."

"His wife's inside," she said. "You can ask her."

"Right, I will . . ." Frank's concentration was slipping slightly, as he stared at the mortal remains of Bruce Lester and wondered if there was something obvious which he'd overlooked; something which might make the question he was about to ask redundant. Or ridiculous. "One thing—is there any particular reason why he's wearing ladies' clothing?"

She smiled. "Not one that has been vouchsafed to me at this particular juncture, no."

"Right." So at least he hadn't missed an explanation which everyone else'd spotted within seconds. That was a relief. "Not that I—you know, not that it . . . I just wondered, that's all."

"He don't look particularly dead, does he?" said one of the uniformed constables, obviously determined to play more than a non-speaking role at the crime scene.

His mate snorted. "Well, I've been here half an hour, pal, and he hasn't breathed during that time, so I don't reckon he's faking it."

Frank saw what the first PC meant, though. There was a certain amount of blood from a scalp wound, but other than that the body wasn't in too grotesque a state. Mr. Lester's dress had ridden up, exposing enormous frilly knickers, but to a uniformed policeman—more used to attending fatal road accidents, or examining elderly people whose deaths by natural causes had gone undiscovered for some time—the present show was comparatively unspectacular.

Frank started to check his watch again, then realised that this might look like a nervous habit—and that it might actually be a nervous habit—so he aborted the operation halfway through. Which definitely looked like a nervous habit.

"You've called the doctor?"

"Yup," said the WPC.

"And you've called Scenes?"

"Frank, I've called everyone."

"Right." So where were they?

"I've called everyone except my granny. I don't suppose she'd be that interested—she's not a cricketer, either."

"Right," said Frank. "I'd better have a proper look inside. Give me a shout when anyone arrives."

The cricket pavilion was beginning to fill up. A uniformed inspector was now on the scene, as well as several more PCs, and some white-suited technicians were just arriving as Frank re-entered the main room. A small group of witnesses was undergoing initial statement-taking in one corner. No sign of the Detective Inspector yet . . .

"Frank—this is Miss Stella Wardle. She reported the body."

"Thanks, Sarge. Miss Wardle, I'm Detective Constable Frank Mitchell, of Cowden CID." Frank took out his notebook, and gestured towards a bench against one wall. "We might be more private over there."

As she settled herself on the bench, Frank carried out an initial assessment—without being obvious about it, he hoped. She was in her early sixties, he reckoned, conservatively dressed, her hair short and mostly grey. Her expression was a little stern—even allowing for the circumstances—and Frank decided he would do best to dispense with opening

9

pleasantries, and get down to business.

"First of all, can you tell me how you happened to find the body?"

"I didn't happen to," she said. "I was looking for it."

That made him glance up from his note-taking. "You knew he was dead?"

She spoke rather precisely, in a crisp North Wales accent which reminded Frank of his primary school headmistress. "I knew he was *missing*."

"I see. And how long had he been missing?"

"Play ended just before seven. We were batting, and I—"

"You were batting?"

She treated him to a sneer which reminded him even more strongly of his old headmistress. "Our *side* was batting. I was scoring."

"Of course. So you batted second?"

"No, we batted first."

Now he was puzzled. "Rather a long innings?"

She sighed. "It's a two-day match."

"Oh, right."

"We won the toss."

"Fine, right."

"Not that I have the slightest interest in the stupid game."

"Right." He turned over a page in his notebook and started again. "So, your innings ended around seven?"

"That's it. Bruce and a girl called Louise Ogden were the not-out batsmen."

"So Bruce came off the field just before seven. Would you say five to? Later than that?"

"Hold on." She stood up and walked away. For a moment, Frank wondered if she was doing a runner—whether he'd just let a murderer walk out the door. When she picked up a bound notebook off a table by the front window and brought it back to the bench, his relief was not inconsiderable.

The scorebook, Frank could see, was highly detailed—though untidily completed—and he wondered why she went to such trouble over a game she claimed to despise. Perhaps her husband was playing. No, she was a Miss. Partner, then?

"Six-fifty-six," she said. "That's when the umpires pulled the stumps."

"So, thank you, we know he was alive then."

"Oh, I think so, Constable. I think we'd have noticed if he wasn't."

Why does everyone have to be a comedian? "He came straight off the field? And what did he do then?"

"He took a cold drink out of his kitbag—"

"Coffin," said Frank.

She uncrossed and re-crossed her legs. "No, he was breathing quite normally."

"I meant—"

"He took a cold drink from his *coffin,* then went off to have a shower."

Impressed, Frank said: "They have showers here?"

"Well, there wouldn't have been much point otherwise, would there? There's only a couple of cubicles, so there's often a queue."

Frank was still looking around, wondering where the showers were.

She pointed. "Through that door at the back—the one you came through a few minutes ago."

"OK, so you saw him head off to the showers, and when did you next see him?"

"When I found him dead."

"Which was about an hour and a half later? So, what made you think he was missing?"

She rolled her eyes. "Well, I was right, wasn't I? He *was* missing."

"Absolutely, I just wondered, in the specific situation of the present circumstances of the—"

Stella Wardle leant towards him. "Do they send policeman on a training course to learn how talk in such a pedantic fashion?"

Frank smiled, and shook his head. "No, Madam. We just pick it up as we go along." *Well, if she was going to be a comedian . . .*

"By the time Bruce went off for his shower, most people had gone."

"I see."

"Most of the other team, that is, and several of ours. Plus supporters, wives and so on."

"Gone home?"

"God, no! Gone to the pub, most of them. Those who were invited, anyway."

"Do you happen to know which—"

"Of course I happen to know. The Eagle, do you know it? About ten minutes away, towards the station."

"Let me go back a bit, here . . ."

"What a surprise."

"Did you actually see Bruce Lester emerge from the showers?"

"I didn't even see him *im*merge."

"So you don't actually know that he went for a shower? As such."

For the first time, she paused for thought. "No. No you're right, I just assumed. I think . . . yes, I think perhaps it was because he was carrying a towel and bottle of shampoo, and going through the doorway where the showers are. Anyway, by the time eight o'clock came around, those of who were left—which was not many—wanted to be locking up, and we began to wonder what had happened to Bruce."

"He couldn't just have gone off to the pub without telling you?"

She looked at him as if he'd put a propeller hat on his head and started reciting nonsense verse. "Well of course he bloody couldn't, he was dead!"

"No, I meant—how did you know he hadn't gone to the pub?"

"His wife was still here. She had the car keys."

"OK, so you looked for him."

"We searched this place—which didn't take long, obviously—then while the rest were sitting around wondering what to do, I took it on myself to search the outside."

"By this time you suspected he might be in trouble? I mean, ill or something?"

"Certainly. He's a bit overweight, he's middle aged, he'd just had an uncharacteristically strenuous afternoon—"

"Uncharacteristic?"

"I don't imagine he took much exercise in the normal course of his life."

Frank made a note of that, and wrote after it: *Coffin??*

"Quite honestly," said Stella, "I thought, you know—heart attack."

"And what made you look for him in the bushes?"

"Because he wasn't to be found anywhere else."

"Of course. And having found him, you called the police."

"Of course not."

"I'm sorry?" God, don't say she wasn't the reporter, after all that!

"I called the ambulance—they called the police."

"Right," said Frank, starting another new page. "And during the day, were there any arguments, which might—"

13

"Not so far as I am aware."

"Or anything which could have—"

"That's the same question, Constable. Thus: same answer."

At that moment, Frank heard a large and singularly inappropriate laugh erupt just outside the pavilion's wedged-open front door. *Thank God for that!*

"You'll have to excuse me, madam," he said, slipping his notebook into the jacket pocket of his uncomfortably hot, dark suit. "My boss has arrived."

DI Don Packham—wearing a linen safari suit, which made up in practicality what it lacked in formality—had already visited the body *in situ*. His first words of greeting to his DC were: "Frank—are you aware the deceased is wearing women's clothing?"

"Yes, sir."

Don leant towards Frank's left ear. "Was he like that when they found him, do you suppose? Or is that uniform branch, having a bit of a laugh?"

He seems cheerful enough, thought Frank. So: it's going to be a long, hot night—but not quite as long as it might have been.

"So, who's still here?"

Frank pulled out his notebook, and flicked a few pages forward and then back. He looked a little flustered, Don thought; but then, if he would insist on wearing a suit on an evening like this, what did he expect? Still, coming from the North, he perhaps hadn't got used to the concept of summer, yet.

"Just four of them left over from the match, apparently. Including Miss Wardle."

"And the rest are at the pub?"

"Uniform are checking."

"The widow's still here?"

"That's her over there, sir." Where Frank was pointing sat a woman being comforted by a young, painfully self-conscious WPC.

"You're joking! Was he very rich, the dead man?"

Frank shrugged. "He was an accountant."

"Ah well, that would explain it. You never see an accountant on a bike, do you?" The newly widowed woman looked a good bit younger than her late husband—even allowing for the latter's current condition; and, given that Don was seeing her at what was presumably not her best, he reckoned she was at least one league above Mr. Lester, in terms of attractiveness. "Shall we nick her now, or leave a decent interval?"

Frank looked across at the woman and frowned. "Nick her?"

"Come on, Frank! Well-off victim, younger wife."

"Ah," said Frank. "Right. Quite a nice pavilion this, isn't it? Well appointed."

"Not bad," Don admitted, though the place was a touch modern for his taste. "Is it municipal?"

"I understand the pavilion itself belongs jointly to various local clubs, who rent it out to other sides when they haven't got a home game. The playing fields are owned by the borough."

"And who is this side, do we know?"

"Not yet."

"Well, never mind, we can do all that tomorrow. Have you got a list of who was present?"

"That new WPC was doing it." Frank called her over.

"Evening, sir."

"Evening," said Don. "I'm told you have a list?"

"No sir," she said. "It's just these shoes."

"Very good," said Don. "The list?"

15

"Sorry, sir." She handed him a sheet of paper. "This is everyone who was still here at seven, when the deceased went to have a shower."

Don glanced at the paper, and handed it to Frank. "Everyone who was still here, according to whom?"

"Well—according to everyone *else* who was still here."

"Fair enough." Don dismissed the WPC, and raised his eyebrows at Frank. "She's a bit saucy, isn't she?"

"She's from Yorkshire," Frank explained.

"We'll have to check whether anyone could have come back in after they'd left. But if not, we're looking at a gratifyingly short list of suspects. Assuming the accountant's death was, indeed, suspicious. Any sign of the—ah, who's this?"

Don could tell that the young woman walking towards them was the doctor—by her purposeful bearing as much as by her medical bag—but he didn't recognise her. Frank clearly did.

"Dr. Sandhu—I don't think you know DI Packham."

The inspector and the doctor shook hands. From her expression, Don wondered if they had, in fact, met before—she was looking at him as if he was familiar. Odd; he usually had a decent memory for faces. Particularly female ones. The minor mystery was solved when she said: "Only by reputation. Pleased to meet you, Inspector."

"Likewise. Sam Walker's all right, I hope?"

"He's fine, Inspector, as far as I know. He's not on the rota tonight, that's all."

"Fine, fine." Don was still wondering when he'd become famous enough for young police surgeons to know him before he knew them. "You've pronounced life extinct?"

"Not all life, Inspector—just that of the man in the frilly knickers."

Is everyone in this bloody place a comedian? Don wondered;

16

then he glanced at Frank, his face straight and his pen upright as he immortalised the doctor's every syllable. *No, not everyone.* "Can you give us a cause of death?"

"One, possibly two, blows to the back or side of the head."

"What with?"

She smiled. "I'll tell you that when you tell me what you find. But a good piece of wood, say, or a small scaffolding pole. Something shortish, and hard."

"It is murder, then?"

"Got to be." She nodded. "Even if you did decide to kill yourself by bashing the back of your head in—or did it accidentally, for that matter, while swatting a wasp—you wouldn't be able to get a proper swing, consistent with the wounds. Autopsy'll tell you the material the weapon was made from, its exact dimensions and so on. But I'm afraid that's all you're getting from me tonight."

"And a fine feast it was, Doctor," said Don, with a generous smile. "Many thanks."

Dr. Sandhu looked about her, and added: "I've never pronounced in a cricket pavilion before."

"Ah," said Don. "You've clearly never been to a Roses Match. They drop like flies there."

"From excitement?"

"From old age."

The doctor laughed, much to Don's delight. Quite a dirty laugh, he thought it was.

"My father always says that diplomacy is war continued by other means," she said, "and that cricket is war continued by the usual means."

"Well," said Don, watching her depart the scene. "She makes a change from old Sam." He clapped his hands together. "Now then: we need the mystery weapon as soon as possible. I wonder if it's worth starting the fingertip search tonight?"

17

"I don't suppose we've got more than half an hour's light left," said Frank. "Might be better to wait until—"

"Sir!"

An overweight PC, who looked as if his tunic had shrunk in the day's humidity, was urgently waving at them from the rear doorway. Outside, in the bushes a few yards from where Bruce Lester had been found, a knot of uniformed officers stood, looking pleased with themselves.

Don looked down at the find which had so excited his colleagues, and he felt his face redden with a mixture of rage and disgust. "We've got to catch this maniac," he said.

"Yes, sir," said Frank.

"I mean, my God, Frank! What sort of animal commits a murder outside a cricket pavilion—with a baseball bat!"

CHAPTER TWO

Beautiful morning, thought Don. This early, before it got too hot, this was when a summer day was at its best. The weatherman on the radio had said, "No good news for gardeners, I'm afraid." *Sod the gardeners* was Don's view; they get rain for at least nine months of the year, let the rest of us enjoy a few days of blue skies.

He and Frank were walking the plot, familiarising themselves with the murder scene by daylight. The search team had restarted its work an hour ago, and there were a few specialists still poking around here and there. Don couldn't stop yawning—he'd only slept for a couple of hours—but otherwise he felt fine. Smelling the grass of the outfield, as a slight haze lifted from it, he couldn't imagine how anyone could fail to feel fine.

"Excuse me, mate—are you the police?"

A short, round man, bald with a neat grey beard, came waddling towards them from the direction of the pavilion. He held out a hand as he reached them; for a second, Don thought he was asking for help conquering a slight rise in the ground, but realised his mistake as Frank Mitchell shook the man's hand.

"I'm Glenn Curtis, I'm the groundsman here."

"Pleased to meet you," said Don. "Looks like you keep a nice pitch, Glenn."

"Oh yeah," said Curtis, "thanks. Thing is, do you know

19

when I'll be able to get my pavilion back? Only, I need to clear up. We're fully booked, all month. Weekdays as well as weekends."

Don smiled to himself. *Groundsman!* He wasn't a groundsman, he was a caretaker—a janitor. If he was a real groundsman, he'd have responded to Don's compliment about the pitch with a three-hour lecture on bounce and drainage, third-day deterioration, and the way that the Meteorological Office conspired against his efforts.

"We're hoping," said Frank, "to clear everybody out by lunchtime. So that the current match can be completed."

That had been Don's idea, and he'd been pleased with how quickly it had been generally accepted. He was looking forward to seeing as many of the suspects as possible in their natural environment.

"Oh, thanks, mate! That is a relief." Curtis looked back at the pavilion and shook his head. Now that the important business was concluded, he had time to spare for expressions of outrage and sadness. "Terrible, that guy getting killed. Awful. I mean, we've had the odd bit of trouble here in the past, but—murder! Never thought I'd—"

"Trouble?" said Frank.

"Yeah, you know. Vandalism. Kids. Just the usual, but you know what they're like these days. Nobody gives a toss about anything."

"No actual violence?"

"Not yet. But I don't mind admitting, I get a bit nervous when I'm working here on my own, at night especially."

"Aye, I can understand it."

"I take precautions, but—anyway, that's not what you're here for. If you don't mind me asking, what was the guy's name that was killed?"

Frank glanced at Don, who nodded. The victim's name

had been released by the press office overnight. "Bruce Lester. Do you know him?"

Curtis shook his head. "Doesn't ring a bell. He was playing yesterday?"

"That's right. About forty, thinning hair, slightly over-weight."

"No, don't think so. I recognised one or two of them yesterday—they've played here before, you know, for proper teams. Bloke called Eddie something? And a girl called Louise. Lovely girl, good wicketkeeper. But I don't think I knew your guy."

They thanked Curtis and let him get on with his groundskeeping—which seemed to consist of walking around the boundary rope with his hands in his pockets. To be fair, thought Don, there wasn't any litter for him to pick up—it had all been collected already by the search teams, and now sat in carefully labelled plastic bags in the properties room back at the station. Every lolly stick and fag packet, unexpectedly given posthumous—if temporary—value. Bit like a Turner Prize winner in an art gallery.

Don and Frank's walk took them parallel to the London Road, and for a while conversation became difficult, against the noise. "So much traffic these days," said Don, as they turned away from the road and back towards the small club car park. "It's all changed so much in just a couple of decades."

Frank said nothing, and from his scrupulously blank expression, Don could see that he had no idea what the DI was on about. Clenching his teeth against a sliver of annoyance, Don elaborated. "I'm saying, when I was younger people stayed in bed on Sunday morning. The streets were virtually deserted until lunchtime."

"What, all morning?"

Don nodded. "People read the papers, had a proper breakfast. Even had sex, possibly, unless they were married. Of course, young people today don't do sex, do they? They do shopping instead. Hence the traffic. Destroy the planet driving to an out-of-town *shopping experience,* buy a load of planet-destroying crap, then destroy the planet driving home again."

"Hmm," said Frank—which, if he had but known it, was not the response most likely to alleviate his boss's irritation.

"Never understood the attraction of shopping as a leisure pursuit. There again, I've never been married. Never understood the attraction of *that* as a leisure pursuit, either." He smiled. "Do you and Debbie go shopping on Sunday mornings, Frank?"

Frank blushed. He's been in CID for two years, Don thought; he should have stopped blushing by now!

"I've arranged for a CCTV check," said Frank, pointing up at a camera mounted on a lamppost.

"Most appropriate," said Don. "A lamppost."

"Appropriate?"

"That's what mobs lynch people from, isn't it? It starts with CCTV spying on law-abiding citizens and it ends with lynchings."

Frank coughed. "I don't know. I reckon CCTV makes people safer."

"Makes people *feel* safer, maybe."

"Feel safer, then—that's a good thing, isn't it?"

"Frank, if everyone stayed at home all day watching soap operas they'd be safe. A twenty-four hour curfew, that'd be safe."

"Right. Anyway, we should be able to tell from the footage who left the ground at the significant period, and if any of them returned."

"Yes, all right," said Don. He found Frank hard work

22

when he was in one of his officious moods. "Let's have a look at the pavilion."

A squat, single-story building, sitting on a slight rise to the north of the cricket pitch, it boasted a small balcony—or whatever you call a balcony when it's on the ground floor; Don wondered briefly if Frank would know, but then realised that he didn't care about the answer enough to be bothered to ask the question. Inside, there was one fairly large room—presumably the location for presentations, and for the essential lunches and teas—with a big window situated next to the manually-operated scoreboard. The small kitchen was through a doorway to the left.

At the back of the main room, a heavy fire door led to three other doors: one for the lavatories and showers, one for the changing rooms, and one for the fire exit. Supply cupboards were bolted to the walls between the doors. Don and Frank, after a quick squint into the first two portals, took the third, from which they emerged onto a strip of roughly mown grass. This, in turn, gave way almost immediately to a thicket of rhododendron bushes, beyond which a high link fence enveloped the entire ground. It was amongst these bushes that Bruce Lester had found his peace.

"So," said Don, "we're assuming that he came in from batting, and went through the fire door, supposedly heading for the showers. Did he get as far as the shower?"

Frank checked his notes. "Autopsy will say for certain, but the doctor said it didn't look as if his hair had been washed, and there were stains on his hands and knees that suggested he hadn't washed. Also, the fact that he was in ladies' clothing—"

"What, transvestites don't wash?" *Was that a sigh, Frank?*

"He wasn't a transvestite. Or at least, he might have been, but I did tell you last night—"

23

"*Yes*, Frank, I was joking. He was still wearing the clothes he batted in. Presumably he wouldn't have got out of his fancy dress, showered, and got back into it. So: he went to have a shower, but for some reason went out through the fire exit instead. Forensics reckon he was killed *in situ?*"

Frank nodded.

"OK, so he came out here—to talk to someone, perhaps, or to have a smoke, or whatever. And at some time, standing amid those bushes, he was hit from behind."

"With a baseball bat."

Don ignored that. "Was he a comedian or a writer?"

"He was playing for the comedians' team."

"Well, that would explain the costume I suppose," said Don. "Unless he was a spin bowler. Some of the twirlymen I've known would think nothing of coming on the pitch wearing filly knickers and a dress."

"He was batting at number eleven," said Frank, "so I suppose he might well have been a bowler."

"Well, if he was," said Don, "he was a spinner." He nodded, firmly. "Fast bowlers don't wear frilly knickers."

Frank declined to comment.

"The widow first," Don had said. "With any luck, we won't need to talk to anyone else."

Anna Lester and her husband had been spending the weekend of the cricket match with a cousin in Harrow—though, as the detectives parked outside the address she'd given them, Don sneered. "This isn't Harrow. This is North Harrow."

Frank didn't need to ask what the difference was: a few grand on the value of the house.

"His cousin or hers?" Don asked.

"His," said Frank, checking his notes. "Same surname."

24

In fact, Frank reckoned as they waited for their ring on the doorbell to be answered, the house would be worth a few hundred thousand, no matter which North London suburb it belonged to, and no matter that it was nothing much to look at. Three bedrooms and a parking space? Pure gold.

The cousin let them in—although, during the introductions, it transpired that he wasn't *the* cousin; the house belonged to another cousin, who was currently abroad. The cousin presently under consideration, Ivan Lester, was a tall, well-built man of West Indian appearance, good-looking, and clearly nearer Anna's age than that of her late husband. These facts did not escape the DI's notice; as Ivan led them through the house, Don nudged Frank and muttered "Aye, aye!" Frank pretended not to notice. He could only hope that Mr. Lester would do likewise.

"She's in quite a state, I'm afraid. The doctor gave her some sedatives, but I'm not sure they did much good."

"You can't know, can you?" said Don. "Without them she might have been twice as bad."

"I suppose that's true."

"Do Bruce and Anna have children?"

"No," said Ivan Lester. "Just as well, perhaps."

The widow was installed in a small conservatory attached to the back of the house, past the dining room. Very nice, Frank thought; he and Debbie had talked about putting in a conservatory. Or moving, maybe.

Ivan gave Anna Lester a peck on the cheek and rubbed her shoulders, then said "I'll leave you to it."

After the statutory expression of condolences, Don said: "We have to ask you a few questions, Mrs. Lester."

She gave a sad smile, and said "To the obvious one, the answer is no."

"No?"

"No, I can't think of anyone who would wish to kill Bruce. He had no enemies. The idea's ridiculous. He was a very mild-mannered man. He got on with everyone."

"Well," said Don, "we'll come to all that another time. What I really wanted to find out today is some more basic facts—your husband wasn't a comedian?"

"No, he was an accountant."

"But I understand the cricket match was an annual fixture between comedians and comedy writers?"

"Yes, something like that. He was—it was his hobby. Comedy. He collected comedy-related ephemera, autographs, that sort of thing. Fandom, they call it."

"You don't share this hobby yourself?"

She dabbed at her lips with a tissue. "Only in the role of dutiful wife."

"But Bruce was also a cricketer?"

"God no, not at all. Hadn't played since school. But he was very flattered to be asked. He'd met the captain through the hobby—Declan Donohue. You know? That Irish comic?"

"And Mr. Donohue asked Bruce to play?"

"That's right."

"Do you know why?"

"I don't know, they must have been short of a man, I suppose. Bruce was delighted, it's all he's talked about all week." The tissue came back into use, and she closed her eyes. "He bought all the kit, you know. A bat, a helmet, all the protective gear. One of those big boxes to lug it around in."

"A coff—" said Frank, turning the word into a cough halfway through, as he realised it might not be the most tactful word to use in the circumstances.

"Did he know many of the other players?"

"I think he knew quite a few of them, to some extent."

"Was there anyone he knew particularly well?"

"Bernie Ponting, he'd known Bernie for years. And Dick Kidney."

"Dick what?" said Don.

Frank could almost see an inappropriate remark forming on Don's lips, so he asked his next question rapidly. "But your husband was on good terms with all these people?"

"Yes, I'm sure he was. He was always on good terms with people." She looked out of the window at the beautiful day. "There was something with Bernie years back, but they got over that ages ago."

"A falling out, you mean?"

She shook her head. "Something to do with fandom. Something trivial. I don't know—all that stuff's a mystery to me, to be honest. I think he knew Stella Wardle too, but mostly by correspondence."

"But Declan Donohue wasn't a close friend—despite inviting Bruce to the match?"

"No, hardly. He'd met him a few times through the hobby, but until he became his accountant, they—"

Don leaned forward. "Your husband was Declan Donohue's accountant?"

"Yes, but not for long. He started doing Declan's accounts quite recently."

Don raised his eyebrows at Frank, who carefully recorded this new information in his notebook. *Well,* he thought: *at least we have two suspects, now.*

CHAPTER THREE

For lunch, they returned to Cowden—to the Eagle, the pub to which most of those involved in yesterday's game had retired post-match. It was Don's turn to buy. He returned from the bar with two cheese sandwiches, a bottle of light ale, and a fruit juice "for the driver." Frank wasn't sure which fruit. The juice was yellow, which seemed to rule in more than it ruled out.

They finished their sandwiches quickly—the food not being of either a quantity or a quality that encouraged lingering—and Don lit his first small cigar of the day.

The DI shook his head, and asked, in affronted tones, "Who brings a baseball bat into a cricket pavilion? I mean, do you know anyone who plays baseball?"

"No."

"Have you ever *heard* of anyone playing baseball?"

Frank Mitchell was not a big fan of rhetorical questions. If you don't want it answered, in his opinion, you shouldn't put a question mark at the end of it. "Didn't one of Marilyn Monroe's husbands play baseball?"

Don's cigar went out, possibly in sympathy with the bafflement which clouded its owner's face. "What?"

"The one that wasn't a playwright," Frank explained.

"Frank, what are you talking about?"

"Marilyn Monroe. I think she was married to a baseball player before—"

"*No,* Frank, I meant have you ever heard of anyone in *this* country playing baseball."

"Oh, right." He took a sip of his fruit juice. Grapefruit? But were grapefruits supposed to be so sweet? "No, I haven't, but there's hundreds of thousands of Americans live in the UK. I bet some of them play. Students, and that."

Don relit his cigar. "Well, I've never seen them."

Oh, well, thought Frank, *that proves it then. If Don Packham hasn't seen them, they don't exist.*

"And yet," Don continued, "when you hear of someone being beaten up or murdered, half the time the weapon is a baseball bat. Gangsters—they're always doing each other with baseball bats. And people rob shops with them. Racist gangs carry them around as standard issue kit. You raid a drug dealer, and—"

"People use them for self-defence, as well. Taxi drivers and what-have-you."

Don dismissed the interruption with a wobbly smoke ring. "What I want to know is, all these sports shops, happily selling hundreds of baseball bats every year, knowing perfectly well that the nearest bloody baseball ground is in Massachusetts, do they ever sell any baseballs, eh? I bet they bloody don't!"

"Maine, surely," said Frank, picturing in his mind the outline map of the USA that they showed on the news when there was an earthquake or a school massacre or a presidential election. "Though I suppose it depends whether you're flying or going by boat."

"My point *being,*" said Don, "what are all these people doing with bats but no balls? Bloody funny game of baseball that'd be." He finished his beer. "Not that it isn't a bloody funny game to begin with. Girl's game, isn't it? Just rounders on steroids."

"Don't know. Never seen it."

"Neither have I," said Don, as if puzzled by the irrelevance of his colleague's remark. "They should be licensed. Anyone caught in possession of a baseball bat, who can't prove to a court's satisfaction that he is a regular baseballer, should be chucked in prison for a month."

"Wouldn't that be," asked Frank, thinking of CCTV cameras and lampposts, "a breach of civil liberties?"

"Bollocks." Don held out his glass. "I'll have the same again."

This time, Frank asked for the fruit by name. "Light ale and an orange juice, please."

"And what's wrong with cricket bats, I'd like to know?"

Frank wrinkled his nose—the orange juice was identical to whatever it was he'd just been drinking. Except it wasn't quite as yellow. "What—for playing baseball with?"

"No, Frank, *do* try and keep up. Not for playing baseball with—we've already established that nobody plays baseball—"

"Except Marilyn Monroe's husband," said Frank. "Though he's probably retired by now."

"I mean, what is wrong with a cricket bat as a weapon? Why can't British criminals use decent British cricket bats to break British people's heads open with?"

It took Frank a moment to realise, from the look on his boss's face, that this last question had been asked with serious intent. He gave the matter some thought; he knew well enough by now that when DI Packham asked him a non-rhetorical question, there was probably a good reason for it. Even if Don himself didn't yet know what it was.

"Maybe it's because of the edge." He essayed a couple of imaginary swings. "With a cricket bat you'd have to be accurate. A baseball bat's rounded, so it doesn't matter where you hit the ball—or the victim's head—because all the surfaces are the same. But a cricket bat, flat on one side, ridged on the other, requires accuracy: if you don't get your stroke just right—"

"You get caught in the slips." Don nodded.

"Or your victim only gets a bruise."

"Good point." Don put his hands one above the other, and stared blankly at the quiz machine in the corner through half-closed eyes. His hands twitched a couple of times. "Yes, you're right. I suppose the weight distribution's different too—a baseball bat is all handle, really, isn't it? Doesn't need any skill—you can't really miss with a baseball bat. Not a target as big as a human, anyway. I think you've got it, there, Frank—criminals use baseball bats because they're not intelligent enough to handle the more sophisticated cricket bat."

That wasn't entirely what Frank thought he'd said, but he let it go with a grunt. It was close enough.

"So," said Don, "the question becomes—could Anna Lester have wielded the bat hard and high enough to brain her hubby?"

"Don't see why not. We've agreed the baseball bat is pretty much a foolproof tool for the job. I'd say she's slightly above average height for a woman, and I reckon Bruce was maybe a bit below. Anyway, I suppose the autopsy will give us some idea of a height range for the killer."

Don snorted. "No it bloody won't, Frank, you know what they're like—they don't rule anything in and they don't rule anything out. *And* they expect you to be impressed by their brilliance while they're doing it."

Its restart slightly delayed, for reasons beyond the control of the organisers, the annual cricket match between the Comedians and the Writers was just about ready to begin Day

Two when Don and Frank arrived back at the ground after lunch. A slightly larger crowd had gathered to watch the game today than had seen its first day, which didn't surprise Don; the murder had been reported on the regional TV and radio news.

"I see the pavilion's still out of bounds," said Frank, as a bearded man emerged from a small car, wearing a tutu. "Can't be much fun getting changed in your car, in heat like this."

"I blame limited overs cricket," said Don. "Hello—what are those two getting steamed up about?"

Two young men stood on the nearest boundary, each with his nose in the other's face. Much jabbing with fingers was taking place. "That's Declan Donohue, the thin guy with the dark hair—I've seen him on TV."

"I don't recognise him," said Don. "What's he been in?"

"He's done some of those late night stand-up shows."

Don was surprised. He wasn't sure why, but somehow he couldn't imagine Frank and his wife staying up late to catch university graduates making satirical jokes about farts. "Do you watch that sort of thing, then?"

Frank smiled. "With a two-year-old in the house, you get to see all sorts."

Never mind surprised; Don was now officially amazed. Should two-year-olds really be allowed to sit up all night watching TV? And if they insist on doing so, do their parents have to stay up with them? Still, none of his business—leave parenting to the parents, they probably knew what they were doing.

"So, is he a big name? This Donohue bloke?"

"I wouldn't think so, not big. Up and coming, I suppose."

"And who's that he's arguing with?" The other man, who seemed to be getting the better of the disagreement, if his smile was any guide, was well over six feet tall, but stocky with it.

"No idea," said Frank.

"All right. Let's go and ask him."

The antagonists broke apart as the detectives introduced themselves. The tall man stuck out his hand. "Good day, Inspector—Eddie Tarr. I'm captain of the Writers." His accent wasn't London; mostly neutral, with a bit of something else in there. Australian, perhaps?

Don shook his hand, then turned to his opponent. This man offered no handshake, but kept his hands deep in his trouser pockets. "And you, sir?"

"Declan Donohue." Don summed him up: Irish, scowl, no manners. He looked forward to arresting him for the murder of his accountant. Don didn't object to scowling, and he was an admirer of all things Irish, with the obvious exception of fiddle music, but there was no excuse for rudeness.

"You're captain of the other lot, I take it?"

"Uh-huh."

"Look," said Eddie Tarr, still smiling, "are you gents at all *au fait* with the regulations concerning substitutes?"

"I know the basic rules of the game," Frank began, "but I'm not really up on the more—"

"Laws, Constable!" Don rolled his eyes. "Cricket doesn't have *rules*—it has laws. Mere games have rules. What is it you want to know, Eddie?"

"He won't let me have a substitute," said Declan Donohue, prompting an even bigger smile from his opposite number. "I've got a man lying dead on a slab, and this little Napoleon wants me to field with ten men!"

Don took out his cigar tin, and passed it back and forth between his right hand and his left. "Well . . . that is a tricky conundrum." He took out a cigar. "It seems to me—"

"Surely," said Frank, "you're allowed a substitute fielder provided he doesn't bowl?"

"Thank you, Frank." Don put his cigar back in the tin, and the tin back in his pocket.

"Exactly," said Donohue, his face red. "Which is exactly what I've been saying for the last half hour!"

Tarr raised his hands. "Ah well, if you say so, Constable—you are the law after all." Don watched him walk away chuckling, and realised that this hadn't been an argument after all—it had been a wind-up. Looking sideways at Donohue he saw that the comic had come belatedly to the same realisation—and wasn't best pleased by it.

"He knew that perfectly well," said Donohue. "He was just being difficult because he had it in for Bruce Lester."

Frank opened his mouth to follow that up, but Don interrupted; *one thing at a time,* he thought. "I understand the murdered man was your accountant, Declan? Is that right?"

Donohue scratched an itch at the back of his neck. "Briefly, he was, yeah."

"And why was that?"

"Because he got killed! I know accountants do sod all for their money, but I'm not employing one who's *dead.*"

Don smiled—and then noticed that there was not the vaguest hint of humour in Donohue's expression. He had genuinely misinterpreted the question. "I meant, why did he become your accountant?"

"I needed a new accountant, that's all."

"What was wrong with your old one?"

Donohue took his hands out of his pockets, finally, and put them on his hips. "Simple: he's in Dublin. I'm in London."

"You've moved over here permanently?"

34

"This is where the work is, sure."

Don took a half-step back, and was pleased to see that Frank was alert, despite the heat. Despite having a tyrannical, precocious toddler who forced him to sit up all night watching surly comedians.

"When did you relocate to London?" Frank asked.

"Full-time, about three months ago."

"I see." Frank wrote in his notebook. Without looking up, he added: "And when did Bruce Lester become your accountant?"

Good lad, Frank! Don was interested to see what Donohue's reaction to this line of questioning might be.

"Same sort of time." *Uncomfortable; definitely.*

"And why did you—"

"Look, can we do this later?" Donohue pointed past Frank, towards the car park. "I'm supposed to be taking the field—the umpires are coming out."

Sorry, son, thought Don; *suspects leave when I tell them to. Not the other way around.* "You're a keen cricketer, Declan?"

"No point being any other sort."

"Where did you learn the game?"

The comic sighed. "I played for a club back home, from the age of about six."

Don was about to make the obvious remark, when Frank beat him to it. "I didn't know they played cricket in Ireland."

He's in a very interrupting mood, today, thought Don. *I must have a tactful word in his ear.*

Declan Donohue raised his eyes to the sky and let out another sigh. "Do you know? I would love it if just *once* I could go to a fucking cricket match in this country without someone saying that to me! There have been cricket clubs in Ireland since the eighteen thirties. We were playing internationals before Test Matches were ever thought of. In fact—"

"I do apologise for my colleague," said Don, shaking his head in sympathetic disgust at Frank's *faux pas*. Donohue, his face almost as flushed as it had been during his disagreement with Eddie Tarr, stalked off. "Let him go," said Don. "We'll talk to him later."

As they watched the Comedians' captain gather his men around him out in the middle for a team talk, a voice from behind Don's left ear said: "Don't worry about him, Inspector. He takes the game pretty seriously. He's always a bit highly strung before a match, and we're not defending a very high total today."

Don turned to greet a wiry man in late middle age, of medium height, with slightly long, salt and pepper hair, and a friendly smile on a weathered face. "Well, you know what Marvin Cohen said?"

"No."

" 'Life is an elaborate metaphor for cricket.' "

"Very good! Who's Marvin Cohen, though?"

"I don't know who he was," said Don. "I don't even know who you are."

"Oh, sorry—Bernie Ponting."

"Don Packham—and this is Frank Mitchell. Were you a friend of Bruce Lester's?"

"I was," said Ponting. "Look—I hope you don't mind, but if you're going to be around for a while, could I ask you to hold onto my mobile for me? I don't want to leave it in the van, it's not very secure. And what with the pavilion being closed—"

"Of course," said Don. "No problem. You couldn't persuade your wife along today, then?"

Ponting's smile froze. "Actually, I'm a widower."

"Ah—I'm sorry."

"Well . . . anyway, thanks very much."

"Shit," muttered Don—then he noticed what he strongly suspected was a *look* being directed at him by Frank. *Better not be,* he thought: *he can wait until he makes sergeant before he starts giving people looks.*

CHAPTER FOUR

"There are all sorts of silly rules," said Stella Wardle. "I mean, even sillier than the usual rules."

She sat on a bench on the boundary, at right angles to the wicket, her scorebook open on her knees. Frank Mitchell sat to her left, Don Packham to her right. The Writers were batting, the Comedians fielding.

"Like the fancy dress," said Frank.

"Exactly. Everyone has to wear women's clothing. Unless they *are* women, obviously. And if you drop a catch, you have to tie a rubber chicken around your neck."

"Really?"

"Yes, *really*." She reached into a floppy denim shoulder bag between her feet. "There you are."

Frank took the comedy chicken from her, inspected it, and handed it back. Don could see from the DC's expression that he wasn't quite sure what he was supposed to be inspecting it *for,* in his role as a detective. "Very nice."

"Very bloody stupid. Typical of men, though, isn't it?"

"I—"

"And if you drop two catches, you have to wear the chicken for twenty-four hours."

"And this is an annual event? The match, I mean, not the—you know, not the chicken."

She nodded. "Been going on for years. Decades. In the old days, it was a big event—you'd get big names turning out, big crowd watching. They use the usual excuse for playing silly buggers."

"Excuse?"

"Charity. That's the excuse for everything in this country, isn't it? If you claim you're doing it for charity, you can behave as ridiculously as you like."

True, thought Don. *And with a bit of luck, you can use the publicity to revive a dying career.*

"But," said Frank, "it's not such a big deal these days?"

"See that for yourself, can't you? Bunch of unknowns and wannabes."

"And accountants?"

Out in the middle, the batsmen scampered a quick run. It might have been three runs, but any natural athleticism the batsmen possessed was considerably hampered by their costume. Wardle made a mark in her scorebook, swore, crossed it out, and rewrote it in a different column. "Case in point," she said, once she'd finished. "Things have got so bad that they even have *fans* playing for them now."

She wasn't wrong—the skills on display would, for the most part, be extravagantly flattered by the description "amateurish"—but it didn't matter, Don reckoned, didn't matter at all. That was the thing about cricket; you wouldn't want to watch a game of rugby or football played by people who couldn't play; you wouldn't voluntarily spend time at a swimming competition or a long jump match if the athletes taking part were useless. But cricket was different. Cricket was such an inherently graceful sport, that nothing could ruin it entirely. That was why even the most urban Englishman sighed with pleasure at the thought of village cricket—whether or not he'd ever actually seen, let alone taken part in, a village cricket match.

It wasn't a bad job he'd got, all things considered—sitting

in the sun, getting paid to watch cricket. If only those two would stop waffling on about irrelevancies and let him concentrate on the game.

"So how do you come to be doing the scoring, Miss Wardle?" Frank asked.

"For money! I certainly wouldn't be doing it for love."

Frank frowned. "So you're a—what, you're a professional scorer?"

"Good God, no! No, I've been in the comedy business one way or another pretty well all my adult life. I started out as a secretary at Broadcasting House, then I got *lured* away from that to work for a scriptwriters' co-operative."

"That sounds interesting."

"Secretarial work is rarely *interesting*," she said. "But, well, I suppose we did represent most of the top writers of the late fifties."

Half-listening—but wholly hearing—Don noticed that Stella Wardle couldn't quite help herself from sounding a tiny bit boastful, no matter how keenly she cultivated her air of blasé cynicism.

"Anyway, that eventually broke up, and I did various jobs in the industry—PA work for stars, producers, and so on."

"So," said Frank, "you know where all the careers are buried."

"Oh, yes, Constable—all the careers, and all the jokes."

"And is that what you do now—PA work?"

She pushed her sunglasses further up her nose. "I'm more or less retired, now. Just do a bit part-time, to get me out of the house."

"A bit of . . . ?"

"I run Declan Donohue's fan club, if you can believe that."

"I see," said Frank. "And does he have a big fan club?"

"Hasn't got one at all. Hasn't got any fans, as far as I know. Not likely to either, with his act."

There was a shout from the field of *Feline waste! Feline waste!* as the ball flew off the handle of the bat, and looped high in the air.

"What does that mean?"

"It means 'catch it,' " Wardle explained. She tutted at Frank's unenlightened silence. "It's what we in the business call a 'joke,' Constable. A pun, or play on words."

One of the fielders ran in to take the catch, but just when the ball was almost in his hands his miniskirt fell down, he tripped over it, and the ball ran away between his knees.

"Very vaudeville," said Stella.

Don agreed. "Cheap material. But his timing's good."

The unlucky fielder regained his feet—and his miniskirt—before trotting over to the scorer's bench. As he got nearer, it became apparent that he was much younger than he'd appeared at a distance; in his twenties, Don reckoned, despite the fact that he was mostly bald.

Without a word, Stella Wardle handed him the rubber chicken. He thanked her with a wide, friendly smile, tied the chicken around his neck by its legs, and jogged back to his position.

"Who's he?" Don asked.

"Jerry Marsh."

"A comic or a fan?"

"Comic. So he says. He's a Yank, not been over here long."

"Oh, I get it," said Frank. "Cat shit."

"American?" said Don. "You'd expect him to play baseball, wouldn't you, not cricket?"

"Same thing, as far as I know. Bunch of stupid men waving their shafts in the air."

"That one's not a man," said Don, who'd just seen the wicketkeeper make a diving, tumbling stop, away to her left. As she stood up and slung the ball down the pitch to the bowler, her long, dark hair escaped from under her cap and the game was briefly delayed while she returned it to captivity.

"Louise," said Wardle. "Louise Ogden. Another fan." The term sounded like a damnation, the way she used it.

"At least this fan can play," said Don. "So, tell me—if Declan Donohue hasn't got any fans, why has he hired you to run his fan club?"

"The more businesslike comics—and these days, that's all of them, comedy is a career nowadays, they probably study it at business school—they set up the fan club before they've got any fans."

"Bit hubristic, isn't it?"

"It's partly for the image, and partly to be ready to go if they do take off." She smiled at him. "Customer service is everything these days, you know. No matter what you're selling."

Comedy as a career, thought Don. He knew she was right; perhaps they didn't study it at business school, not quite, but he'd read about youngsters leaving school, enrolling in drama college, doing a course in stand-up, and then taking their acts up to Edinburgh. And no doubt the drama schools did a Business Studies module, even if the business schools didn't yet offer one in Knob Gags and Custard Pies. Maybe he was just being nostalgic, but surely you couldn't create great comedy on such a structured foundation? Although, come to think of it, such people presumably weren't interested in great comedy—their career plans probably involved abandoning stand-up by the time they were twenty-five, and making their fortunes fronting game shows and doing voiceovers for ads.

True, the Monty Python lot started at university—but they hadn't studied *comedy*. No, they were all wasting taxpayers' money pretending to study medicine.

"The Goons didn't learn their craft in college," he said. "They fought World War Two, instead. As career plans go, persuading Hitler to invade Poland is pretty radical." She didn't respond, except by giving her lips a vaguely contemptuous twist, so he added: "I suppose you must have known all the greats of the post-War generation?"

"I met most of them," she admitted.

"You'd have met Tony Hancock, of course?"

Stella Wardle didn't reply.

"The best of them all," Don continued. "Wasn't he? The man who bridged the fifties and sixties, the radio and TV eras. The little man with the big pretensions, the ordinary loser who—"

"All I really remember about Hancock," she said, "is that he was once sick on my shoes outside a theatre in Bournemouth, when he was even drunker than usual."

"Oh," said Don. Could that *honestly* be her sole abiding memory of the greatest comic talent this country ever produced? If so, hers could not have been a very happy life.

"They were the most expensive pair of shoes I'd ever worn." She turned to look at Don. "And I'd bought them that day."

"Dear oh dear," said Don—and then realised that sounded as if he was doing a rather poor Hancock impression. "How about the Goons? Did you have much to do with that lot?"

"As little as possible. At least two of them were certifiably mad, and one was a professional Welshman with an incontinent larynx. I can't stand people who burst into song every few minutes. Peter Sellers was the only one of that lot I had any time for. At least he knew how to act the gentleman." She sniffed. "He wasn't one, but he knew how to pretend, and that's all that matters."

Her verdict on the troupe which had just about invented modern comedy seemed a little harsh, Don reckoned—even allowing for the trauma of spoiled shoes and inappropriate warbling. And meanwhile, what was wrong with Frank?

"You want to get some linctus for that cough, Constable?"

"Yes, sir," said Frank, his voice cracking slightly. "I will."

What a miserable woman, thought Don. Still—he'd most likely never get a chance like this again, to talk comedy with someone who'd met so many of his heroes. "Of course, everybody still reveres Hancock and Spike Milligan and that lot, but half the old shows are just forgotten, aren't they? What was that thing with Peter Ustinov and—"

Wardle turned to face him fully—or as fully as it is possible to face someone when you're sitting next to them on a bench—and said: "You're not a *fan*, are you, Inspector?"

"Me? Well, I—"

"I will never understand this pathetic need men have to make a *hobby* out of everything. If they've got that much spare time, why don't they spend it on real life? You know? Wives, families, that sort of thing. Relationships. *Communicating*. Instead of obsessing over fifty-seven different varieties of trivial crap. They say autism's a disease, but as far as I can see it's just a neat, one-word definition of maleness!"

"Yes—" Don began.

"Or anal retentive—that's two words, but just as accurate."

"Yes, I'm aware that that's the fashionable view," said Don, confident that his "fashionable" sounded ever bit as filthy a swearword as her "fan." "But I can't help feeling the world would be a better place if more people opened their lives to enthusiasm. And if we're entering the realms of gender-based generalisations, then I've often wondered why women feel so threatened by the idea of men being interested in something other than their immediate lives."

"Evolution, I expect," said Frank, who seemed to have got over his coughing fit.

"*What?*" said Wardle.

"What are you talking about, evolution?" said Don.

"If the male is off somewhere, taking an interest in things, then from the female's point of view he's not doing his job—which is staying in the cave, guarding her young from tigers—thus reducing her chances of passing her genes on."

They both looked at Frank for a moment, in silence. Don recovered first; he'd made a career out of recovering first. "Besides, being interested in comedy is more than a hobby, isn't it? These fans, as you call them, are helping to preserve our cultural history."

"Oh, balls—they're just a bunch of carrier bags."

"Carrier bags?"

"Little men," she said. "Greasy little men in anoraks, carting around plastic bags full of their pathetic treasures. It's got sod all to do with cultural history. If it wasn't comedy, it'd be something else—science fiction or railways or stamps. Or bloody *cricket*. Anything with plenty of unimportant detail in it that they can all get obsessed about."

Well, thought Don; perhaps he'd drawn out this witness enough for one day. It was a good technique, but no sense in overusing it. Silly old cow. "Was Bruce Lester a carrier bag?"

"Bruce? King of the carrier bags. He was a self-confessed collector of ephemera."

"What sort of ephemera? Autographs?"

"Oh, that's beginner's stuff for the true carrier bag. He had everybody's autograph by the time he was fifteen, I'm sure."

"So what else?"

She waved her fingers dismissively. "He collected playbills, old copies of the *Radio Times*, original scripts, even holy relics."

"Holy relics?" said Frank.

"Oh *God,* yes! He had a Groucho Marx cigar stub, a receipt from a hotel in Aberystwyth made out to Arthur Askey. Anything imbued with the saliva or sweat of the gods."

He wasn't going to admit it to this woman, but Don was willing to say it in the privacy of his own head—that really did sound a bit . . . well, a bit pathetic. "Well, I never . . . is a collection like that valuable?"

"Who knows? Seems to me these days there are enough loonies on the loose to make everything in the world valuable. Have you ever looked at one of those auction sites on the internet? Everything's worth something, even if it's completely worthless."

"I'm surprised Eddie Tarr isn't opening the batting," said Don. "Captain's privilege, I'd have thought."

"He's a bowler. Wasn't bowling yesterday, though—carrying an injury."

"Injured during the game, you mean?"

She shook her head. "No, he came in with it. Don't know where he got it. Hope it was from a woman."

An umpire's call of *No ball! Bring on the bottle!* returned their attention to the cricket.

"What's that all about?" Don asked.

"A bowler who delivers an illegal ball has to take a shot of booze. Another of their *amusing* little rules."

Sure enough, Don saw, the errant bowler—a large, grey

man in his late fifties—was surrounded by laughing fielders as he swallowed a tot of Cuban rum. *At least it's the real stuff,* Don noted, *not the usual Bacardi.*

"Who's the bowler?"

"Dick Kidney."

"Dick Kidney?" said Don. "What sort of name is—"

"Is he a good bowler?" Frank said.

"I don't think he can be," said Wardle. "He played for the team a few weeks ago, got through most of a bottle on his own. Had to go and have a lie down. I was surprised—I would have thought your lot would have harder heads, with all the free drinks you must get."

"Our lot?" said Don, though he thought he knew what she meant.

"Oh, didn't you know?" Her smile was at its broadest, and most insincere. "Dick's a copper."

"Really?" Don kept his tone light, as if unconcerned at the idea that a suspect in a murder case might be a serving officer of the law. "In London?"

"No, I don't think so—up North somewhere." As if aware that this detail somewhat reduced the explosive power of her bombshell, she added: "I wonder why he didn't make himself known to you, last night or this morning."

Don—who was wondering exactly the same—explained. "Protocol. Wouldn't do to be pushy on someone else's patch."

She laughed openly at that. "Oh, I see."

"He's another fan, I presume? Another carrier bag merchant?"

She wrinkled her nose. "Actually, he's not the worst of them. He at least does know a bit about his subject, which makes a change."

"His subject being?"

"Robb Wilton. He's writing a book about him, apparently."

Frank said, "Who?"

"I'll tell you later," said Don. "Before your time."

"Before *your* time, Inspector," said Stella, peering sideways at Don with something almost approaching interest. "Before mine, pretty well."

"One of the greats, though," said Don. "Not forgotten by those who remember. I must have a chat with Constable Kidney."

Again, Wardle smiled—which Don was by now sure was an unconscious signal that she was about to engage in mischief. "Pity you can't have a chat with Bruce."

"Oh?"

"Yes, I believe he had more than a passing interest in Robb Wilton's life and times, too." *No doubt about it,* thought Don; *she is enjoying herself.* "Now you must excuse me," she added. "I need to concentrate on the scoring. I am being paid for it after all, albeit very poorly."

"We'll leave you to it," said Don.

"Was that a four or a six?" she asked, peering at the field, trying to make out the umpire's signal.

"I think it was a single," said Don.

"From a leg bye," added Frank.

"Oh *shitholes,*" said Stella Wardle, as she scratched at the scorebook with her biro, before turning it sideways so that she could scribble in the margin.

CHAPTER FIVE

On Monday morning, Frank picked up the DI at home—having received a late call from Don the night before. "Just remembered, Frank—you haven't got my current address."

"Haven't I?"

"Well, I very much doubt it. I didn't have it myself until Saturday."

Frank was expecting the A-Z to lead him to the usual North London back street, where he'd find Don in a decent but dull bedsit, either—depending on mood—stumbling around unshaven in an ill-fitting dressing gown, or else in the kitchenette, engaging in acts of culinary extremism with an industrial-sized frying pan.

He wasn't expecting . . . this place.

There *were* bedsits in Pinner, that ancient village and modern suburb on the outskirts of Harrow, but Don's new address was not one of them. It was an architect-designed, split-level, detached house with a horseshoe drive, surrounded on all sides by manicured lawns.

He checked the address he'd written down three times before daring to enter the drive. There was no mistake; this was it. Unless Don had been having him on. No—Don didn't do practical jokes. And people who knew what was good for them didn't do practical jokes *to* Don, either.

Well, after all, Frank thought—*all houses are architect-designed, aren't they?* Who else was going to design them?

Inside, the house was spacious, well-lit, if a bit unlived-in. Mind, it would be, wouldn't it? If he'd only just moved in. The entire contents of Don's previous gaff would probably fit into the lobby here. Frank wanted to ask him about it—how come he'd moved up in the housing market so dramatically, so suddenly—but the DI seemed a little quiet this morning, so Frank didn't want to risk any conversation which might lead to . . . well, which might lead anywhere, really. *It's always safest to be safe,* his granddad used to say.

"Nice place," he commented instead, leaning against a counter in the pine and chrome kitchen as Don dragged a portable electric shaver over his cheeks.

Don grunted. "If you've got a phobia against hot water, it's a dream."

Oh, great. One of those days. "Hot water not working? You should get a plumber round to that."

"Really? A *plumber,* you say? I thought that brain surgeon I called in last night looked a bit out of his depth."

"I've got a Yellow Pages in the car if you want to—"

Don put the shaver down on the breakfast counter. "Is that what they pay you for, Detective Constable? Solving people's plumbing problems?"

So Frank dropped it. Perhaps Don really did have a hot water phobia. Or a plumber phobia.

They got in the car and drove south, quite slowly. Frank had no idea where they were going, but after three years of working with Don Packham he was used to that. A destination would emerge in the fullness of time. Unless Don went into one of his real Downs. *In which case I'll just drive him home and dump him on the doorstep. He probably won't notice.*

"That list came through, sir—it was on my desk this morning."

"You've been into the office?"

"Well—yes." *Didn't he want me to?*

"What did you want to do that for?"

"Well—it's where I work."

Don gave a puff of laughter. "It's where I work too; you wouldn't catch me going in there. Anyway, what list?"

Frank steered the car around a small roundabout. For the second time in ten minutes. "From the CCTV—comings and goings from the cricket ground. If we compare that list with lists of who was there, taken from witnesses at the scene—"

"Yes, yes, Frank, I do know how it works. I used to do a bit of detecting myself, you know, before they decided to retrain me as a typist."

Frank took one hand off the wheel to cover the sudden return of his chronic cough. *Honestly!* DI Packham was probably the only officer in the Met who was not overburdened by paperwork. Mind, he would be, if Frank ever got transferred. Luckily, Frank didn't object to paperwork. He'd never understood the way cops moaned about it; they were still getting paid the same rate, weren't they, whether they were outside knocking on people's doors or inside wearing their fingerprints out on a keyboard? It's a job: they give you stuff to do, you do it, then you go home. Where's the problem? Still, this was not a viewpoint he was foolish enough to express out loud, other than to Debbie. The party line was that all police officers were action-starved adrenaline addicts who resented every single second they spent sitting on a swivel chair, when they could be out in the dark getting stabbed. Anyone who said different was a weirdo or a poofter, not to be trusted as a team-mate. As if anyone who bag-carried for Don Packham could be trusted, anyway!

"Yes, sir. So, what it comes down to is, we've got a suspects list. Given the timings, there's only eight of them could have killed Bruce Lester."

51

"Right. Well, you can list them for me over breakfast." He pointed through the windscreen. "There's a transport café up here on the left. Turn right past the mosque, and it's the road after the new health centre."

"Oh God," Frank muttered.

"What?"

"Oh, good. I am feeling a mite peckish as it happens."

He was a bit disappointed, in the hot, crowded café, to hear Don order tea and toast. Frank was pretty certain the DI hadn't breakfasted at home, and he associated loss of appetite in Don with depression. That and abstention from smoking.

"Do you want an ashtray?"

"What for? I'm not smoking, am I?"

"No, sir. Right." Ah, well—at least Frank himself would only have to have a cup of tea and a bun, rather than one of Don's legendary seven-course gut-busters.

"Where's this list of yours, then?"

Frank took out his notebook. "Right. Well, if all the statements are correct, and the CCTV scanners got it right, and if—"

Some of Don's tea sloshed onto the table as he banged down his mug. "Just give me the list, Frank, for God's sake!"

"Right you are, sir. OK: eight people. Declan Donohue, comedian; the captain of the Comedians' cricket team—"

"Him," Don interrupted. "He did it."

"OK," said Frank. "Why?"

"Miserable sod. No sense of humour."

"Ah. Right. Well, just in case it's not him, there's still Stella Wardle."

"She did it."

"Oh yes?"

"Sarcastic old bag."

"OK. Then there's the widow, Anna Lester."

"*She's* the one. She was having it off with that cousin of her husband's, didn't want a divorce, this way she gets the man *and* the dosh. Money and sex in one package—she did it."

Which was interesting, Frank thought; Don wasn't joking about Anna Lester, or venting spleen—he was proposing a serious, and obvious, avenue of inquiry. Did that mean he'd already made his mind up?

"Next on the list, in no particular order, we have Jerry Marsh. The American comedian? We saw him at the game yesterday."

"Yes, I remember him," said Don. "We'll arrest him later."

"On what charge sir?"

"Baseball bat."

"Ah yes, of course." Frank pretended to write those words next to Marsh's name, and was rewarded with a slight twitch of Don's lips. Not a smile, you couldn't call it an actual smile, but it at least suggested that Don was making an effort to pretend that he and his colleague were in the same room at the same time, having a conversation. With each other. "Dick Kidney. Police Constable Dick Kidney."

Don nodded. "We'll arrest him, too."

"For?"

"For being a copper. I bloody hate coppers, always have."

A van driver leaned across the gap between their adjacent tables, and said: "Me too, mate."

Don toasted the driver with his tea. "Right on, pal."

Frank lowered his voice. "Bernie Ponting."

"Speak up?"

I'm not blushing, thought Frank, annoyed at the small but unmistakeable twinkle in his boss's eye. *I'm drinking hot tea on a hot day, that's all.* "Bernie Ponting," he said, at the same low volume. "The one who had us looking after his mobile at the match."

"Put him down as a probable stroke definite."

"Will do. Any particular reason?"

"Well, how was I supposed to know he was a widower?" Don looked hurt. "Trying to make me feel bad like that."

"Then there's Eddie Tarr, captain of the Writers."

Don patted at his pockets—although he didn't seem to know he was doing it. Frank hoped he was looking for his cigar tin. "What was his accent?"

"Sounded slightly Australian, I thought," said Frank. "New Zealand, maybe."

"Yes, I thought so, too."

"So it was him then, was it?"

"Almost certainly. What's that—seven?"

"Seven. And number eight is Louise Ogden, the wicketkeeper."

"Must be her," said Don. He'd stopped patting his pockets now, but instead he was twiddling the first two fingers of his right hand, tapping them against the thumb, as if knocking a small ash off a small cigar.

They're in your shirt pocket! "Why her?"

Don spread his hands out, as if the answer was so obvious that he was a little disappointed to hear the question. "She's gorgeous."

"Right, of course. Well, that's our lot. The surgeon says the murderer would only need to be of ordinary build and strength to deal the blow, could be male or female."

Don was visibly unimpressed. "Typical vague rubbish. I'll tell you what—one day, just as an experiment, I'd like to tell one of those useless sods that amongst the suspects is a one-legged elephant. Could such a suspect have put the poison in the butler's teapot? Bet you anything they'd say yes. Rule nothing in, rule nothing out, that's their motto."

"No doubt," Frank agreed. "Everyone interviewed so far, by uniform or CID, has been asked whether there was anything during the match itself, or on that day generally, which might have led to argument."

"And everyone says not."

"Everyone says not."

"So, if true, that means the cricket match was an opportunity only, not the source of a motive."

"I suppose so." Frank finished his tea. He reckoned—he couldn't be sure, you could never be sure—but he *reckoned* Don was ready to roll. "So, who do we start with?"

Don thought about it. "Where does that rozzer ply his filthy trade?"

"PC Kidney? York."

"How long would it take us to get there?"

Frank did the sums in his head. "Three hours? Four."

"Right, then." Don stood up. "You give him a ring, while I have a pee. Oh, and Frank?"

"Yes?"

"If his sergeant answers, and wants to know what it's about, be sure you only tell him what he needs to know, all right?"

"Yes, sir."

Halfway to the gents, Don added: "That his officer is a leading suspect in a brutal baseball bat slaying."

The drive made Don feel better. It was hot in the car, of course, but there was a decent breeze through the passenger's window once they got onto the motorway, and more importantly, he'd tuned the radio to Radio Four Long Wave, **Test Match Special**. There was something quite comforting about listening to ball-by-ball commentary of the England cricket team undergoing a batting collapse; something timeless. They'd been winning a lot lately, England had, at home and abroad. Which was good of course, encouraging, but a bit . . . unnatural.

"At least they lasted into the fifth day," said Frank, as another English wicket fell.

"True. They wouldn't have managed that a couple of years ago." He'd felt a bit rough this morning, thought maybe it was sinusitis, but it was probably just an allergic reaction to that stupid house, with its horrible stripped pine floors. When had posh people decided that not having a carpet was a sign of class? Probably explained the lack of hot water—it wasn't a plumbing problem, just a lifestyle statement. Anything the plebs can afford can't be worth having.

When they stopped for lunch at a miserably antiseptic roadside restaurant, Don asked Frank what sort of comedy he and Debbie liked. He assumed that any such opinion in the Mitchell household would be a joint one.

To Don's surprise, Frank seemed a little uncomfortable—a little reluctant to commit himself to an answer. Did he have a shameful secret? Was he a closet **Are You Being Served** fan? Surely he wasn't going to nominate that horrible American thing about the trendy young skeletons, who live in lofts and dance around fountains? The one that was written by a computer, acted by automata, and directed by an actuary.

Then again, fair enough—Frank was right to be cautious. There couldn't be any question more intimate, more revealing of inner character, than "What makes you laugh?" It's like asking someone: "Who are you, really?"

"Well," said Frank, eventually, "I've been watching a lot of Bilko lately." Don's amazement must have shown on his face, because the lad blushed, turned his attention to his burger, and clearly regretted speaking.

"No, great," said Don. "Great stuff—I'm just surprised you've even heard of it, that's all. I mean, it was old when I was young!"

"They've been showing the repeats lately, in the afternoons. Debbie started watching it—you know, with Joseph."

Don felt his mouth drop open, but he couldn't do anything to prevent it. "*Joe* likes Bilko?"

"Debbie thought it was good, so she started taping them for me."

"Well," said Don, "as in all matters, I find Lady Mitchell's taste—and that of the Mitchell scion, indeed—to be exemplary. Phil Silvers; one of the giants. Seminal stuff. Almost the equivalent of Tony Hancock over here—half a century later you still see acts young enough to be his great-grandson which are based on him, even if they don't know it."

"They're pretty funny shows," said Frank.

"It's strange to think that American television used to be good, isn't it? When you look at the crap they send us now. Must be twenty years since a US show made primetime over here. And their comedies are the worst of the lot."

"Oh, I don't know," said Frank, "I don't mind **Friends**."

"Right," said Don. "Eat up. We're not on holiday."

CHAPTER SIX

It wasn't a view that Don was likely to share, he was aware of that, but Frank didn't really see why Dick Kidney should be subjected to more embarrassment than was strictly necessary—so he'd arranged for them to meet the PC at a pub of the latter's choosing.

Even from the almost-deserted car park, it was obvious why Kidney had picked this particular place. A large, open-plan, nineteen seventies building, it stood—or slumped, at any rate—on the extreme southern outskirts of the ancient city of York, so that if you didn't know better you might almost have suspected it of belonging to the extreme northern outskirts of Goole.

Don chuckled as they got out of the car. "You don't think Brother Kidney is ashamed to be seen with us, do you? If you checked the coordinates of this dump on a map, it'd turn out to be in a place called: Nowhere, Middle Of."

"I don't think we'll have much trouble finding a table," Frank agreed.

He was right. Monday lunchtimes obviously weren't a peak hour for drinking in these parts. Looking at the tatty state of the furnishings and fittings, Frank rather thought that the Friday night of a Bank Holiday weekend wouldn't be a peak hour in this sad hole.

"Open-plan," Don sneered. "Totally unplanned, and only half open." They soon spotted their prey, sitting alone at a corner table, in plain clothes, with a half pint of mild. Don treated him to a firm handshake and a hard look. "This your local, is it?"

"Just a convenient meeting place, Inspector. I thought I'd spare you the one-way system."

"Very thoughtful. Frank—what are you having?"

Sticky from the journey, Frank decided to risk the DI's disapproval and ask for a half of lager. Don compensated for his colleague's lack of taste by quizzing the elderly barman for several minutes about the choice of bitters. Eventually, he settled for a pint of something Frank had never heard of, and they sat down opposite Kidney.

"So, Dick," said Don, without preamble, "we've had a long journey on a hot day; do you want to do us a favour and tell us why you killed Bruce Lester?"

Kidney smiled. "I should have thought that was obvious."

"Yes?"

"Because when I get away with it, it'll make CID look like berks."

Don's slow, considering nod made Frank think that his boss found such a motive entirely believable. Which, come to think of it, knowing the way lifelong plods felt about detectives, it quite possibly was.

"You're not a York native, Dick?" said Don. Frank, too, had noticed the middle-aged constable's flat, catarrhal, Midlands accent.

"No, I'm from Birmingham, originally. I thought we all sounded alike to you southerners?"

Don tut-tutted. "You'd better not call young Frank, here, a southerner. He's a Geordie. As far as he knows, Birmingham's on the Isle of Wight."

Dick Kidney seemed to notice the DC for the first time.

"How long you been in CID, then, youth?"

"Couple of years."

"You don't miss it, then?"

"Miss what?" Frank asked, though only for form's sake—he'd heard this old gag often enough to know the punch line off by heart.

"Being a police officer," said Kidney.

"The question is," Don said, "will *you* miss it, when you're banged up for murder?"

Kidney was unrattled. It'd take a bit, Frank reckoned, to rattle this old timeserver. "You'll have to get your skates on if you want to arrest a cop for this murder, Inspector."

"Oh? Why's that?"

"I get the pension in seventy-eight days." He lit a cheap cigarette from an expensive lighter. "You've not nicked the wife yet, then?"

"Any reason why we should?" Frank asked.

"Come *on*, have you seen her? And you've seen poor old Brucie?"

"We have," said Don, "but to be fair to him, he wasn't at his best when we saw him."

Kidney shook his head. "Hadn't been at his best for years, mate. Mind you, credit where it's due, he did have his day."

"Really?" Don leaned forward, and Frank knew why: this was the first interesting thing Dick Kidney had told them—whether or not he intended it to be.

"Certainly! Time was, he never went short of girlfriends." He drew on his cigarette, then added: "Surprised you, haven't I?"

"We never met him," said Don. "Not when he had all his hair; not even when he had all his head. But, yeah, I wouldn't have had him down as a ladies' man. I'll give you that."

"Years back, I'm talking about. He had some money in his

pocket, he was a nice bloke. Dressed well. He was never exactly good looking, but he wasn't ugly."

"So what happened?"

"I don't know." Kidney tapped the ash off his cigarette, onto the floor. The ashtray on their table, Frank noted, was cleaner than the carpet beneath their feet. "What happened to Brucie? I reckon he was allergic to middle age."

Don rewarded him with a sharp laugh. "Allergic, you say?"

"Yeah, that's my diagnosis. Allergic to middle age—it made him swell up, you know, made his hair fall out. Caused unsightly distensions to appear around his waist, beneath his chin, under his eyes." He pointed to his own sallow wrinkles, and winked at Frank. "You've got all that to look forward to, son. Middle aged acne, they call that."

"So Bruce got married?" Don asked.

Kidney took a swig of his weak beer. "Best thing to do, eh? If your share price is dropping, sell out while you've still got some assets."

"His assets being . . . ?"

"He was still a nice bloke. He still had money in his pocket. He still wasn't ugly."

"So, no more girlfriends after that?"

Stubbing out his cigarette, and exhaling his final drag, Dick Kidney shook his head. "Oh, that'd all stopped anyway—I mean, well before he got too old for it."

"Well before?"

"Years before."

"Five years? Ten?"

Kidney shrugged. "Twenty years ago?"

"Do you know why?"

"Usual reason," Kidney said. "He met some woman, fell in love with her."

"You're not talking about his wife?"

Finishing his beer, Kidney said: "No, no. Before Anna—few years earlier. I don't know, there was some woman, it all went wrong, whatever."

"How do you mean," said Don, "went wrong?"

"I don't know the details. Brucie and me, we didn't have that sort of relationship. But anyway, after that he was on his own for quite a while. Until he met Anna."

Don sent Frank up to the bar for refills. While he waited for the drinks—a generic cola for him, this time; he wouldn't risk another beer, and he didn't fancy an overpriced glass of orange-yellow pulp—Frank wondered if the interview hadn't, perhaps, drifted slightly off topic. If the young widow was their favourite suspect—which she had to be, because young widows always were, by definition—then surely it should be her love life they were asking about, not her husband's?

When he got back to the table, Frank found the two men talking about cricket—specifically, about their native land's apparent inability to produce spin bowlers of world class. PC Kidney's relaxed posture suggested that the conversation in Frank's absence had been wholly unrelated to the murder inquiry. *Say what you like about DI Packham,* Frank thought: if he asks a junior officer to assist him in conducting an interview, it's not just because he doesn't fancy driving. Maybe that was partly why Don was so unpopular in CID—because (as he himself had been heard to say) he thought the phrase *superior rank* was rhyming slang.

"Well done, Frank. There we go, Dick, one horrible half of stagnant rabbit piss. Get that down you."

"Cheers." Kidney took a sip and pantomimed his enjoyment. "Good stuff, is mild. What they used to drink all the time in the old days, workers in heavy industry—they didn't trust the water."

"What's that you've got there, Frank? Fruit juice?"

Frank wasn't entirely sure that the DI would acknowledge the existence of cola—generic or otherwise—so he nodded.

"Good man," said Don. "Blackcurrant, is it? Lots of vitamin C—that'll help you through all those late nights." He leant back in his chair and busied himself with his pint, his eyes telling Frank that it was the DC's turn now.

"Dick," said Frank, placing his drink carefully on a virginal beer mat, so as not to leave rings on the heroically scarred table. He'd had one sip of the slightly fizzy black liquid, and decided that one sip would probably be adequate. "From what you've told us, it's obvious why Bruce married Anna. But why do you think she married him?"

Kidney lit another cigarette before replying, then held his lighter out to perform the same service on Don's small cigar. "Have you seen their house?"

"Not yet," said Frank.

"Lovely place." He smirked, but then thought better of it, and waved a hand in front of his face as if to sweep away his lapse into cynicism. "No, I'm being unfair—basically, they were very fond of each other, I'd say. Fair enough, he could be a bit dull, could Bruce—but then which of us can't? We've all got our favourite hobbyhorses that we bang on about *ad nauseam,* haven't we? When all's said and done."

"Absolutely," said Don, and Frank was momentarily silenced, so impressed was he by the DI's diplomacy. Don Packham, it could not be denied, had plenty of hobbyhorses that he was more than happy to bang on about *ad nauseam*—but it did help that he threw them all out and got a new lot in, at least once a month.

"He was a nice guy, though," Kidney continued. "Friendly, decent sort. I'll miss him, that's the truth." He raised his glass as if in toast—an unconscious gesture, Frank thought.

"You'd known him for quite a while?"

"Oh, God yeah! *Centuries*. Him and Bernie Ponting. You met Bernie yet? When I was still living back in Brum, this was. There was a meeting, they were trying to get funding to build a statue to Tony Hancock." He raised his eyebrows at Don. "Did you know Hancock was born in Birmingham?"

Don laughed. "Went south bloody early though, didn't he?"

Kidney wagged a finger—only half-jokingly, Frank thought. "Maybe, but he never lost touch with his Brummie roots."

"As it happens," said Don, "I've seen the statue."

"*Have* you, now?" Dick Kidney gave the DI a small salute. "Good on you. Made the pilgrimage to Birmingham specially, did you?"

"Something like that. Don't tell management, mind— they seem to be under the misapprehension that I was there to attend a seminar on Community Policing in the Digital Age."

"Well, you did right. But I'm talking about late seventies, early eighties. Back then, it was basically just a bunch of Hancock nuts trying to get people to take notice. I just went along out of curiosity, I wasn't an active fan in those days."

"But Bruce was?" Frank asked.

"Oh yeah, he was into all that. Had been since school-days."

"And you became friends?"

"Well, we saw each other around, you know. I got into comedy fandom after that, and we'd quite often meet up at conventions, collectors' marts, that sort of thing."

"I understand," said Don, "that your special interest isn't

Tony Hancock, but Robb Wilton. He was a Scouser, wasn't he?"

"I'm surprised you've even heard of him," said Kidney, his warmth towards the London cop growing almost palpably by the minute.

"I should think so! My granddad used to do impressions of him during Christmas dinner." Don crumpled his face, and tugged nervously at his left earlobe with his right hand. " 'The day war broke out, my missus said to me . . .' "

"Not bad," said Kidney, and Frank was fascinated to see how the lugubrious, world-weary PC—a typical cop waiting for his pension, shocked by nothing, impressed by nobody— was transforming before Frank's eyes into an animated enthusiast. It was a trait Frank had noted before in hobbyists: people who stumbled through their daily grind, scarcely aware of their surroundings, only to light up like Christmas trees at any vague scent of their peculiar passion.

"I've not really heard of this Wilton guy," Frank said. "What's so special about him?"

"Ah, well," said Kidney, thoroughly enlivened now, clearing a space for his elbows on the table, his eyes fixed on Frank's, "you have to understand the times he lived in."

"Which were?"

"Well, eighteen eighty-one to nineteen fifty-seven, those are his dates, but the *key* dates are nineteen thirty-nine, forty. World War Two's just started, so you've got Britain, right, at war with the mightiest military machine on Earth, entirely alone, no help coming from anywhere—and who do you suppose the best known voice in the whole nation belongs to?"

The answer to that was obvious from context, Frank reckoned, but he played along. "Winston Churchill?"

"No—Robb bloody Wilton! Churchill hadn't really got into his stride yet—in terms of being a wireless personality, I mean—but the whole country used to listen to Robb Wilton. And he was this middle-aged music hall comedian—well, I say comedian, he wasn't like a regular stand-up." Kidney took a quick mouthful of beer to wet his whistle. "He was basically a monologist, if you know what that is."

The only person Frank could think of who might be so described was his Uncle Charles, who had been known to go on at some length about the Labour Party leadership's iniquitous role in the great pit strike of nineteen eighty-four to -five. But he didn't want to interrupt the flow, so he nodded.

"Right. Well, Wilton took on the persona of a Home Guard volunteer, right? And he did these broadcasts which were like, basically, taking the piss out of everything the country was doing to get ready for the German invasion."

"Doesn't sound very patriotic," said Frank.

"Ah, but it *was,* you see! Because that's the British way of dealing with things, isn't it? If you're scared of something, you have a laugh at it. So what Wilton was saying, basically, to the nation was—don't worry, just because we're all alone in the world, and Nazi parachutists are going to be dropping out of the sky like dandelion seeds any moment, that doesn't mean we're not still living in the same country we've always lived in. See what I mean? We're not going to start taking ourselves seriously, or giving respect to those in authority, any more than we ever have over the last thousand years."

"Right," said Frank, "I see what you—"

"We'll just muddle through, sort of thing, like we always have before. Plus which—he was bloody funny. Terrific timing. Best ever. Better than Hancock, and that's saying something."

"Right," said Frank, whose intimacy with the works of the late Tony Hancock was only slightly greater than his knowledge of this Wilton geezer. "That's very interesting."

66

"They're still funny if you listen to them today, his Home Guard monologues. Tell you what, mate, I'll lend you some tapes."

"We'd appreciate that, Dick," said Don. "Mind you, all those old comics were great, weren't they? They don't build 'em like that any more, more's the pity."

"You can say that again," said Kidney.

Don said, "You're writing a book about him, is that right?" At that, Frank fancied he detected a slight deflation in the burly cop's exuberance.

"Planning to, yeah—been talking about it for years. Once I'm retired, I reckon I'll get down to it."

"Was Bruce Lester also interested in Robb Wilton?"

"His interests were more general," said Kidney. Frank noted his dismissive tone; and noted Don noting it, too. "I used to go all over the country trying to pick up stuff about Wilton. Especially tapes. Reel-to-reel, off-air in the beginning, then later on cassettes. Of course, it's all MP3s, now."

"Is it?" said Don. "Yes, I expect it would be. Yes indeed." Frank buried his smile in his cola—a kindness he immediately regretted as the flat, warm, sugary liquid hit his tongue. "And you'd meet Bruce on these excursions, yes?"

"Now and then. Occasionally, if there was some big convention on or something, Bruce and I would share a car, or share a hotel room. To cut costs, basically. Not that he needed to, really, but I think he liked to have company."

"He was a gregarious man, then?"

"Well . . . not exactly gregarious. Quiet fellow. Friendly, though, with those he knew. And a good sort. Wouldn't hurt a fly." Kidney smiled, and Frank couldn't help smiling back; there was something so transparently genuine about his pleasure in recalling his friend. "Except—he was *ruthless* about his collections! He really was. If he set out to acquire something special, say something that didn't show very often—"

"Didn't show?" Don asked.

"It's what collectors call it—a rarity that hasn't turned up in a sale for a long time, they'll say 'It hasn't shown for years'. Anyway, if Bruce was after something like that, no matter what the competition, he'd get it. You could count on that."

"You're saying," said Don, "that Bruce Lester, nice bloke, accountant, comedy fan . . . he could be a tough guy when he needed to be?"

And with that, the last remnants of PC Kidney's fit of zeal left him. "I'm not making any particular point. I'm just saying he was keen on his hobby."

"OK," said Don.

Kidney drained his glass and stood up. "And now, Inspector, if you reckon you can spare me—I'd best be getting on. My shift starts soon."

"Of course," said Don. "And you've got that one-way system to cope with."

After the handshakes, in the car park, Don thanked Kidney for his help.

"No problem," said Kidney. "But understand—if you want to interview me formally, under caution, I will require notice so that I can ensure the attendance of my solicitor and my Federation rep."

"Naturally. Those are your rights."

"Nothing personal, Inspector. It's just that I know from experience that all detectives are untrustworthy bastards."

On the drive south, Don said: "He's a nostalgic, Frank, that's what PC Kidney is at heart. And like most nostalgics, the nostalgia he feels is actually for a time before he was born."

Frank grunted, to signal that he had taken on-board Don's

elegant paradox. The DI appreciated these little touches, Frank had learned.

"It's not so much the comedy with him," Don continued. "That's just to give it a focus. It's really about what he imagines the world was like when his parents were newlyweds. Everybody ate roast beef, nobody spoke foreign, or made strange noises in weird temples. People left their doors unlocked at night, and on those rare occasions when a kid might give cheek to a policeman, the jolly bobby would clip him around the ear hole, and then cycle off home, content in the knowledge that another career in delinquency had been satisfactorily curtailed."

Frank couldn't honestly say he remembered Dick Kidney saying any of that, or even hinting any of it. But as long as Don was enjoying himself, he wasn't going to interfere. *Seems like the art of the monologue is not entirely lost.*

"What Dick and his type conveniently forget, of course, is that back in his Golden Age, most of the country couldn't *afford* roast beef—or parsnips, come to that—and the nineteen forties had just about the highest rate of child murders ever recorded in this country. That's the trouble with the British, Frank. We're very fond of golden ages, but it never seems to occur to us to think that it might be nice to have one ahead of us instead of behind us."

"Right," said Frank, and concentrated on his driving.

About an hour later, Don asked him: "What is an MP3, then? I saw you smirking, you might as well enlighten me."

"You can download speech, songs, music, whatever, and store them on your computer."

"Can you really?" said Don. "Oh well, I was miles off. I thought it was one of those forms we have to fill in when we clip hooligans around the ear hole."

CHAPTER SEVEN

It was early evening by the time they re-entered London, England had lost the cricket, Don had closed his eyes many miles back—though he opened them occasionally to assure Frank that he wasn't sleeping—and Frank himself was trying to work out what he should do.

The thing was, Don had asked Frank to drive him home, so that he could change his shirt. They weren't finished for the day; they'd be working this evening. Fair enough, Frank wasn't bothered by that—he didn't like it, in fact he rather disliked it, his evenings at home with Debbie and Joseph meant a lot to him. But after all, he'd chosen to join CID, knowing full well that the hours were what some of his colleagues called "one-way flexitime"—the one-way being, naturally, the bosses' way.

It wasn't working late that bothered Frank. It was Don; what to do about Don.

The obvious thing to do—since Don didn't have any hot water, for whatever reason—would be for Frank to invite the DI back to his place, where he could have a shower. They could have a sandwich, cup of tea, and get back to work. Heaven's sake, Frank could do with a quick brush-up himself. Driving Don, instead, to a showerless house made no sort of sense. The only problem was . . .

What it was, was that Don hadn't yet visited Frank's place. Never been inside. Never met Debbie, except on the phone, or young Joseph. It'd just never come up. Or, if it had come up, one or the other of them had steered away from it. And the whole thing was starting to prey on Frank's mind. He wasn't sure why exactly, but the longer it went on, the more it seemed to mean. Don not coming to Frank's house was beginning to take on *significance*. Though what it signified—well, Frank had no idea.

He liked to keep his lives separate, as far as possible. Not fanatically, it wasn't an obsession, it was just that work was one thing, and his home—his house, his wife, his kid—they were something else. Couldn't go on forever like this, though. The longer it was before Don's first visit, the bigger a deal the whole thing was going to become. They'd end up with a formal dinner party, all jackets and ties and different wines with each course. It'd be a nightmare. It'd be like a bloody royal visit. And then, it wouldn't stop there: Don would be obliged to ask them to his place in return, and so on and so on forever. They'd never have a night in again as long they lived!

Really, this was the perfect opportunity to break the ice. This wasn't a social thing, that was clear, this was just a sensible convenience.

So. He cleared his throat. "You know what, Don? If you like, we could stop by my place—quick shower, you know, get a sandwich or something."

"No, you're all right, thanks for asking. We haven't really got time. I want to try and do another interview tonight."

"Fine, yeah, sure, no problem, right. If you're sure, you know, but the offer's there."

"I appreciate it, Frank, but better not this time. Another time."

"Right you are. No problem." Frank wasn't sure if he was relieved or not. He wasn't sure how to tell, really. He wasn't used to having things prey on his mind; he wasn't practised in it. Didn't want to be, either.

"Unless," said Don, "obviously, if you need to pick up a—"

"No, no, that's fine—I keep a spare shirt and that in the boot. Overnight bag, you know."

"Very sensible," said Don. "Good thinking."

That's Don, all right, thought Frank; *he thinks an ever-ready bag is an excellent plan, but he wouldn't dream of following it himself.*

As Frank pulled into Don's drive, the DI leapt out of the car. "I won't be a second." He got halfway to the front door, then turned back. "I'm sorry, Frank, I wasn't thinking. You probably want a pee, don't you? Glass of water, whatever."

Frank's discomfort was growing by the second, but the fact was he *did* want both those things. "Thanks, right. I'll just get my bag."

He wasn't going to mention it—if Don didn't offer an answer, Frank wouldn't risk a question—but he couldn't help noticing that there really was almost no furniture in the place.

In turn, the two detectives used the loo, changed their shirts and socks, drank blissfully cold water from the tap. "Right," said Don. "Give Louise Ogden a ring. I feel ready for her, now."

On the way out, Frank paused.

"What?" Don asked.

"Aren't you going to lock it?"

Don shook his head. "Haven't got a key."

What the hell is going on?

"You coming, Frank?"

One small living-room, and—Frank assumed—an even smaller bedroom, made up Louise Ogden's rented Edgware flat, along with a galley kitchen and a bathroom consisting of a shower stall, lavatory, and sink. A glorified bedsit, to be honest, with only a partition wall promoting it to two-room status. Still, these days, even this much space would be expensive beyond a lot of people's reach.

It was untidy—or rather, a bit chaotic, a busy person's place, the home of someone who mostly used it to run in and out, dump stuff, pick stuff up, and occasionally sleep. But only briefly, before rushing off to the next adventure.

Don, perhaps tired from the drive, or the lunchtime beer, had been a bit quiet in the last hour; but he perked up nicely in Ms. Ogden's company. She was, Frank acknowledged, very good-looking. Indian features and colouring, very dark, long hair. Just Don's type—though, to be honest, Frank couldn't imagine many women who wouldn't be.

She opened the door wearing soft Indian trousers, a biker's leather jacket (not for show; the crash helmet, Frank saw, sat on her coffee table), and under the jacket a Sachin Tendulkar t-shirt, bearing a picture of the world's most popular and revered sportsman, the Little Master himself, above the slogan: "Cricket is our religion, Tendulkar is our god."

"Demi-god, perhaps," Don said, as they sat down, with some quite astonishingly bad instant coffee. "But for my money, Rahul Dravid's the backbone of the Indian side."

"I suppose you're right," she agreed, her South London accent strong. "But there's something different about Tendulkar. I visited India last year for the first time, and it's extraordinary—he really *is* like a god over there."

"So I've heard."

"Yeah, but hearing and seeing—believe me, it's two different things. I can't describe it, but if you imagine the most famous footballer in England, or the biggest film star in America, and then—well, I was going to say double it, but really that doesn't get anywhere near." She pushed her hair back with her fingers, and Frank, watching Don out of the corner of his eye, hoped the DI wasn't going to faint. "For instance, half the billboards have got his face on them, half the adverts on TV."

"Well," said Don, "you are talking about a place where you get an audience of a billion for any big game."

"That's right! He's by far the most important person in the country. Inspector—"

"Don."

"Don, I'll tell you, it was so exciting being in a place where cricket *matters*."

"Must be," said Don, with a rueful smile. "If you did a random survey of twelve-year-old boys in this country and asked them who the current England cricket captain was, I wonder how many would be able to tell you?"

She shook her head, sadly—though the bouncing of her hair somewhat undermined the solemnity of the gesture. "Football!" she said. "Soccer has eaten the world, hasn't it? Outside the Indian sub-continent, it's the only sport that matters any more. Bloody stupid game."

Don nodded. "Quite. Any sport which routinely ends without a score after ninety minutes should be banned by parliament. I wouldn't mind, but it's not even as if we're any good at it in this country."

Frank scratched his right wrist with the fingers of his left hand, allowing him to sneak a look at his watch without anyone noticing. He knew how Don operated—talking to people, engaging in apparently irrelevant chat: "the old dialectic." It wasn't even a technique, in all honesty, it was just the way Don was. Fair enough—but it *had* been a long day. Frank was tired, sweaty, hungry, thirsty . . .

"Ah," said Don. "Constable Mitchell's subtle body language is designed to remind me that we are not paid to sit around talking cricket on overtime. I'm afraid we must move on to less delightful matters."

How did he know? Frank resolved not to make that mistake again.

"Oh, yeah—poor old Bruce." Louise Ogden's mouth turned down at the corners, and she shook her head again. This time, her hair stayed still. "It's hard to imagine anyone wanting to kill him. I can't help feeling—I don't know, maybe it was mistaken identity or something?"

"Interesting idea," said Don. "So, if you were going to kill someone at that cricket match, who would it be?"

Frank saw the moment of shock in her face. But she recovered quickly. "I couldn't kill *anyone* at a cricket ground. It'd be sacrilegious."

She offered Don a smile which he returned only briefly.

"Did you know Bruce well?"

"No, not really. Only met him a couple of times, in fact."

"Where did you first meet him?"

"Well," she said. "More coffee?" Both men were quick to assure her that the first cup had met all their immediate caffeine needs. "I'm a freelance studio manager, that's my living, and I've always been interested in old sound recordings."

"You mean like collecting old radio shows?"

"Not exactly. It's not the shows themselves I'm into, it's more the technology. What I do—on the side, I mean, just as a sort of hobby—is I like to track down old recordings, on acetate or tape or whatever, and renovate and preserve them."

"Conservation work," said Don. "Like Save the Whale."

"Just the same," she said, smiling and nodding. "Except nobody harpoons off-air tapes. But what they *do* do to them is bad enough."

"How do you mean?"

75

"Well, I don't know if you've heard about this, but for years and years, well into the nineteen eighties, the BBC—all the broadcasters, but the BBC had most to lose—they used to just junk old recordings to make shelf space for new ones."

"Unbelievable," said Don. "Cultural vandalism."

"You're not kidding! Some of the most famous moments in radio and TV history ended up in skips in BBC car parks. And that's just the stuff we know we lost—imagine all the *obscure* treasures that must have been lost forever."

"Terrible," said Don. "So, through this you met—"

"Sorry, yes—I got side-tracked. Bruce Lester. Well, he phoned me a couple of months ago—"

"Sorry," said Frank, "how did he get your number?"

"Oh, I don't know—someone in comedy fandom, presumably. Maybe Bernie Ponting or Dick Kidney, I know both of them quite well and I think they were friends of Bruce's."

"Right. So, Bruce rang you . . . ?"

"Yes, he wanted to know if I'd heard a rumour about a lost Robb Wilton recording that was supposed to have turned up in someone's attic."

"And had it?"

She shrugged. "Not that I knew of. But that sort of thing does happen, it's not uncommon. That's the great irony of it, you see. The BBC got rid of all this priceless stuff, and now they're running around the world, desperately trying to get it back—mostly, from listeners who illegally taped it off-air years ago!"

"Of course," said Don, "it's all MP3s these days, isn't it?"

"Um—yes." Ogden seemed to have lost her place. "Sorry, what was the question?"

"You've answered it," said Don. "Tell me, how did you get into all this? Have you always been a comedy fan?"

"I'm not, especially. I got into fandom through an old boyfriend. To be frank, I find all that fan stuff a bit—dull, really. Most of these old comics they go on about, my *mother* wasn't born when they were famous! But my boyfriend, my ex-boyfriend, was very into it, and I soon realised it overlapped very well with my interest in conserving old audio stuff."

"Do you sell the tapes you restore?" Frank asked.

"Oh, no." She looked away. "That would be illegal."

Frank wasn't convinced by her denial, but a slight shake of the head from Don told him that it wasn't a matter they were interested in pursuing. "So it's just a hobby?"

"Yeah, that's about it. It puts my professional skills to good use. I enjoy the challenge—the technical challenge, you know? People bring me some grotty old bit of reel-to-reel, and I fix it up. It's like magic."

"Do you do the work here?" Don asked, looking around at the tiny flat.

"Oh no! No, I rely on the generosity of my employers." She smiled, exposing her lower teeth: *aren't I a naughty girl?*

"Ah," said Don. "Not that they are necessarily aware of how generous they are, right? And when you're not restoring crackly old tapes, you're playing cricket."

"Not as often as I'd like. I belong to a few teams—you know, pub sides and so on. But not everybody's cool about having a woman behind the stumps."

"You don't play for any women's teams?"

She made a scornful noise with her lips. "I'm not really interested in women's cricket."

Thinks she's too good for it, Frank decided; *and maybe she's right.*

"How did you get called up for the Comedians' team?"

"I think it was through Dick. Dick Kidney, yeah? He knew that Declan was looking for a wicketkeeper." She made an apologetic face at Don. "No offence, not being ageist, but wicketkeepers need to be young, to have young knees—all that crouching. Apparently the last bloke they had, he got down all right, but he couldn't get back up!"

"Dear oh dear," said Don. "Geriatric bloke, was he? Over thirty?"

His tone, Frank noted, was more flirtatious than sarcastic. Louise Ogden evidently picked up the same message, as she giggled. "I'm not saying he was old, Don, just that he was old for a keeper. The other side's keeper, on Saturday, he was only in his early thirties, maybe thirty-five, but he was having a lot of trouble dealing with their skipper's bowling."

"Eddie Tarr? He's quick, is he?"

"He is quick, actually. Though I wouldn't say it to his face—he fancies himself quite enough as it is."

"I have to ask you the obvious question, Louise," said Don. "Do you have any idea who might have killed Bruce Lester? I know you've already said you can't imagine a motive, but—"

"Well, that's right—I mean, Bruce? You know, he's just not the type to get himself killed. Unless it was a mugging, or something. He was just a really sweet bloke."

"Sweet?"

"Yeah! You know, he was sort of . . . chivalrous. Like I said, I didn't really know him, but that's how he struck me. Kind. A gentleman."

"And as far as you know, he hasn't had any disagreements, however minor, with anyone who was at the match?"

She looked away; Frank followed her unfocussed gaze, to a poster on the wall: "Free the Miami Five." She saw him looking, gave him a small smile, then turned back to Don, and said firmly: "No. He seemed to get on with everyone."

"All that talk of India," said Don, as they walked back to

the car, "made me hungry. You up for an Indian, Frank?"

Frank took a bit of persuading, but Don persisted. It was all too easy, as he knew as well as anyone, to neglect mealtimes when you worked CID hours. He had a responsibility to ensure that the lad ate properly. Surely that was included in the Detective Inspectors' Mission Statement? If not, it bloody should be. Besides—no fun eating curry on your own.

"Come on, mate—my shout, I'm buying."

"Well . . ." said Frank, looking at his watch.

Him and his watch! He was in danger of developing a full-blown neurosis there. "I'm only thinking of Debbie. And Joe, he'll be asleep, won't he? They'll both be asleep, most likely. You don't want to wake them up, do you, banging around in the kitchen, the fridge door opening and closing, the whoosh of the gas as the kettle goes on . . ."

"All right, all right," said Frank. "Have to be quick, mind."

Quick, indeed! That was the trouble with this country—everybody ate their meals as if they were taking part in speed trials. You wouldn't get Italian detectives bolting their food. Or French. Or Indian, for that matter.

Don prided himself on knowing most of the Indian restaurants within an hour's drive of . . . well, of wherever he happened to be. And tonight, he knew just the place.

It was quite a large restaurant, and Don visited it as often as he could—partly because the food was sensational, and partly because, due to the place's location, a damaging distance away from the nearest pub, cinema, or office block, it never seemed to be more than a quarter full. Great chefs deserved full houses, and Don was intent on doing his bit to support the culinary arts.

The waiters knew the DI, and showed him to a secluded table far from both the kitchen and the lavatories. He ordered

Indian beer and two kinds of *poppadum,* and then began to study the menu in earnest. Frank read his menu for precisely twenty-two seconds, and then put it aside. *Better nip that in the bud,* Don told himself.

"Look, this is my treat, Frank, all right? I'll order for both of us, yeah? You won't be sorry."

Frank shrugged. "Sure."

Ten minutes passed, during which Don made notes on a paper napkin. Eventually, he called the waiter over. "Listen, you haven't got it listed here, but could the chef possibly do us some *matar kofta?*"

The waiter smiled and dipped his head. "Of course, of course. No trouble. Anything you don't see, I told you before, you just ask."

"Excellent," said Don, rubbing his hands. "In that case, one *matar kofta,* please, one *Kashmiri alu dam,* a *dal sag,* and a *sambhar,* some of those mushrooms—the ones I had before?"

"Of course."

"Lovely. One *muttor panir,* some spicy cauliflower, I can't remember what it's called . . ."

"Yes, *gobi kari.*" The waiter turned to a fresh page in his notebook.

Don ordered a few more dishes, and then turned his attention to sundry breads, chutneys, and rice. And two more beers.

"One more, thanks," said Frank, pointing to his car keys. "And some water."

The meal arrived with impressive rapidity—even the customised items. "There you are, Frank—fast food doesn't have to be made from factory floor sweepings."

"Bloody hell," said Frank, as two waiters covered the table with a succession of steaming, and in some cases sizzling, metal vessels. "Are we expecting company?"

Don inhaled, then stretched his neck to another area of the table and inhaled again. "You're going to enjoy this, Frank. Lentils, mushrooms, fried pea balls, spinach . . . where's the *aloo sag?*"

"You've not ordered any meat, then?"

Here we go. Don folded his arms on the table, and prepared to enlighten the youngster. "Let me guess—you're a chicken tikka man?"

"Tandoori lamb, mostly."

"Whatever. The point is, Frank, you don't sit in a high class Indian restaurant like this and order meat."

"Why? What's wrong with the meat?"

"Nothing's *wrong* with it, Frank! But you wouldn't go into a French place and order roast beef, would you?"

"Well . . ."

"Course you bloody wouldn't! And if you were in a restaurant called—I don't know—the Stars and Stripes, you wouldn't ask for a quiche, would you? You'd have steak, and ribs and . . . well, more steak and . . . and . . ."

"Potato skins," said Frank.

"What?"

"Potato skins. American delicacy, I believe."

"Potato *skins?* No, no, Frank—you've got that wrong. What do they do with the rest of the potato, build houses out of it?"

"Served with sour cream, apparently," said Frank.

Oh, well, thought Don, *no point arguing with him when he gets a bee in his bonnet like this. He'll only turn pouty.* "Have it your own way, Frank—my point is, when in Rome eat spaghetti. This is one of the oldest, most elaborate, subtlest cuisines in the world, and it's based on vegetables and pulses. Not bloody chicken."

It took almost as long to serve themselves from all the

small dishes as it had for the food to be cooked. It was worth it, though—the sheer range of tastes and textures, colours and aromas, singly and in combination, had Don uncertain whether to eat the food or kneel before it in respect. At first, he tried to infect Frank with his enthusiasm—"Try a bit of that, you've never had aubergine like this before"—but all the DC ever said in response was, "Aye, very nice," so after a while, Don gave up.

There was far too much food, as it turned out—no doubt because Frank wasn't eating his proper share. "If I'd known you were on a diet, I'd have taken you somewhere expensive."

"No, no," said Frank, "it's all very nice. Just a bit filling."

Over a cup of aniseed tea, once the plates had been cleared away—Don had decided against *halva* or *barfi*, because if there was one thing he wasn't, it was a glutton—Don lit a small cigar, and said: "Well, do we have any idea at all why Bruce might have been murdered, early days though it is?"

"Well," Frank replied after, Don noted with approval, a considerable pause for thought, "I suppose we can say there's three areas where a motive might arise."

"Go on."

"Right. There's comedy fandom, cricket and—well . . ." He shrugged, and added: "The rest of his life."

"Yes, good summary. I don't think it's the cricket. We're agreed that the cricket match was simply an opportunity for the killer?"

"In which case, I'd go for the 'rest of life' category—broad though it is."

"You don't fancy fandom?"

Frank grimaced. "I know what you always say, Don—nothing's too slight a motive for murder—but we haven't really seen any boiling passions so far, have we? Just a bunch of pretty harmless hobbyists."

Don signalled for the bill. "Fair enough. We'll see if we can get some boils out of the rest of our party." He paid at the till, to save the waiter's feet, having left a fiver at the table for a tip. Indian food, even of this quality, was so absurdly cheap; he shuddered to guess what the wages were like.

Next to the till sat a bowl of cardamom pods, to aid digestion and sweeten the breath. Don's digestion required no assistance—his stomach was as happy as a sleeping cat—but the seeds of the pungent spice left a perfect final taste in his mouth, as he chewed on them during the walk back to the car.

"Must do this more often, Frank. Most enjoyable."

"Yes," said Frank. "Thanks very much. Very nice."

Very nice! Miserable little bugger, thought Don. *I just hope he's in a better mood tomorrow.*

CHAPTER EIGHT

"Where do we keep the mouthwash? It isn't in the bathroom cabinet."

"Mouthwash?" Debbie put a bowl of instant porridge in the microwave and set the timer. "I don't think we've got any. Put it on the shopping list if you like. What do you want it for?"

Frank cupped his hands over his mouth and nose and exhaled. "I can still taste that curry."

"That's not bad breath—that's indigestion."

"I don't usually get indigestion from Indian food."

"You don't usually eat that much Indian food. Or any food." The microwave pinged. Debbie took out the bowl, stirred the porridge, and reset the oven. "Certainly not at that time of night."

"I know." Frank sipped his second cup of tea, checked the time on the kitchen clock: no hurry. Sit down and drink his tea slowly, that'd sort out any indigestion. "I had to eat it, Debbie. I had to eat my share—Don would have been really offended if I hadn't. There was enough left over to make a takeaway for two, as it was."

Debbie giggled, and Joseph joined in. "You'll have to go down the police gym and develop your stomach muscles. Your belly's not big enough to cope with CID portions."

"You're not wrong."

The phone on the wall rang. Mr. and Mrs. Mitchell exchanged glances. The microwave pinged again, and

Master Mitchell said, "Orridge."

"Frank—don't pick me up at home today."

"Right you are. Any particular reason?"

"Because I'm not *at* home, so it would be a futile exercise. Even by police standards."

Frank mouthed to Debbie: *He's not sounding too good.* Debbie rubbed her stomach and mimed an immense belch. Joseph laughed so hard porridge came out of his nose.

"Where shall I meet you then?"

"Hampstead Heath."

Frank waited. In vain. "Could you be a bit more specific, sir? The Heath's a big place."

"All right, hold on." The phone line transmitted traffic sounds for a few moments, then Don was back on: "Junction of East Heath Road and Well Walk. Do you know it?"

"I can find it."

"Right. Quick as you can."

"Hampstead Heath?" said Debbie.

"Orridge," said Joseph.

Frank shrugged, and gulped the last of his tea. "Don't ask me."

Sitting on a bench, his back to "the lungs of London," Don was unshaven, wearing a linen jacket with no tie. If it wasn't such a ridiculous idea, Frank might almost have thought that the DI had slept the night here. He took his time getting out of the car, trying to work out a suitably neutral greeting. In the end, he settled for "Morning, sir. Have you had breakfast? I'm sure there's a café—"

"Breakfast? Frank, we're working on a murder inquiry. If you want to have breakfast I suggest you do it in your own time."

"Yes sir."

Don wanted to interview "the Yank," but didn't have his mobile phone with him. Frank had his, of course—but then he'd spent the night at home, whereas . . . *No, no: best not to follow that thought.*

"Hello, Mr. Marsh, this is Detective Constable Frank Mitchell of Cowden CID. DI Packham and myself would like to talk to you about . . . That's right, yes . . . Absolutely, yes, we wondered whether it would be possible to . . . Yes, that'd be perfect. Will you be at your home address, or . . . I see. Yes, I see, no that'd be fine . . . Absolutely . . . Yes, I know it—we'll be there in just a few minutes. Yes, that's right . . . Yes, thank you, Mr. Marsh, we'll see you shortly."

"Well?" said Don.

"Yes, he's available to see us right now. In fact—"

"At home?"

"No, sir—Hampstead Heath."

Don's irritation expressed itself through a baring of his teeth and a closing of his eyes. "Not *us*, Frank—Jerry Marsh, where is Jerry Marsh?"

"Hampstead Heath, sir. As it happens—"

"Frank! Why do you keep waffling on about Hampstead bleeding Heath?"

"Because," said Frank, slowly and with some force, "Jerry Marsh is, at this moment, waiting for us at Whitestone Pond."

"Whitestone Pond? The Whitestone Pond that's by Hampstead Heath?"

"That's the one, sir."

"But that's only a couple of minutes away."

"Quite, sir. So we'll leave the car here, shall we?"

Seeing Jerry Marsh in men's clothing for the first time, Frank decided that he didn't look much like an American; too thin. Whether or not he looked like a comedian, Frank wasn't sure. He was young, maybe mid-twenties, but that didn't mean anything these days—the middle-aged gag-crackers who'd dominated TV comedy in Frank's early childhood were long gone. The lack of hair helped; gave him a bit of distinction.

"You're not working today, Mr. Marsh?" In fact, *Mister* Marsh—Americans liked formality, they didn't go in for the first-names-with-strangers thing like the British; Frank'd read that somewhere—Mr. Marsh didn't look too well today. A bit pale, a bit drawn.

"No, well, I'm a comedian—not much call for morning comedy, people seem to associate comedy with the hours of darkness. Don't know why. Like sex."

For a horrible moment, Frank thought that was a question. "I—right. You're working tonight, are you?"

"Matter of fact, yes. Got a little gig at a pub in Kilburn."

From his beaming smile, it was obvious that this was a matter of great delight to the young comic, so Frank congratulated him.

"Thanks! I am pretty pleased, I must admit."

"Can't be that easy, getting work in a foreign country?"

"Well, you know, I've only been living here a short while. Nobody knows me in London. Not that I was exactly on the cover of *Time* magazine back home, but I'd built up a bit of a circuit at least over the last few years."

"And where is home?"

Before Marsh could reply, Don—who had been sitting silently beside Frank on a wooden bench, staring into the water of the man-made pond—got up, and began to stroll around the pond's perimeter. Marsh watched him for a moment, then asked Frank: "That guy—he is with you, right?"

Frank said "Yes," and didn't enlarge.

"OK," said Marsh, with another big smile.

He seemed a friendly guy. Frank wasn't an idiot, he knew that these casual American smiles didn't really mean anything—they probably smiled as they mugged you, over there—but even so: at least they made the effort. They must find the British very surly by contrast.

"I'm originally from Iowa—a real small town, you wouldn't have heard of it. Not many people in Iowa have heard of it. But recently, I've been living in Los Angeles."

"What made you move to Britain?"

"Ah, you know—I don't know. This and that."

No smile now, Frank noted. And the American was definitely trembling, slightly. It certainly wasn't from the cold; probably a hangover—must be a lot of late nights in his business. "Such as?"

"Well, my wife's English, I guess she was missing the old country. So, you know, we thought maybe we'd try it over here for a couple of years. See how it goes."

"Bit of a risk with your career, I'd have thought?"

"Not necessarily. There's a *lot* of comedy over here. Seems to me it's your biggest industry! Radio, TV, stand-up—the radio scene particularly, is easily the biggest in the world. Lot of opportunities in radio here."

There's something else. Frank was as sure as he could be that there was another reason for the move to London. He ought to pursue it; Don would have, if he was up to it. He wasn't sure how, though, so instead he said: "So, tell me, what do you find is the worst thing about living in London?"

Marsh looked serious. "In fact? *That.* Negativity. At first I thought it was modesty, but I'm beginning to think it's almost the opposite. British people—I mean, some British people seem to take a pride in . . . I don't know . . ."

"Being negative."

"Yeah, listen—you're trying to investigate a murder, you don't want to hear some guy who's only been in town ten minutes shooting his mouth off!"

"No, I know what you mean. We do enjoy complaining in this country." Something Frank had seen on a nostalgia documentary a while ago came back to him. "There was a catchphrase during the war, from a radio comedy programme, as it happens: 'It's being so cheerful as keeps me going.' "

"Yeah?"

"Yeah, but the joke was, it was always said in a really miserable voice."

"Right! I like it. No, all I meant was—if you'd been the visitor, and we'd been in America, the question would have been what do you like *best*."

"Which is?"

"Oh, man—lots of things. The general atmosphere, for one thing. So cosmopolitan, so mixed. And it's a lot more relaxed over here. Fewer rules, less formality."

"Than L.A.?"

He shrugged. "Well—than where I grew up, certainly. And people earn more, work shorter hours, take longer vacations. More importantly from my point of view, in comedy there are far fewer taboos—in fact, I haven't discovered *anything* yet that you can't make jokes about in this country."

"I suppose that's true." *Not sure it'd be on my list of the Top Ten best things about the UK, but . . .*

"And since you ask, the *worst* worst thing about London is real estate prices—I guess that's down to population density, it's so incredibly high compared to the US, but the price of a tiny flat here would buy you a decent spread where I come from."

"I know," said Frank, with deep feeling. "It's awful, isn't it? And it's getting worse."

"I mean—the equivalent of half a million bucks, for some little place? And that's not for a palace, that's just a family home, miles away from the city centre!"

"I know. There's people with good jobs, decent wages, can't even get a toe on the property ladder. It can't go on forever, but there doesn't seem—"

"Oh, and the showers."

"The showers?" Frank would quite happily have talked about house prices for the rest of the morning. On showers, by contrast, he had no firm opinion.

"There's this thing called *water pressure?* I can only think it's considered vulgar over here. But hey, who cares—I'm getting used to taking *baaaths* like a proper Brit."

Don, having completed his circuit of Whitestone Pond, arrived back at his starting point. Jerry Marsh smiled at him. "Hi, how you doing? Nice spot this, isn't it? We were just talking about—"

"How well did you know Bruce Lester?"

"Ah—Bruce? OK, right. Not well at all, really. I just met him for the first time on Saturday."

"The day he died," said Don, looking right into Marsh's eyes from close range.

Marsh took a half-step backwards. "Right, right. Maybe had one conversation with him, that's all."

"About what?"

"About cricket."

"Cricket?" said Don. "That's a subject you know a bit about, is it?"

This time, and despite the sneer on Don's face and in his voice, Marsh stood his ground. "I'm not an expert, Inspector, but I do follow the game."

"Really? You've got into it very quickly, haven't you?"

"In fact, no, I started following it in the US." This time,

Frank thought, Marsh's smile was less innocent. "Take a guess, Inspector, how many cricket clubs you think there are in the USA?"

"At a *guess*," said Don, "I'd say roughly none."

"Well, there you go, you see—you'd be wrong. There are about six hundred."

"Six *hundred?*"

"Sure. You know, depending on how you do the math, you could argue that the US is the tenth biggest cricketing nation."

"How long has this been going on?" Don demanded—sounding, to Frank's ears, considerably more like a policeman than he usually did.

"Cricket in America? Since the eighteenth century. Matter of fact, the first international sporting fixture in the modern world was the annual Canada vs. USA cricket match. And you know why the head of state in the US is called the President? Because John Adams, who was a keen cricketer, said if it was good enough for cricket clubs, it was good enough for the new republic."

"So," said Frank, "you played cricket in Iowa?"

Marsh held up his hands, as if in surrender. "Admittedly, there's not a *lot* of cricket in the Midwest. There's some, but it's mostly in the major cities. Especially New York. Also, Silicon Valley—anywhere where there's a lot of immigrants from the Indian subcontinent. But it also has quite a following among young black men in L.A. You ever hear of that cricket team out of Compton? Made up of ex-gang members, homeless men, run by a social worker."

"No, I don't think so."

"Well, they toured the UK a while back. See, cricket has an appeal because it's seen as a black man's sport—it isn't owned by the white corporations."

"Is that how you got into it?" Don asked.

Marsh's smile was bigger than ever; not only did he refuse to take offence, but he was, Frank reckoned, pleased to have prompted such a reaction from the DI. "No, with me it was working in showbiz—on the fringes, in my case, but in that whole industry there's a lot of ex-pat Brits and Aussies. Some of my friends began to get interested in cricket, too. Few years ago, there was a bit of disillusionment with baseball, people felt it'd become too commercialised, lost touch with its roots. Cricket's attractive because it seems still to have some sense of the importance of doing things the right way."

"What," said Frank, "even after the events of recent years?"

"You put enough money into a sport, you'll get corruption. That's a given. But yeah, even so, there's something about cricket . . . you know that quote from CLR James? 'What does he know of cricket, who only cricket knows?' It's more *connected* than other sports."

"So you're an ex-baseball fan?" Don asked.

Marsh shrugged. "Still am a fan, I guess."

"Do you play baseball much?"

The customary smile was replaced by a frown—of irritation or of puzzlement, Frank couldn't tell. "Baseball? No, I don't play baseball."

"You've played it in the past, I suppose? You must have played at school."

"Well, you know, there were a lot of sports on offer at my high school—American football, soccer, basketball, track, you know . . ."

"And which did you prefer?" asked Don. Frank understood his persistence on this point: the fact that the murder weapon was a baseball bat had not been released to the press, on the off-chance that the perpetrator wouldn't realise it had been found, and so would be more careless about disposing of evidence linking him to it. Unlikely to work, but standard procedure. The police were pursuing various means of trying to trace the ownership of the bat, on the working assumption that it had been brought into the pavilion in a cricket bag. All the suspects would be asked if they'd agree to having their fingerprints taken, for elimination purposes. Any who refused would soon learn that "voluntary" doesn't mean the same as "avoidable."

Jerry Marsh spread his hands. "I was never what you could call a jock. Hey, I was on the debate team, though—taught me everything I know about how to time a line."

They weren't going to get anywhere on that, Frank reckoned—and, as Don seemed to have lost interest again, he decided to bring the interview back on track.

"So you only met Bruce that once, and the only thing you talked about was cricket?"

"Pretty much. I mean—I don't know, the weather, maybe. Nothing of consequence."

"Did he seem nervous to you, or worried, or anything like that?"

"No, not that I could tell. Except—yeah, I got the impression he was a bit nervous about batting. Especially against Eddie Tarr—he's quite a useful quick bowler; gets it up above eighty mph a fair bit."

"And how did you come to be on the cricket team?"

"Oh, that was Declan. We were on the same bill not long ago—my first gig in London, in fact—and he was checking the cricket scores on Teletext. So we got chatting about cricket, and he said did I fancy a game."

"Which you did."

The smile returned to Jerry Marsh's face. "Sure. I didn't

think it was the time to mention that I'm a cricket *fan,* not a cricket player."

"I see," said Don. "But you were willing to play the part of a *jock* on this occasion?"

Marsh made a sheepish face. "Listen, Inspector—you know what the secret of good comedy is?"

Don began to say, *Timing,* but only got as far as the first syllable, before Marsh interrupted him.

"Networking."

CHAPTER NINE

"Like this," said Don, taking a couple of hopping steps forward, pointing his left elbow down the hill, then wheeling his right arm past his ear. "You never see anyone doing that any more, do you?"

"Not really," Frank agreed. Having finished, for now, with Jerry Marsh, they were walking down Heath Street towards Hampstead High Street, in search of a cup of something.

"When I was a kid," said Don, "every schoolboy in the country used to do that all the time, from spring until autumn." It was true, Don thought; Frank was wearing a fixed smile, clearly embarrassed to see his senior officer engaging in bowling practice in public, but it was true. Dawdling along a corridor between lessons, jogging up to join the lunch queue, walking to the bus stop at the end of the day. Coming out of morning assembly: that was what Don remembered the most. A great mass of boys, pouring out of the school gym, and every single one of them delivering an imaginary cricket ball at an imaginary wicket. Unsynchronised, of course; it was more or less an involuntary action. What must it have looked like, from afar or above? The teachers would occasionally call out a *Mind what you're doing, boy!* or a *Keep moving, there!* but they couldn't really complain, because they'd all done it themselves in their day.

But you never saw it now. Perhaps if you went to a school where most of the kids were Asian—well, maybe. More likely, they'd all have mobile phones clamped to their ears, or they'd be pecking away at handheld computer games.

"Of course, this was back when a quiche was still a flan. Didn't you do it when you were a lad, Frank?"

"I don't remember, really. It was more of a football area, where I was."

"Newcastle? Yes, I suppose it would be. Here we are—coffee shop."

Coffee shop! Whatever happened to cafés? These horrible coffee shop chains—American, or even worse, fake American—they were just cafés with bumped-up prices, designed to take money off people who couldn't even quench their thirst without permission from a style guru.

Frank was looking at a menu. A bloody *menu* of different types of coffee! Don wasn't fooled—it all came out of the same tin, everybody knew that.

"Right," said Frank, "I think I'll have a—"

"The emperor is naked," Don interrupted. "Yes please, love—one coffee and one tea, please," he told a thin girl with a big earring in her lower lip.

She slumped one hip and one shoulder, narrowed her eyes, and opened her mouth. Don knew what she was going to say: did he want mocha, latte, espresso, rumbaba, tutti-frutti, zigga-zag-hey . . . she was going to run through the lexicon of dragooned hipness. But he also knew how to deal with these people.

The girl's eyes met his. She hesitated, and was lost.

That's all it takes. Keep the smile rigid, the eyes unblinking, show them you're not afraid. And aim to convey just the *tiniest* hint that you are not wholly unfamiliar with the inside of a psych ward. It never fails.

"One coffee, one tea," the girl mumbled.

"Lovely."

"Three pounds eighty."

Don blinked. "Three pounds eighty?"

"Three pounds eighty."

"Have you got a knife?" said Don. "I thought I might just cut out one of my kidneys and give you that, instead."

Frank leant past him, holding out a five-pound note. "This is on me."

At the table, Frank was quiet, and Don hoped he wasn't still sulking about whatever it was he'd been sulking about last night. "Coffee all right?"

"Fine, thanks," said Frank. "How's the tea?"

Don looked at the small cup of tepid, greyish liquid, with the tea bag still in it, its string hanging over the rim. "I'm sure it will be absolutely delicious."

He began patting his pockets until he found what he was after: breakfast. He'd only taken one sizeable bite from the Mars Bar when an officious young man who was entirely hairless other than an almost microscopic goatee bustled over.

"Sir, sorry, you can't eat that in here."

"Why not?"

The man put his hands on his hips. "Well, you didn't buy it here, did you? How would you like it if—"

Don crammed the entire remaining portion of the Mars Bar into his mouth, shoved the wrapper down the front of his trousers, and grinned at the goatee boy, widely and brownly. "Can't eat *what* in here?" he said, with—he flattered himself—excellent diction, given the circumstances.

The man twisted his mouth in disgust, and flounced off.

"I'll tell you right now," said Don, after a few hearty swallows, "you're leaving a tip over my dead body."

"Right," said Frank.

"Now then. What do you reckon, have we met the murderer yet?"

"We've met all of them, haven't we? The suspects."

Don chuckled. "Yes, fair point." He was feeling quite cheerful, really. That long walk last night had blown some of the cobwebs away, as he'd hoped it would. He was dying for a decent cup of tea, but the chocolate bar had been most enjoyable. "All right then, different question: do we have a sense of the *shape* of the case?"

Frank looked a bit blank—but as if he was trying. That was fine; that was all Don asked. That people at least tried. "What I mean is—the dynamics of the group. What is the centre of this group of people? Is the victim at the centre?"

Frank sipped his coffee. "Not much at the centre, as far as I can see. It's a pretty loose group, isn't it? Half of them don't know each other well at all."

"True."

"Inasmuch as they have a centre, I suppose it's the Irish comedian, Declan Donohue."

Excellent! "Not Bruce Lester?"

Frank shook his head. "Doesn't seem like it, does it? Declan seems to be the only one who's connected to all of them."

"OK," said Don. "I think you're right. So—give him a bell. Find out where he is, and tell him we're on our way round to see him now."

Frank checked the number in his notebook, and keyed it into his mobile, while Don played with the string of his tea bag. He could tell from Frank's end of the conversation that Donohue wasn't as keen to see them as they were to see him.

"What?" said Don.

Frank moved the phone away from his mouth and hissed: "He says can it wait?"

Don snatched the phone. "Of course it can't bloody wait! We're investigating a murder. State your location immediately. Right." He gave Frank his phone back. "Looks like we might get some lunch, after all."

Despite the giant screen TV, currently tuned to a one-day domestic cricket match, the suburban pub in Cowden wasn't busy. Not surprising, thought Don—who had time to drink beer and watch cricket on a Tuesday morning? Apart from comedians and coppers, obviously.

Declan Donohue was in a ringside seat, drinking lager. Don's already less than elevated opinion of him dipped further: an Irishman drinking lager instead of stout! Disgraceful. Don loudly ordered, and then ostentatiously savoured, a pint of draught Guinness. And a fruit juice for Frank. A yellow fruit juice.

Donohue didn't acknowledge the arrival of the detectives—even when Don had gestured at him, to ask if he wanted a refill, the comedian had looked straight through him—but as they pulled up chairs to join him in the TV area, the cricket broke for a furniture advert, fronted by a lumpy Scots comic in his late twenties.

"He stole most of his act from me," Donohue informed them, without taking his eyes off the screen.

"Really?" said Don.

"Oh yeah. That stuff with the curtain? I was doing that five years ago."

Yes, thought Don, *and Morecambe and Wise were doing it thirty years ago.* To be fair, though, the ad was quite funny. Not that you'd know it from watching Donohue's reaction; beyond a slight nod of acknowledgement at the punch line, he didn't so much as crease his cheeks. *Why do humourless people become comics*, Don wondered; *was it the same rogue gene that turned child-haters into schoolteachers?*

The game resumed on the TV—with three consecutive boundaries off a man recently promoted in the press as England's next strike bowler—and the Irishman's eyes still hadn't strayed from the screen.

"Right, Declan—how did you first meet Bruce Lester?"

And *still* the bloody eyes didn't move! "When I first relocated over here, my then-agent thought it would be a good idea for me to attend a convention of comedy fans."

"And was it? A good idea?"

"If you like spending a whole day with a load of pathetic fans, clutching carrier bags and getting orgasmic over fifty-year-old copies of the *Radio Times*, and you don't mind not getting paid for it—yeah, brilliant idea."

"You're not a comedy fan yourself?" Frank asked.

Donohue snorted. "Hobbies are for people who haven't got lives."

Or, thought Don, *they're for people who take an interest in life.* "But you got on all right with Bruce?"

"He wasn't as mad as most of them, I suppose."

"You wouldn't say you became friends, then?"

Still engrossed in the cricket—or else still trying to display such an engrossment—Donohue shrugged. The question, his shoulders said, was an irrelevant one.

"So how did he become your accountant?"

Ah-ha! Eye contact, at last. "I think it was his idea, far as I remember. He was probably thrilled at the idea of having a client who was in the business, you know. Being a fan."

"Or to put it another way," Don translated, "he did your books on the cheap. Yeah?"

Donohue's gaze drifted back to the match. "His fees weren't as excessive as most."

"Are your accounts complex?"

Donohue busied himself draining his glass. "How should I know? That's what I pay an accountant for."

He stood up, squeezed past them, and headed to the bar to buy himself a drink. Himself, only; he didn't offer to get one for the detectives.

"Not short of a bob or two," said Frank, watching Donahue peel a tenner of a fat roll of banknotes.

"Possibly. Could just be that he doesn't trust banks."

"Hello, he's dropped one," Frank said, as the comic bent down to pluck a piece of paper off the floor.

"No, he hasn't. Too small for a banknote." Don laughed and shook his head. "Bet you anything that was a receipt."

"Receipt for what? You don't get a receipt for a pint of lager."

"Receipt for anything," said Don. "Doesn't matter what for—I reckon he collects them." Frank still looked blank, so Don added: "So he can claim them as expenses against taxes. Most people don't bother with receipts, do they? They just litter them. So, you pick up one for, say, thirty quid's worth of petrol, and bung it in with yours when you're doing your tax return."

Even before Donohue had resumed his seat, Don attacked him with another question. "Why did you call him up for the game on Saturday?"

"Him?"

"Bruce Lester."

"Oh, right. I don't know, we were short of players. That fixture's been running for years, but these days it's hard to find proper players. Not like the bloody football game, they all turn out for that."

"Yes," said Don. "Taking over the world, isn't it? Soccer. Just wait until the Indians get into it."

"Nah," said Donohue. "If you ask me, the soccer craze has

peaked. It's not as fashionable as it was even a year ago. Over-kill, yeah? Overexposure."

"I hope you're right." Donahue was still transfixed by the TV. *How can anyone who loves cricket be so bloody rude? It's not as if he's an Australian.* Without trying to disguise what he was doing, Don shifted his chair so that he was between the comic and the screen. "You couldn't get enough writers and comics to make up the teams, so you decided to rope in some fans."

"Sure."

"But why Bruce? Was he a keen cricketer?"

"Not as far as I know. Tell you the truth, I only rang him because he was someone I knew who knew a lot of fans. Asked him if he could suggest a couple of names."

"And he suggested himself?"

"I should have known he would." Donohue's curled lip expressed his opinion of Bruce Lester's pathetic eagerness to mingle with his idols.

"But it was definitely down to you that he took part in the game—it's because of *you* that he was there?"

"If you want to put it like that."

"Therefore, if you'd wanted to arrange an opportunity to kill him, this would have been a good time to do it."

That remark, apparently, was worth taking one's eyes off the action for—at least, briefly. "Oh, do yourself a favour, In-spector! Why would I want to kill him?"

"Well, at the moment, Declan, we can't see why anyone would want to kill him. That's the thing. Can you?"

Declan Donohue, straining his neck just slightly to see past the DI's head, swore at something he'd just seen on the giant screen. "See, England are never going to get into the big time in international cricket until county bowlers learn how to bowl aggressively for more than one over at a time. You don't catch the Aussies going all defensive like that, just when the opposition's starting to hurt."

"You reckon?"

"Bloody basic, that is."

Don stood, and put his hands on his hips, making himself as big a visual anti-aid as possible. "Do you know, or can you guess, why someone might want to kill your accountant, Declan?"

"No." Deprived of his cricket, Donohue crossed his arms, then uncrossed them and drank some lager. "Dull little man—surely you've got to be at least a *bit* interesting to get yourself murdered?"

"He didn't have any hidden side to his life, as far as you know?"

"I doubt it."

"What about his wife?" said Don. "Have you met her?"

"Yeah, I think so, once or twice."

"And what do you make of her?"

"I don't make anything of her."

"What do you mean—she was as dull as him?"

Donohue thought about it, but not much, and his reply when it came was as dismissive as anything they'd heard him say so far. "I mean that he was my accountant—and she wasn't. That's all I know about her."

Though he was glad to see Don so obviously back in charge of the investigation, so energised again, Frank couldn't help feeling, as they walked back to the car, that the DI was running ahead of himself a little.

"I still don't see that we've got a motive for him."

"Money," said Don.

"Has he got any money? I mean, sure, comedy is a big business these days, but Declan Donohue's just an up-and-comer, he's not a star."

Don was hearing no cavillations. "His accounts, Frank—we've got to see about getting a look at his accounts."

Frank could just imagine how such a request would go down with the superintendent. "But on what grounds? OK, so you reckon he's fiddling his taxes, bumping up his expenses with receipts for stuff he hasn't bought. But we've still got the same problem, there's not enough money involved to make it worth killing for. Surely?"

"Comedians," Don said, "are notoriously tight-fisted as a breed. They're always being done for tax evasion."

"But Donohue hasn't been done for tax evasion, has he? You're talking about comedians who earn a fortune."

"Only a matter of time," Don insisted. "Here we have someone who collects abandoned till receipts, *and* a comic who hires a comedy fan on the cheap to do his books. I'm not saying he's a big-time crook, what I am saying is that he is *mean.*"

The greatest sin imaginable, Frank knew, to someone as recklessly generous as Don Packham. "But lots of people are—"

"I mean *really* mean. Ingrained in the psyche. Clinically tight. Unable to help himself, forced by his nature to fiddle every available penny—even if it is only pennies. For all we know, he might have killed Bruce just so he didn't have to pay his accountancy bill."

They reached the car. As Frank undid the passenger door, Don repeated, even though Frank couldn't hear him: "Only a matter of time."

CHAPTER TEN

"I'm getting fed up with this bloody weather, Frank. Bloody sunshine all the time, it's not natural. It's been going on for almost a fortnight, it's ridiculous."

Frank kept his *"Hmm"* noncommittal. It was hot in the car, true enough, even though they were sitting with all the doors and windows open. But wasn't this DI Packham the same one who'd been rhapsodising the heat wave just a few hours earlier?

Don seemed astonished at Frank's response. "Well, I don't know—perhaps you like the heat. Some people do. Each to his own, I suppose."

"Hmm," said Frank. "I've been thinking—don't we really need to speak to someone who actually knew the victim? I mean, knew him better than as a casual acquaintance."

"It would help, yeah. Who are you thinking about, the widow?"

"No, someone a bit more objective. Well—objective, assuming he or she isn't the killer, of course. A friend."

"Doesn't PC Knob Liver come into that category?"

"Kidney said he'd known Bruce a long time—he didn't say they were real friends. We're looking for quality of relationship, not quantity." This was one part of the CID job—and of working with Don, in particular—that Frank would never grow tired of. For all the differences in their ranks, wages, experience, and ages, when they sat like this in private, discussing tactics and approaches, they were equals. One's opinion was as valid as the other's. That was something Don had made clear from their first days together.

"OK," said Don, "so who fits that bill?"

"Only Bernie Ponting, that I can see. Two people have told us that Bernie and Brucie go back a long way. As for how well they knew each other—we'll have to ask him."

"Right you are, Frank. Get your mobile buzzing."

Bernie Ponting's mobile was in his jacket pocket, and his jacket pocket, it turned out, was hanging on a door handle in the admin office at Cowden Animal Rescue Centre.

"Animal rescue centre?" said Don, when this information had been conveyed to him. "What's he doing there?"

"Don't know," said Frank, starting up the car. "Rescuing an animal?"

"In *this* heat?" Don seemed personally affronted. "This is not the weather to be pulling horses out of bogs, Frank."

They found Ponting cleaning out dog pens with a mop and a bucket of disinfectant. He seemed to be doing a decent job of it, too, his work-earned muscles pushing and pulling the mop handle, then squeezing its head in the perforated wringer on top of the bucket. What with his build— he wasn't far off being a small man, but very obviously strong with it—and what Frank reckoned was an East End accent, the overall impression would have been of a tough guy, if it wasn't for the earlobe-length hair, and the crinkled smile.

He pulled off a red washing-up glove to shake hands with the detectives. "Hello, gents—listen, hope you don't mind meeting here?"

"Not at all," said Don.

"Only, we have a rota, you see, and I wouldn't want to let

them down. It's not like this place is exactly overstaffed, if you know what I mean."

"I knew this place was here," said Frank, "there's a notice on the board at the station, but I never realised it was so big."

"Expanded recently," said Ponting, propping his mop in a corner, and shrugging into his lightweight jacket. "Mind, it's expanding all the time—officially or unofficially. But this whole block we're in now, this is new. Opened about six months ago, space for two hundred cats and fifty dogs. And it's full already."

"Bloody hell," said Don.

"Oh, yeah. Over-full, in fact. We have to turn away more than we can take in. And it's not just cats and dogs." Ponting stepped out into the corridor, and Don and Frank followed him, to an accompaniment of barks, yaps, and low, moaning howls. "Down there, we've got a vivarium for the reptiles."

"You get a lot of those?" Frank asked.

Ponting sighed. "Hell of a lot. People buy these exotic pets, and most of them end up dumped. If you ever feel the need to adopt a chameleon, let me know. Or a Vietnamese pot-bellied pig, or a chinchilla, or indeed just about anything short of a giraffe. Down here," he said, moving along, "is the main cat block."

Frank and Debbie planned to get a cat, when Joseph was a bit older. They'd seen this thing on TV, or it might have been in a magazine, some research that the two main factors determining the mental health and intellectual abilities of a child were whether or not it grew up with pets, and whether or not it read for pleasure—especially comics, for some reason. These two things, so the experts reckoned, were more important than socio-economic background, parenting, and diet put together. So, a cat and a subscription to the *Beano* were both on the agenda. He'd know where to come, anyway.

"I call that one John Cleese," said Ponting, nodding towards a large, thin ginger cat alone in a cage.

"John Cleese?"

Ponting chuckled. "You remember the Ministry of Silly Walks? Watch this." He put his fingers up to the bars of the cage, and made encouraging noises with his tongue. The two detectives smiled in recognition as the old ginger tom came over to see what all the fuss was about, with an exaggerated, high stepping gait. "Got a couple of pins in his legs, see, where he got run over. You mustn't laugh out loud, mind— he doesn't realise he's comical, and knowing cats he'd be bloody annoyed if he found out."

In the next cage sat a longhaired female, with a face like a bulldog that had lost an argument with a sledgehammer. Don couldn't tell how much of the ugliness was down to injury, and how much was natural to the breed. "Let me guess," he said. "Les Dawson?"

"Could be!" Ponting laughed. "Actually, I call her Doberman—"

"Like Private Doberman," said Frank.

"Exactly. But let's be honest, with a face like that, she could be named after almost any comic of the last hundred years. Trouble is, see, we don't kill 'em—no euthanasia, except on strict medical grounds, that's the policy. Not like a lot of shelters, who cull animals that they can't find a place for. People like to hear that when they give donations, but there's another side to it."

"How do you mean?"

"Well, it means a lot of animals stay here for years, when they might be better off getting a decent death. Have a look at this poor bugger, for instance, two cages down."

Frank did so, and then leapt back in alarm as the cage's inmate lunged at the bars, spitting and snarling. Did cats snarl?

Well, aye, this one bloody did.

"Covered with scars," said Ponting, "almost hairless, filthy temper, can't stand humans—or cats—"

"And he's only got three legs," said Don.

"Least of his problems. I mean, be honest, we're never going to re-home that, are we? No-one's going to adopt that. You could advertise him in *Devil Worshippers Monthly*, and you'd still get no takers. But he's not actually suffering you see, not in any medical sense, so we can't put him down. The poor old bastard just stays in that cage, getting older, creating a log jam."

"Does seem daft," Don agreed.

"There's a lot to be said for a merciful end. Unfortunately, the old dear who started this place off, in the nineteen sixties, was religious, so it's in the terms of the legacy." He shrugged. "Still—you do what you can. Same as your job really, you know you can never get it all sorted out but that's no reason not to make a start, is it?"

"Isn't it?" said Don, who was staring—rather morosely, Frank thought—at the three-legged cat. "Are you sure about that?"

"Course I am—there wouldn't be any sense getting up in the morning otherwise, would there?"

"My point exactly."

Right, thought Frank. Time to move on. "How long have you worked here?"

"I don't actually work here," said Ponting. "I'm just a volunteer—been doing it for a few months, now."

"So what do you do for a living?"

"I'm a general builder, by trade."

"You've always been in that game, have you?"

"Just about. Born into it, you could say. My dad was a plasterer, but I didn't fancy that." Their tour of the rescue centre had brought them to what Frank assumed was a staff room. Ponting switched on the electric kettle.

"Why not?"

"You ever seen an old plasterer? You haven't, because it's a young man's game. It's like being a fast bowler at cricket— you reckon the rewards are worth it when you're a kid, but you end up half crippled by the time you're forty. So I was apprenticed to an electrician originally, learned a bit of most trades, ended up self-employed."

"You run your own firm?"

"Coffee all right? Only instant, I'm afraid." He poured boiling water into three mugs emblazoned with the CARC logo. "My own firm? Well, not as grand as that, really—no permanent employees, just me and whoever I can drum up. And that's getting harder and harder—all the kids these days want to go to university and do media studies instead of learning a trade. Here you go." He distributed the coffees. "Fine, good luck to 'em, but when they grow up and have their own houses and their water tank springs a leak, they're going to have to go on a waiting list to get it fixed—and take out a second mortgage to pay for it."

Don grunted, though Frank wasn't sure whether he did so in response to Ponting's remarks, or to the heat of the coffee.

"Now, their children," Ponting continued, "bet you anything, none of *them* will go to university—they'll all go into trades, because that's where the money and status will be. Comes round goes round, doesn't it?"

"You're a busy man, Bernie," said Frank. "Building work, helping out at this place, comedy fandom . . ."

"Well, I'm more or less semi-retired these days. I've done well enough out of it. For years, I worked more or less nonstop. I did the fanzine, but apart from that I just worked. Had some great years during the last property boom."

In his own way, Frank thought, this bloke was just as up and downy as the DI. Big difference was, he seemed to recover from the dips in his mood very quickly, and return to his underlying cheerfulness. Less dramatic than Don—who tended to recover quite quickly from being cheerful, and go back to being miserable. "You don't work so hard these days?"

"Yeah, well, I got married, and—"

"You got married?" said Frank, hoping that the final word of the sentence—*late*—was not audible in his voice. Late and not for long; hadn't he said the other day that he was a widower?

"Yeah, I got married a couple of years ago, so I took it easier at work. Anyway, I wanted to spend more time on the fanzine."

"You publish a fanzine?"

"Yeah, the *Cachinnation Times*." Ponting's enjoyment of Frank's blank look was blatant, but good-natured. "Look it up, Constable!"

Frank smiled. "I will. So how long have you been doing that?"

"Oh, Lord . . . seems like forever. I started it in the early eighties. Of course, it was a real fanzine then, four pages, run off on a Gestetner."

"A what?"

"You're too young! Your boss might know what I mean." He smiled at Don, who emitted another grunt in reply. "It was a duplicating machine, sort of like a photocopier, in the same way that a bicycle is sort of like the space shuttle. You had to type everything onto a stencil, which you then put on the drum of this machine, where it would usually tear—you repaired that with what we called 'corflu,' correcting fluid. Then you cranked the drum with a handle, and sheets of paper were fed around the drum one by one, and the ink was pressed through the holes in the stencil to make an impression on the page."

"Sounds laborious."

"It was, yeah—but it was great fun. You'd get a bunch of mates together, including someone who knew how to fix the bloody thing when it broke down, which was quite frequently, mainly because we were always using cheap ink and paper, you'd get in a few cans of beer, and you'd have what was known as a 'pubbing party'—pubbing as in publishing." He shook his head, in affectionate memory. "They were great machines, really, even though it does sound as if I'm talking about something from an earlier geologic age. You'd end up with ink all over your hands, took days to wash it off. All over your jeans. Then you'd have to staple the pages together, put them in envelopes, address and stamp the envelopes, take 'em down the post office . . . Thing is, you really felt like you'd *made* the fanzine, you see what I mean? Made it from scratch."

"Real hands-on stuff," said Frank, thinking that the whole process sounded like a very strange way to spend your spare time.

"It's all much more sophisticated these days, of course. I've got a couple of copies of the latest issue in my bag, back at the cat block. I'll give you one before you go. But I miss the old Gestetner; it was a revolutionary piece of kit in its time, you know. There's something very democratic about a machine like that, relatively cheap, simple to operate and repair—free speech, made concrete. I don't suppose they make 'em anymore."

"How do you do the *Catsi*—the *Cashe*—the fanzine now, then?"

"On the computer. Can't deny it, DTP makes life a lot

easier. But it's still a labour of love, doesn't make any money."

"Was it through your fanzine that you met Bruce?"

Ponting shrugged. "Don't know. Could be. I've known him for years."

"How long, would you say?"

"Well . . ." He scratched the back of his neck. "Twenty years? Bit more, maybe."

"Sometime in the early eighties."

"Round then. Organised comedy fandom really took off in the late seventies, early eighties. Mostly around Hancock and the Goons, and then of course **Hitchhiker's Guide to the Galaxy** brought in a real explosion of younger fans. Before that, there wasn't much chance to meet fellow fans, except by chance."

"So you reckon that's when you'd have met Bruce?"

"Most likely."

Frank risked a sideways glance at Don. He didn't want to be obvious about it, because Bernie Ponting seemed to be the sort of man who gave you his full attention in conversation. His eyes were fixed on Frank in a way that was almost intense. Perhaps, Frank thought, because he was so interested in what he was talking about. Anyway, Don looked a bit glum, but not depressed, exactly; attentive enough.

"And were you good friends, you and Bruce?"

Ponting tugged at his lower lip. "Well . . . when we were both young and single we spent a lot more time on the hobby, and we certainly saw a lot of each other back then, yes. Less so as the years went on, you know—how it goes, isn't it?"

"You didn't have a falling out, then?" Was this the right moment to ask that? Or should he have kept it until later? Either way, he hoped Don was still listening.

The builder stiffened, Frank thought, and then made a

shooing gesture with one hand. "Well, any hobby or interest group, you get a lot of fierce feuds and wars that wouldn't mean anything to anyone outside." He raise his eyebrows, and added: "Or much to anyone *inside,* come to that."

"And was there something like that between you and Bruce Lester?"

"Listen, there's something like that between everyone and everyone else at some stage! That's just fandom for you. It means nothing."

In for a penny, Frank thought, and was about to pursue the matter, when Don interrupted.

"Was he a goer back then?"

Visibly offended, Ponting said: "I beg your pardon?"

"Bruce," said Don. "When he was a young man. Was he a one for the ladies?"

"Not especially." He took the mugs over to the sink in the corner of the small room, and began to rinse them out. "Not that I'm aware. Normal young man, that's all."

"And you, Bernie?" said Don.

With an obvious effort—obvious to Frank, at any rate; he had to assume it was obvious to the DI, too—Ponting recovered himself. "Look, lads—I cannot imagine who might have murdered poor old Bruce, or why. Cannot imagine it. But one thing I'm sure of: he wasn't bumped off by his mistress or his cheated wife. All right? He just wasn't the sort, he was a happily married accountant."

"Cuckolded husbands have been known to commit murder," said Don.

Ponting barked a short laugh. "Well, don't look at me, Inspector—I'm a widower, remember?"

"He was just a quiet, happily-married bloke—that's what you're telling us?"

"I'm sure that's what everyone's telling you." He held out

his hands, as if in reconciliation. "Look, I realise you have to go through a man's life like you're sifting through the rubbish, of course you do when the guy's been murdered. But I can tell you now—Bruce was what he seemed. His life would look the same from the inside as it did from the outside."

"And yet," said Don, "he had at least one enemy, didn't he? Because someone beat him to death with a blunt object."

"Not necessarily."

"What do you mean, not necessarily?"

"I've been thinking—it's hard not to. Maybe someone else was in trouble, and Bruce intervened. Sort of thing he might do."

"All right. In that case, why hasn't the *original* victim come forward?"

"I don't know. Maybe whatever they were up to wasn't as innocent as it looked to Bruce. Maybe he or she has got a good reason not to speak up."

"Where's that magazine you promised us, then?"

Ponting opened his eyes wide at the change of subject. "Magazine?"

"You said you'd give my colleague a copy of the *Cachinnation Times*."

"Oh, right—sure. Come with me, we'll go and get it."

"That's what I like to see," said Don. "A man of his word."

CHAPTER ELEVEN

Frank and Debbie were at home, on the sofa, watching cricket highlights on the TV, with the sound down. A few hours earlier, Don had decided that they might as well call it a day. Or, to be precise, what had happened was this: they'd tried to ring three of the witness-cum-suspects, one after the other, and none had answered their phones.

At which point, Don said: "Sod this. If they don't bloody well *want* to be arrested for murder, then they can suit themselves. I'm buggered if I'm going to forswink myself."

Frank, at least, was watching the cricket highlights. His wife was reading the *Cachinnation Times*, and reading out odd bits of it to him. "It's very professional," she reported. "Covers a broad range of stuff, too. Old comedy, current comedy, British, foreign—TV, radio, stand-up, everything."

"What is it, gig reports?"

"All sorts. Reviews, interviews, profiles, features. Just like a Sunday supplement, really, but all about comedy."

Not that Debbie Mitchell had any particular interest in comedy, not as a hobby or area of study; she liked it well enough *as itself*, as comedy, but that was as far as it went. It wasn't something she thought about when she wasn't in its presence. She did, however, have a great love of magazines. All magazines. The previous weekend, her dad had visited, and when he'd gone they found that he'd left behind, in the loo, a magazine about steam trains. Debbie, who had never in her life seen a steam train and had absolutely no desire to do so, read the paper from cover to cover.

To an extent, Frank felt the same way about the cricket highlights. He'd watch any TV sport, more or less, but he had rarely if ever watched cricket live. Or even live on television. He preferred the highlights show: six hours of play, boiled down to half an hour's TV, not only made the game seem to move faster—more importantly, it made it seem less intense. That was something he found slightly uncomfortable about cricket: its intensity.

A Test match was played for six hours a day, five days in a row. And nowadays, since the big money came in with the boom in Indian TV rights, most professionals were playing close to non-stop, year round. There could surely be no other team sport on the planet that demanded that kind of stamina—or the same degree of concentration. The rhythm of the game was such that it was very easy for a player to lose focus momentarily—and the nature of the game was such that as soon as he did lose focus, he stood a very good chance of losing his team the game. Or ending up in hospital. It was no wonder that, whenever Frank happened to glance at the cricket news on Teletext or in the paper, he saw that half the space was given over to discussing the latest crop of injuries.

"Elaborate metaphor for cricket," indeed! He'd said to Don, "That doesn't quite mean anything, does it?"

Don had given him a rather pitying look. "Just because it doesn't mean anything doesn't mean it's not true. Have you never listened to a piece of jazz?" Which didn't mean much, either, as far as Frank could see.

Too *intense*. Sport shouldn't be like that—it shouldn't matter so much. As far as Frank was concerned, sport existed to be televised, so that people like him and Debbie, hard-working people, could let their minds go blank for a few hours before bedtime. Cricket, uniquely as far as he knew, attracted followers who were more like religious adherents than fans. They treated it as if it had some philosophical, even spiritual, basis. But it bloody didn't! Not only was life not a metaphor for cricket, but cricket wasn't even a metaphor for life. It was *just a game.*

But highlights were all right. He liked highlights: cricket reduced to wickets taken and runs scored and dropped catches—cricket reduced to the status of a game. None of that unsettling, soul-searching stuff in the long bits in-between.

During the ad break, he went to fetch their big English dictionary. There were two words he needed to look up; he only knew how one of them was spelled, but he could probably guess the other. He'd won a prize at junior school for dictionary use, and every Christmas he tried to think of a way of asking whether his mother still had the certificate, without adding to the general hilarity of the table. He hadn't yet come up with a suitable form of words.

He found what he was looking for, cleared his throat, and said: "I must say, my colleague Mr. Don Packham was feeling somewhat forswunk this afternoon."

Debbie said nothing for a moment, didn't even move, but her eyes gradually lost their focus, and then, slowly, her hands holding the *Cachinnation Times* sank to her lap. "Was he, indeed?"

"Oh, aye," said Frank, "indeed he most certainly was. As forswunk, one might almost say—or at least, as my granddad might almost say—as forswunk as a Scouse rent collector on New Year's Day."

She thought about it briefly, then she threw the magazine at him. "Go on, then, give me the dictionary, Ginger-Nut."

"You give up, do you?"

"Just give me the book—don't stand there cachinnating like a hyena."

"Oh, very good! I see I'm not the first person to consult the dictionary tonight."

The cricket had ended, and been succeeded by a sitcom, which Frank also watched with the sound down. It was a US import, quite trendy but with very low viewing figures. The colour looked all wrong, all unconvincing yellows and oranges, and the action seemed to consist mostly of people with expensive hair standing around an enormous sofa, pulling faces at each other. Why did they stand around the sofa? Why didn't they *sit* on it? If they'd wanted something to lean against, Frank reckoned, they could have bought a billiard table for the same money.

He was fed up with Frank going goggle-eyed every time he saw that bloody house in Pinner, so Don called first thing and said that today he would do the driving. Then he phoned Eddie Tarr, so that by the time he picked Frank up from outside his ticky-tacky house on his revolting young-married-professionals housing development, a meet had been arranged, a destination decided. No messing about this morning; no time for Frank's dawdling. Let's get on with it.

It was another beautiful day, another lovely, sunny morning; been a while since they'd had a summer as good as this. You heard people moan about it, but Don, for one, was determined to enjoy it while it lasted. Only one cloud on the horizon: he did wonder if he was developing hay fever, because last night he'd had the definite feeling of a cold coming on. Could you catch hay fever in your forties? Never mind; all gone now.

The address Tarr had given them was in south London, not far from the Oval. "I'll be there until lunchtime," Tarr had said, but Don wasn't clear whether it was his home address, or workplace, or what.

In the event, finding it took Don and Frank some fairly intense scrutiny of the *A-Z,* a lot of snail's pace reversing and kerb crawling, and finally—to their considerable disgust—asking a plod on patrol. The address wasn't a building, or even a street: it was an alleyway.

Don began to suspect a wind-up, and was on the verge of issuing a general alert, naming Eddie Tarr as a fugitive from justice, when Frank caught sight of the man himself. The big bowler wasn't hard to spot, being the only person over five-foot-five in a roughly circular mob of kids gathered at the far end of the alley.

The children were of both sexes, and of every skin colour known to mankind. Don would be the first to admit that he was no expert on the ageing of children, but he guessed that most of them were around ten or eleven years old.

"It's a cricket school," said Don. "Look—they're doing catching practice."

As soon as he saw them, Tarr marched forward with his big right hand outstretched. Hearty handshakes were exchanged.

"This is an idyllic scene on a July morning, Eddie," said Don.

"Well, it's not quite ye olde village green, but it's not bad."

"What are they playing on?" Frank asked, watching the youngsters taking turns to bowl at a batsman—or batgirl, in fact—guarding her wicket at the end of a strip of some coloured substance taking the place of a grass pitch.

"Great, isn't it? It's one of these new portable, all-weather, roll-up pitches. We got it with a Lottery grant. They're revolutionising cricket for kids."

"I can imagine," said Don.

"In the inner cities, there aren't many open spaces, right? And of course, cricket needs more space than most sports. And tarmac is dangerous, plus you don't get a realistic bounce from it. Not to mention, in the nineteen nineties, the government sold off half the bloody sports pitches so their mates could build burger bars on them."

"Right," Don agreed, "as part of a conspiracy with their lizard masters so the next generation will be too fat and unfit to resist when the invasion from outer space comes."

"This is what we've heard," said Tarr.

Frank turned away, but not before Don had seen the expression on his face: he obviously thought they were both mad. Don wondered if perhaps he should get a flashing light he could put on his head whenever he was joking, just to help poor old Frank keep up.

"The result being," Tarr continued, "that you have the crazy situation of thousands of kids living within spitting distance of the bloody Oval, going through their whole childhood without ever picking up a bat. And half of them are Asian."

"Just the ones that would be most likely to take an interest in the game."

"Exactly. Anyway, this stuff is the answer—it's an all-surface wicket, roll it up and put it anywhere, with a predictable bounce. Very authentic cricket experience."

"And you coach them?" said Don. "Well, good on you. Admirable work."

"Ah, it's great fun. I love it. Anyway, I'm a bit crook at the moment, so I'm pretty much on the bench as far as playing myself goes."

"You're a fast bowler, I believe?"

"When I'm not injured I am, yeah. Got a bit of a side strain just now, that isn't clearing up as fast as I'd like."

"Bad luck."

"Goes with the territory. You think about it, quick bowling has got to be the most unnatural thing you can do as a sportsman. The human body just isn't designed to do that! Puts a stress on every part of you, from the ankles, the knees, the hips, the back, the shoulders, the neck . . . You know what they say: you don't have to be crazy to be a paceman, but you do have to be an idiot."

"Still," said Don, "better to be the one propelling the leather, than the guy at the other end, receiving it. I know batsmen wear plenty of protective gear these days, but even so—you get a bump on the head from a hard object at that speed, and you're going to know about it."

"Yeah—when you wake up, anyway."

"Are you Australian, Eddie?" Don asked, and noted the bowler's delight at the question.

"Not technically, no. Spent a couple of years in New South Wales as a teenager—my mum was a nurse, and she was working over there—that's where I got into cricket. I like the Australian style, they understand what the whole idea of sport is."

"Which is what?"

"To win! That's how they play over there, from the tiny kids upwards."

"And that's how you play, is it? Captaining the Writers' team against Declan Donohue's Comedians?"

"You bet. Why bother, otherwise?"

"And did the Aussies teach you sledging, too?"

Tarr smiled. "Mate, don't think I'm boasting, but when I bowl, when I'm on form, I don't need any verbal assistance to unnerve the opposition."

"Still," Don persisted, remembering Eddie Tarr winding

up Donohue the other day, "they're supposed to have invented it, aren't they? The Aussies. It's an Australian expression, apparently—supposed to refer to the fact that the abuse they give the batsmen is as subtle as a sledgehammer."

"They certainly are masters of it, I can't deny that. One game I played in over there, this one batsman was just leaving every ball, wouldn't hit anything. Eventually, the bowler went down the wicket to him, and said, 'If I bowl you a fucking piano, could you play that?' "

Don gave the old line a slightly bigger laugh than it deserved. "My favourite is where the wicketkeeper asks the batsman why he's so fat, and the batsman replies—"

" '—Because every time I sleep with your missus, she gives me a biscuit.' Yeah, great one."

"Yes, quite," said Don, who was a little put out to discover that Tarr's competitive spirit even extended to finishing other people's gags for them. "And was it while you were in Australia that you got into comedy?"

"In a way, yeah. Bit ironic, really. When we first moved over there I was a touch homesick, and Australian radio plays a lot of old British comedy shows. I got into them in a big way, and I started writing my own scripts for fun. Then when we came back to UK, I was at uni and there was a **Round the Horne** club, so I joined that. Sort of progressed from there."

"Are you still involved in fandom?"

"Not really. I make a living writing material for comics, now."

"Really?"

Tarr pulled a face. "Well—*ish*. It's an up and down business."

There were obvious similarities between comedy and cricket, Don thought: they both relied on rhythm, timing, and a blend of subtlety and strength. "Would I have heard of any of the comics you write for?"

"You'd have heard of one of them all right. Declan Donohue—though you'll never get him to admit it."

"No?"

"No! They all like to pretend they write all their own material. But they can't, once they get on radio or TV. It all gets eaten up too fast."

"So you're too busy for fandom now."

"That's about it, but some of the fans, they think I'm a bit of a turncoat—you know, abandoned the purity of fandom for the life of a filthy pro!"

"That must annoy you," Frank said.

"Hell, no, I couldn't care less. Some of those guys need to get a life, you know?"

"Did you know Bruce Lester well?"

Tarr sighed, and made an effort to look sad. "A bit. He'd been around fandom for years by the time I got involved, so I saw him here and there. We weren't big buddies, or anything."

"Have you seen him recently," Don asked, "apart from at the Comedians' match?"

"No, not recently."

"What sort of person was Bruce? How would you describe him?"

Tarr blew out his cheeks, and lifted his shoulders. "Mate, I don't know what to say. Very ordinary geezer, really."

"Friendly?"

"Yeah, nice enough."

"One or two people have said he was maybe a bit dull . . . ?"

Another shrug. "I suppose so—he wasn't the most thrilling person I've ever met. Not the sort you'd expect to get murdered, that's for sure." He paused, to shout some instructions at the cricketers. "How long you been batting, Vinita? Come on—everybody bats, everybody bowls, everybody fields. Keep it moving!" He turned back to Don and added, as if in afterthought: "You're sure he was definitely not killed by a stranger—you know, a mugger or something?"

"We're as sure as we can be."

"So it was someone at the match that killed him? Jeez, that's a weird thought."

"He didn't have enemies, as far as you knew?"

"No."

"You never heard any suggestion of—you know, playing away?"

"What, a bit on the side?" Tarr looked sceptical. "I wouldn't have thought so. Old Bruce was very much the monogamous type, I'd have said. Matter of fact, he once told me that he'd only been in love twice in his life, and he'd married one of them."

"Did he?"

"Yeah, like, you know, being an accountant, he reckoned a fifty-percent success rate, that wasn't too bad."

"How did you come to have such an intimate conversation with him? From what you've said, I wouldn't have thought you were that close."

"Well—I was having troubles of my own at the time, and I suppose he was just cheering me up, empathising, sort of thing. Like I say, he was a friendly kind of guy. Besides, it was at a Comedycon—a convention, yeah?—and we'd both had a few beers."

"What about his wife, did you ever hear of her going over the side?"

This time, Tarr's denial was emphatic. "No, not at all. They seemed pretty close. I mean, he pretty much worshipped her and she—well, I guess she liked being worshipped."

Don suddenly remembered something that had come up in a couple of interviews, and which at the time they'd dismissed—and it made him wonder whether they'd been asking the wrong question: did Bruce have any enemies. Maybe someone else had enemies, and Bruce Lester had somehow ended up in the middle of it. In some ways, that would make more sense than a nice guy with a solid marriage getting himself murdered on, as it were, his own account.

"What about the other people who were at the match that day, Eddie?"

"What about them, how?"

"Amongst that group, are there are any particular enmities?"

"Oh boy! OK, well . . . sharpen your pencils, guys. For a start, Declan can't stand anybody."

"Why not?"

"He's a *comic*, that's why not! Well-balanced, gregarious personalities do not become comedians, that's just fact."

"OK, but that's a bit general, isn't it?"

Tarr made a show of thinking about the question—and, Don thought, a show of being reluctant to answer it. "Stella Wardle makes out she's a monster, and it's true she hasn't got a very long fuse, but she gets on well enough with most people. Except Declan—I don't think she rates him very highly. Louise—the pretty little wicketkeeper?"

"I know who you mean."

"I wouldn't say she's got it in for anyone specifically, but she doesn't like men much."

"Why's that?"

"Usual reason, I guess. I don't fancy her for a murderer, though—altogether too frigid."

Actually, Don had meant *What makes you think that?*, but Tarr's misinterpretation was just as enlightening as any other answer might have been. "She must be pretty tough, I suppose, to play wicketkeeper in a men's team. That's got to be the most dangerous job on the field—get a deflection or an odd bounce, and you could up end up with split lips, chipped teeth, broken nose, broken ribs, whatever. Still, maybe Louise is good enough to avoid injury."

"Don't know about that. I call her the Ancient Mariner."

"Ancient Mariner?"

"Because she stoppeth one in three."

Don hoped the jokes he sold his clients were better than the ones he used against his acquaintances. "Is that it?"

"Just about. Everybody else rubs along OK, when their paths cross. I wouldn't say anyone out of that lot is great friends with anyone else."

"What, none of them?"

"Well, Dick and Bernie both know each pretty well, I guess, and they both knew Bruce."

Finally, thought Don; Eddie's decided where to point the finger. "How would you say the three of them got on?"

"Cordial, is probably the best word. Not big buddies, especially, just people who'd known each other a long time." He opened his eyes wide, as if the implications of what he was saying had just that minute entered his innocent head. "But, hey, listen—they were all on speaking terms. I never saw anything to suggest otherwise."

"And you?" Don asked. "How about you?"

"Me?"

"Anyone in the group you've had a falling out with, or just don't get on with?"

He must have prepared this answer, surely, Don thought—and yet, Tarr took just a moment too long to reply. First he looked over his shoulder at the cricket kids, opened his mouth to shout at them again, and then changed his mind.

"Mate, I'm a pace bowler—I'll yell abuse at people out in the middle, it's what you do. But other than that . . . I'll be frank, none of those people mean enough to me one way or the other for me to have a row with any of them."

Don didn't reply, just stood there with a slight smile on his face. After a silence lasting a few seconds longer than was comfortable, Tarr said: "Listen, I've got to get back to the kids—they'll start playing footie with the helmets. OK?"

"Sure, we'll let you get on, Eddie. When's your next match? You, I mean, not the kids."

"No idea—this bloody injury could ruin me for the whole season. I play for a club side, usually."

"Pretty serious stuff?"

"We take it seriously."

"They'll be missing you, then. So how did you get the injury?"

Eddie Tarr looked away, and it was clear that he was struggling with anger. "Oh, just one of those things. Got it in the nets! I'll tell you, I sometimes think practising is more dangerous than playing."

"But you still turned out for the Comedians' game."

"Oh sure," said Tarr. "I couldn't bowl though—we'd have thrashed them if I had!"

"Well, anyway," said Don, "I'm glad to see it hasn't shattered your confidence."

CHAPTER TWELVE

Frank was due in court—giving evidence in a distraction burglary—so Don wandered off in search of some brunch. He let
Frank take the car.

"Don't worry, if I need to go anywhere I'll get a bus."
Frank was almost out of his sight, when he shouted after him:
"Frank! They do have buses south of the river, do they? Ones
with wheels, I mean?"

In fifteen minutes of strolling—or it may have been more
than that, he wasn't really counting—Don passed any
number of intriguing ethnic eateries; restaurants, snack bars,
and bistros from just about every country he'd ever heard of,
and not a few that he hadn't. But he wasn't in the mood for
eating on his own, not proper eating. There was very little
point in experiencing something new if you didn't have
anyone to talk to about it. Instead, he went into the next de-
cent-looking sandwich shop he came across, bought a cheese
and pickle French bread and a can of ginger beer, and found a
bench under a big tree, at the edge of a tiny park. The whole
place was smaller than an out-of-town supermarket: a loose
circle of wooden benches, punctuated by litter bins, surrounding a patch of browning grass, which had at its centre a
small duck pond. Well, the *ducks* looked normal size, but the
pond was no bigger than a self-assembly backyard swimming
pool.

It was hot, but there was a breeze—enough to carry the

smell of the ducks to Don's nostrils—and the shade of the tree was welcome.

Taking advantage of this moment of calm, he tried to organise his thoughts so far about the murder of Bruce Lester.

Bruce did, indeed, seem an unlikely victim—but then, who wouldn't be, with the exception of fully-fledged gangsters? Despite what the media would have you believe, thought Don, murder is still a relatively uncommon crime in the United Kingdom. Most victims of violence outside the home are young and male. If you're middle-aged, white, and an owner-occupier, even if you're male, you have much less chance of getting killed by a stranger than you have of being asked by your teenage daughter's best friend to scrub her back for her while she showers after a sweaty game of netball. (As it happened, both rare fates had befallen acquaintances of Don's—and he knew which one had left him most open-mouthed with disbelief. Which just went to show that statistics are only statistics, but a juicy divorce is a joy forever.)

Bruce, however, was murdered by someone he knew. *What a miserable thought.* Bad enough to be killed by a stranger, but to be killed by someone you thought was a friend . . . Or someone you *knew* was an enemy? Pointless, of course, to say that Bruce didn't seem the sort to have enemies. You could be the friendliest, kindest, most easygoing bloke on Earth, and still upset someone enough to get killed—it doesn't take much. If there was one thing Don had learned in his professional life, it was that homicide is the very least of crimes.

Burglary takes planning, armed robbery takes guts, blackmail takes ruthless forethought—but you can kill someone in less time than it takes to light a cigarette, without trying, without design, without conscious intent, except during that single, flashing moment of anger. Almost every killer Don had ever met had been crippled with regret within a few seconds of the act.

Burglars are nasty and heartless, blackmailers are pure evil—but most murderers aren't even criminals. They're merely people who've done the most terrible thing it is possible to do. From a purely functional point of view, most detectives agreed, pursuing and prosecuting murderers was a scandalous waste of resources, since the chances of them re-offending—with or without a prison sentence—were something like zero. By contrast, nobody had ever heard of a mugger who only mugged once.

He unwrapped his sandwich. It was still a bit early, but in this heat the thing would bake if he didn't eat it soon. He was just about to take a first bite of his lunch, when a young woman, with a baby in her arms, nodded to him, shyly, as she sat at the very edge of one end of his bench. He could see why she'd chosen this bench—others were unoccupied, but this was the only one in full shade. Of course, if he'd known he was going to be sharing it, he wouldn't have positioned himself in the middle of the seat. He'd have taken one end, and she could have had the other, and any late arriving third party would have been able, quite legitimately, to sit in the centre of the bench.

Now what was he to do? If he stayed where he was, surely he'd make her nervous—a woman on her own, and a middle-aged man. But if he shuffled his bum along the wooden slats away from her, didn't that look equally weird? Rude, even?

Then he had a brilliant idea. *Brilliant!* He stood up, walked to the nearest litterbin, into which he deposited his sandwich wrapper, and when he returned to the bench, he causally sat at the opposite end to where the young mum was sitting.

Once more, Don prepared to eat.

"I'm sorry about the whiff."

"Sorry?" said Don.

"It's this one," said the mother, nodding at her burden. "She needs changing, but I've left all her stuff at home. Enough to put you off your lunch, isn't it?"

Don had only the vaguest idea what she was talking about, but—yes—there was a bit of a pong. Still, wasn't her fault: the mother or the child. Only nature, after all. He decided to put her mind at rest.

"Don't worry about it, love," he said. "The reason babies stink is to remind you not to eat them."

That seemed to do the trick. The young woman stared at him for just a moment, and then leapt up and scurried away at some speed; presumably to fetch from home whatever "stuff" it was that she needed.

At his third attempt, Don succeeded in getting a mouthful of cheese and pickle. As he chewed, he reflected on the lack of helpful physical evidence in the case. Their best hope was that once they had a chief suspect in their sights, they'd somehow be able to tie him or her to the baseball bat. This wasn't going to be easy. Forensically, the murder weapon carried plenty of traces of its victim, but none of its wielder. Tracing ownership of the bat from the retailer's end of the equation was simply impractical: it was, Don was assured, a common make of bat, sold in sports shops all over the UK— and further afield; no reason why the killer shouldn't have bought his bat in France, or Peru. Routine inquiries were continuing, but Don held out little hope for them.

The trail would have to be followed in the opposite direction; when the police knew, or thought they knew, the killer's identity, they would try to find evidence at that person's home, or other addresses, which tied him or her to the bat. Always assuming the killer was daft enough to have left a sports shop receipt sitting on his dining room table.

Put that to one side for now—too depressing. Don was expecting a call about the post mortem any time now; maybe that'd give him something.

So far, he only really fancied two suspects: the widow, obviously. As always. And Declan Donohue—financial misdoings had ruined plenty of showbiz careers before, and Declan seemed the sort to get into that kind of bother. As for the others—he couldn't see anything. He and Frank didn't really know the *victim* yet, that was the problem.

His mobile rang: it was the DS who'd attended the post mortem. Don's mouth was clogged with French bread, so that he was reduced to grunting.

"You all right, sir?"

Grunt.

"I said—are you all right, sir?"

Grunt!

". . . Mr. Packham?"

Oh, for God's sake! He took a swig of lukewarm ginger beer, swilled it around his mouth, swallowed urgently and uncomfortably, and finally managed to say: "Yes, yes, I'm perfectly all right. I'm having lunch, if that's permissible. Give me your report . . . Yes . . . Right . . . Ah, now that is interesting, thank you."

Very interesting. Given the time, Frank should be finished at court. Still, he didn't want to risk causing the DC's phone to ring while he was in the middle of giving evidence. The courts tended to take a rather sniffy attitude about that sort of thing.

Never mind—this was a perfect opportunity to figure out how to use his new phone. There had been nothing wrong with his old phone, but a couple of months ago, he'd been walking down Tottenham Court Road, after having lunch in

the falafel place on Charing Cross Road with an old girlfriend, and he'd seen this thing in the window. It was a mobile
phone with a built-in digital camera, so you could take a
photo and send it to someone—assuming, of course, that you
knew someone who'd got a phone with the same facility.
Until now, he hadn't got around to exploring his new gizmo,
beyond the basics. He'd send Frank a text message.

He knew within the first five minutes that he didn't know
how to do it, but it took another twenty minutes of frustration
before he accepted that he never would know how to do it.

"Bloody thing!" Don stood up and hurled the useless
phone away from him, like a fielder returning a cricket ball
from the boundary. It landed in the shallows of the pond, very
nearly killing a sleepy duck in the process. He was immediately struck with guilt: a man of his age, polluting a duck
pond with his technological waste.

"Oh, for God's sake . . ."

He rolled up his trouser legs, and waded in. The phone
was quite easy to locate; it was only a matter of finding a duck
with a bump on its head, and searching the water for a few
feet in each direction. Don was amazed—not necessarily
pleased, but certainly amazed—to discover that the phone
still worked. He called Frank, and left him a voice message
telling him where to meet up.

He was tempted to just go home; he felt exhausted, and
wet of foot. In retrospect, he should have taken his shoes and
socks off when he rolled his trousers up, but then hindsight is
a wonderful thing. No: he couldn't go home. He didn't want
to set Frank a bad example.

Press on. Like the man said: I can't go on—I go on.

As he parked the car, Frank was disturbed to see Don
standing by the side of the road holding his socks and shoes in

his hand, with his trousers rolled up, and a face as clouded as the sky was clear. Looking in a temper. *Oh God, has he finally flipped?*

"Everything all right, sir?"

"Everything all *right*? A bloke's been murdered and we don't have the faintest idea who did it—yes, everything's lovely."

"I meant . . . right, sir. Yes. Where to?"

Don got into the passenger seat, his movements a little ginger. "I've phoned Anna Lester, she's back home in Bristol, and she's expecting us."

"Bristol? Right sir."

"Well, get driving then, Frank—long way to Bristol."

"Yes, sir." Frank got driving.

"We've got something interesting from the PM. Bruce Lester had bruising and other marks on his hands, which indicate a fist fight."

"A fight? But I thought the evidence from the scene was—"

"That there was no struggle, exactly; the assumption is that Bruce's killer attacked from behind, without warning. That still stands."

"Oh, I *see*," said Frank, after a moment.

"Yes!"

"The fight injuries are nothing to do with his death—he already had them."

"The exact phrase is: 'Not necessarily contemporaneous with the time of death, and on balance thought not to be so.' "

"But they're not old wounds?"

"Not more than a week or so before he died."

"So, shortly before he was killed, Bruce was involved in a fist fight—with his killer, presumably."

"Presumably," Don agreed. "Unless he was in the habit of

bare knuckle scrapping against all comers."

They arrived in a verdant Bristol suburb late in the afternoon. The Lesters' house was detached, double fronted; well set back from the road. Not flashy, Frank felt; modest but prosperous. As they got out of the car, he was relieved to see that the DI no longer had naked feet. Driving along the motorway with Don holding his shoes and socks out of the window to dry them was not the most embarrassing thing Frank had done since he was seventeen, but it would probably creep into the top ten.

Again, it was Cousin Ivan who opened the door to them. This brought, inevitably, a licentious eyebrow-waggle from Don, which Frank again ignored. Why shouldn't a cousin offer comfort to a widow?

Ivan Lester led them to the patio at the back of the house, where Anna Lester soon joined them. She was carrying a tray of tea things, and a plate of jam tarts. Don dug into the latter with such abandoned enthusiasm, that neither Mrs. Lester nor Frank (Ivan had made his excuses and withdrawn) felt able to eat even one tart, for fear of trespassing. Bit embarrassing, thought Frank—but on the other hand, probably a good sign as regarded the DI's mood.

"When Bruce's body is released, I'm going to have him cremated, and scatter his ashes here in the garden—he loved it out here. It was his favourite place."

"It is lovely," said Frank. It was: very neat. Shrubs, roses, well-clipped lawn. Just what a garden should look like, in his opinion.

"Thank you. Bruce didn't often want to go out, when he wasn't working. He was happier to spend his time off out here. Not that he was much of a gardener, that's more my province. He just liked sitting, enjoying it—something gardeners almost never do, I'm afraid."

136

Don washed the final jam tart down with his third cup of tea, and cleared his throat. "We're trying to get a clearer mental picture of Bruce—what sort of person he was, why someone might have wanted him dead."

"I still can't believe it." She seemed to be past the crying in public phase, Frank reckoned, but her eyes weren't what you'd call bone dry, and she tended to stop speaking and swallow noisily several times per sentence. "*No-one* would have wanted him dead. He was such a . . . harmless man."

"Everyone speaks very highly of him. How did you first meet him?"

"We worked at the same firm. This was in nineteen eighty-nine—we married in nineteen ninety."

"You're also an accountant?"

"Oh, no—it was just a secretarial job."

"Do you still work there?"

"No, I haven't worked since we married. It was a dull job, we didn't need the money—anyway, we were hoping to have children. Didn't work out that way."

A few moments of silence passed, broken only by Anna Lester's swallows and throat-clearings. When Frank couldn't stand it any longer, he spoke—which earned him a discreet, admonitory headshake from Don.

"Will you go back to work now, do you suppose?"

"I don't know. I haven't thought about it. I don't suppose so—what would I do? I haven't worked for years; I'm out of touch. Why would anyone employ me, instead of some pretty little girl straight from secretarial college?"

Don asked, "You'll be able to manage without working?"

"Yes." She seemed to find the question somewhat peremptory, as, Frank was sure, she was meant to.

"Back in nineteen eighty-nine, when you first met Bruce, did you know his comedy friends? People like Dick Kidney,

Bernie Ponting, Stella Wardle, and so on?"

"Stella, no, I don't think I ever met her in those days. Dick, yes. I knew him a bit. Bernie and Bruce were good friends before I came along, but less so later. That sometimes happens, doesn't it? One friend gets married, and the other feels—I don't know, a bit excluded perhaps."

"At the time you first knew Bruce, were either Dick or Bernie married?"

"Both divorced. Both been that way for years, I think." She made a sad face—politely sad, in contrast to the personal, ineradicable sadness which it temporarily replaced. "Lot of it about, I'm afraid—divorce."

Don paused for a moment, and then said: "What first attracted you to Bruce?"

Her irritation at the question was blatant; as if, Frank thought, she'd been asked it too many times, in too many ways. "He was a very attractive man, Inspector Packham. Kind, generous, gentlemanly."

"And did he have many girlfriends before you were married?"

She put down her cup, and gave the DI a look of genteel loathing. "He was a very attractive man." She added, to make sure the dense copper had got her drift: "Physically attractive."

"Of course, he was a little older than you."

"Less than ten years older, actually. Not so very much."

"So he'd had previous girlfriends."

"Naturally."

"And after you were married . . . ?"

"Ours was not that sort of marriage. We were happy with each other." She struggled to free a handkerchief from her skirt pocket, but didn't quite make it in time to prevent a mixture of salt, snot, and mascara running onto her chin. Her quiet sobbing had hardly started before her late husband's cousin appeared, and steered her into the house.

"Right on cue," said Don. He looked like a cat about to pounce.

Frank understood that the weeping woman might well be a murderer—and the caring cousin might be her accomplice—but also, she might not be. Either way, she might well be a grieving widow. He reckoned she deserved a few minutes respite from DI Packham's sledgehammer insinuations.

"While we're here," he said, "why don't we have a look at Bruce's collection? That should give us a picture of the deceased."

"Good idea. Go in and ask permission."

The widow agreed, tearfully but readily, and the cousin escorted them to the top of the house, where a large, comfortable, loft conversion housed the ephemeral remains of Bruce Lester's life. One of his lives, at any rate. Display tables and filing cabinets took up most of the space. Some particular treasures were displayed on the wall, behind glass, individually lit. This was a serious collection, even Frank could tell that—not some overgrown schoolboy's daft hobby.

"You were very keen to get in here, Frank," Don remarked, once they were alone. "Closet fan, are you?"

"You're always saying, 'Find a man's passion and you'll learn all about him.' "

"I do wish you wouldn't quote my wisdom back at me," said Don. "You're only trying to catch me out." He looked pleased, though.

"Would you prefer if I didn't listen to it in the first place? That could be arranged."

"Hello, look at this."

Frank looked: a filing cabinet labelled Robb Wilton. Inside, not memorabilia; but press cuttings, notes, photocopies and internet printouts. All carefully filed and classified. "Isn't that the same guy that—"

"—That Dick Kidney's spent his entire life researching a book about. Yes, it is."

"Interesting. This stuff could be notes for a book, couldn't it?"

But he'd lost Don's attention—or Robb Wilton had, or both of them had managed it between them. Don was moving from one table to another, from signed photograph to framed theatre bill, with the same air that Frank had seen people adopt in museums or art galleries. Or come to that, the sort of ancient churches that you dragged yourself round when you were on a European holiday. No doubt about it, his posture was *reverent*.

"He's got some marvellous stuff here, Frank. Marvellous! Look at that—the Crazy Gang. And he's got Bob Hope here, signed 'To Bruce.' Wonder when he got that; outside the London Palladium, by the look of it."

"Very nice."

"Bloody hell—there's a cigarette case here that used to belong to Sid James! And an original **Radio Active** script; I'd forgotten them. Hilarious show, that was."

Frank did his best to take an interest. "How about that, then? A bowler hat, as worn by Benny Hill, it says here."

"Benny Hill?" Frank gathered from his tone that Benny Hill's relics had no place in this holy temple. Well, he'd tried. "We'll have to come back here, Frank, have a proper look round."

"I wonder what she's going to do with it all now?"

"The widow? Good point. We'll have to ask her if there's a will."

Anna Lester, somewhat recovered, told them that of course her husband had made a will. "I'll photocopy it for you, if you like." They did like.

"Have you read this?" The will, dated 3rd September 2000, seemed short and to the point.

"Yes, of course."

Just before they left, Don asked one more question. "Was your husband a violent man?"

From her face, Frank could see she didn't know whether to be baffled or affronted. "Certainly not!"

"As far as you know, he hadn't been in a fight lately?"

"Lately? I don't believe he ever had a fight in his life."

"The wounds," Don said to Frank, once they were back in the car, "might well not have been obvious to her, if he took care to hide them."

On the drive back to London, Don was in a cheerful mood—his brief exploration of Bruce Lester's collection had set him up for a few hours, Frank reckoned.

"Tell you what, Frank—how about a slight detour? While we're in Bristol, we really ought to have a look at Archibald Leach's statue."

"Who was he, then—one of the Crazy Gang?"

"The Crazy Gang? Frank, have you never heard of that great Bristolian comic actor, Archibald Leach?"

Frank knew perfectly well who Archibald Leach was. He did watch quiz shows, after all. But it didn't do any harm to feed Don his lines. Occasionally.

CHAPTER THIRTEEN

Not far from London, Don said: "Of course, Hitler locked up all the comedians, you know."

"Did he?"

Frank sounded a bit weary, Don thought. Better keep him talking; don't want him dropping off behind the wheel. "Oh yeah: communists, trades unionists, comedians. Those were Hitler's priorities." He received a sudden, unbidden mental picture of a concentration camp full of clowns in full dress. *It's been a long day,* Don decided; too much car work always tired him out.

"Is that right?" said Frank.

"Same with all totalitarian regimes. You take the Hollywood witch hunts, in America. If you look at the list of screenwriters they persecuted, I'll bet you more than half of them were comic writers. That's what I'm saying, Frank— comedy is, by its very nature, anti-authoritarian. 'Whatever is funny is subversive.' That's a quote."

"Who by?"

"I don't *know*, Frank, do I? If I had known, I would have attributed it. I wouldn't simply have said it was a quote. Do you want me to drive the last bit?"

"What? No, no, not at all."

"You sure? You sound a bit dopey."

"I'm fine, thanks, fit as a baker's log. Carry on with what you were saying, it's most interesting."

"Well, you only have to think of the impact **The Goon Show** had when it started in the early fifties. A lot of people were horrified—they'd not long fought a war, they'd got a socialist government busy dismantling the empire, the class system was taking a battering from every direction, deference was deeply unfashionable, and then to top it all the BBC's been hijacked by a bunch of demobbed soldiers, with long hair and beards, taking the piss out of Churchill and the royal family, and generally spewing forth anarchistic jokes and explosive sound effects over the dear old wireless. Of course, the young generation loved it."

Frank didn't comment, and—although he seemed to be awake—Don did consider giving him a quick nudge in the ribs. Then again, he *was* a Northerner: probably safer not to make any sudden moves.

As it turned out, Frank wasn't dozing, but thinking. "So what you're saying," he said eventually, "is that Bruce Lester can't have been the sort of bloke everyone said he was, because he was interested in comedy?"

The lad had a knack—and this wasn't the first time Don had become aware of it—for making the most complex and subtle insight sound like either a clumping truism or a ridiculous generalisation. "What I'm *saying*, is that having seen the victim's home—having breathed in the air of his passion, his comedy collection—we now have a clearer idea of the kind of person he was."

"Right. And he was a subversive?"

Give me strength. Any minute now, Frank'd be reporting the dead man to the Special Branch. "You don't want to be too literal about it, Frank. My point is simply that, although from outward appearances Bruce might have seemed very straight, very much a man in a suit, in fact there was more to him. In his internal life, I mean."

143

"Because he liked comedy?"

"Because he was *fascinated* by comedy. He must have been of a generally liberal personality. For instance, you can't be a Jew-hater or a queer-basher, can you, if you draw your heroes from the world of comedy. See what I mean? If you remove all the half-Jewish homosexuals from the list of great comedians, you'd be left with just about enough to fill a phone booth."

"But nobody ever said he was anti-Semitic or homophobic, did they?"

"I'm speaking *generally*, Frank." Which, Don realised, was like telling Frank you were speaking Iroquois. Backwards. "I mean that I can't see Bruce being a typical example of the middle-aged, suburban professional. For someone to have such a deep interest in comedy, and especially in the anarchic comedy of the post-War period, it must mean that he's someone who doesn't feel entirely bound by society's rules, no matter what face he presents to the world." The car swerved; not violently—in fact, quite smoothly—but it swerved nonetheless. "You all right, Frank?"

"Dead hedgehog."

"Where?"

Frank gave him a look. "On the *road*."

"Oh yes, I get you. Very sad. Very sad. Beautiful animals. Except when they've been squashed by cars."

"In America," said Frank, "they keep hedgehogs as pets."

"Hedgehogs?" said Don, perhaps a little too loudly for such a confined space. "Hedgehogs live in hedges. How can they keep *hedgehogs* as pets?"

"Well, they do."

Oh dear, here we go again. Who feeds the poor lad this nonsense? "What do they feed them on, then—potato skins?"

"Don't know. But they keep them as pets. It was on TV."

"But that would be monstrously cruel!"

"Well," said Frank, "lots of people in this country keep pythons as pets."

"Yes, but only idiots."

"Tarantulas, too; they're wild animals, same as hedgehogs."

Don shook his head, though he tried to do it discreetly. "Frank, you know, you don't want to believe everything you hear about the Yanks. A lot of it's just anti-American propaganda."

"I do realise that, yes."

"They're human beings you know, same as us." Don lit a cigar. "In many ways."

"Sorry," said Frank, "I interrupted you. Or the hedgehog did."

"I'd more or less finished, I think. I just wanted to say, really, that we mustn't *assume* that Bruce Lester was as he appeared—a nice enough, slightly dull, happily married accountant. There's as least one side to him which wouldn't necessarily be obvious to people he knew professionally—the comedy fandom; perhaps he had other hidden facets to his life, too."

"You think *he* might have been having an affair, not his wife."

"It's a possibility."

"In that case, which of the suspects could be the husband? Donohue's not married. Kidney's divorced. Jerry Marsh *is* married."

"Yes, he did say 'wife,' didn't he? Not 'girlfriend.' Unusual, that, at their age. I mean, nobody gets married any more, do they?" Frank said nothing. Don glanced at him, and saw that his cheeks were flushed and his jaw muscles clenched. Concentrating on his driving, presumably. "Well obviously, that can't be literally true."

"Obviously," said Frank.

"After all, if nobody's getting married, then how come we still have the highest divorce rate in Europe? And they say a quarter of all households in the UK are single occupancy. But you know what I mean—young people don't get formally married."

"Don't they indeed?"

"You know full well they don't. So how come Jerry Marsh has a wife, not a girlfriend?"

"They got married in America, didn't they? I imagine it's all a bit more conservative over there. Besides, it'd make the paperwork a lot easier."

"Paperwork?"

"For when they moved to the UK. If he's living here with his British wife as a permanent resident, presumably he can work here as long as he likes."

"Is that right?"

Frank shrugged. "Don't know, I'm only guessing. I can get it checked if you like."

"No, it's not important. Where were we? Bernie Ponting's a widower. What about Eddie Tarr?"

"Lives with his girlfriend. Don't worry, he's not another one of these young married freaks."

"Hello," said Don, who'd lost interest in the search for a notional cuckold. He'd just remembered Bruce Lester's will. "This is intriguing . . ."

A few minutes later, he heard Frank say: "What is?"

"The will leaves most of everything to the widow, as you'd expect and hope. A few charity and family bequests, details of where his collection goes—"

"Where does it go?"

"Mostly museums and what-have-you, but here's the interesting bit . . . he's left a bottle of wine to Bernie Ponting,

146

'With regrets that I was not a better friend.' He's specified which bottle, too—Chateau Unpronounceable, nineteen eighty. Now, what the hell's all that about?"

"We did hear there was some falling out, years ago. Maybe it's that. Sounds like it was a bit more significant than we've been led to believe, but . . ."

"A lingering resentment . . . yes, that could get you killed. Right, Frank: first thing tomorrow, we'll have another chat with Bernie. You arrange that and then pick me up."

"From home?"

"Of course from home! Where else would I be?"

They drove with only their thoughts to distract them for a while, then Frank said: "How did they know they had long hair and beards?"

What? "What?"

"If it was on the radio, how did people know the Goons had long hair and beards?"

There was silence for half a mile, until Don said: "Are you sure you don't want me to drive?"

Woken early on Thursday morning by Joseph climbing into the marital bed, Frank decided he might as well get up.

Over his tea and muesli, he wondered if Don was right to see infidelity as the likeliest motive for Bruce Lester's murder. He knew, of course, that having sex with someone other than your spouse was a common enough activity, and that its repercussions were frequently to be detected amongst the wreckage caused by violent crime. But still, he'd never quite understood it—like, what was the *point?* If you were married, what would be the point of having sex with someone else?

Probably best not to mention this to Don, he thought.

Meanwhile, what about the wounds found in the post

mortem indicative of the deceased having had a fight in the days before his death; that must be significant, surely? No matter how much of a secret rebel Don reckoned Bruce was, Frank couldn't believe he was a man who had many fistfights.

As soon as it was late enough to be decent, he rang Bernie Ponting, and arranged to see him at his home that morning. First, he had to pick up Don.

He had a nasty few minutes when he arrived at Don's place, since there was no reply to the doorbell. He had just about reached the peering-through-the-windows stage when the man himself turned into the drive. *I'm a bloody good detective*, Frank thought; *didn't even notice the car was gone.*

"Look at this lot, Frank!" The DI was struggling to close his car door with his knee, as his arms were overloaded with a portable cassette recorder and about thirty cassettes. "I'd forgotten I'd got these—been up all bloody night looking for them."

Frank tried to think of a way to ask the question: if you've been up all night looking for them, how come you've just come home? "So where did you find them?"

"Oh, I knew they were in the lock-up," said Don, "it was just a matter of figuring out which box."

Lock-up? What lock up? In CID, they spent half their time executing search warrants on dodgy lock-ups. "What are they?"

"Comedy tapes," Don said, manoeuvring himself into Frank's passenger seat, and then depositing his burden in the footwell. As Frank belted himself in and started the motor, Don sorted through his treasures. "I've had some of these twenty years or more. Some of them I taped off-air, when I was a teenager. Taped some of them from friends' albums. Tell you what, I even bought one or two of them. Now, what do you fancy—Bob Newhart? Bit of Tom Lehrer?"

Neither name meant anything to Frank. "Whatever you think."

By the time they arrived at Ponting's house in Uxbridge—not far from the world's busiest airport, and also not that far from open countryside—Frank had heard just about all he ever wished to hear of Tom Lehrer. *Incredible, the stuff that used to pass for comedy!* It's not funny, it's just horrible.

"There's plenty of money in building, then," said Don.

The house looked to have four or five bedrooms, and stood on a decent-sized plot. Parked in front of it were a van, with Bernie Ponting's phone numbers painted on the side, and a BMW saloon. Not a new BMW, but still a BMW. Twenty thousand quid's worth easy, Frank reckoned.

Ponting seemed happy enough to see them, remembering their names and chatting cheerfully as he made them coffee. He gave them—well, Don really—a guided tour of his office, which was where he produced the fanzine. The builder and the detective enthused together over the contents of various back issues, while Frank stood to one side, trying not to look bored. Mel Brooks he'd heard of, but who was Carl Reiner? And why did anybody care?

"Why comedy, Bernie?" Don asked, after Ponting had pressed an armful of back numbers on him. "I mean, what was it turned you from a consumer into a fan?"

"Good question; not sure if I can give you a complete answer. But there's something about comedy . . . it's like the pop music of your teens, comedy gets under your skin, somehow. Actually, we asked this question in the fanzine some time ago—let me see if I can . . . Yes, here we are. This is what one of the readers wrote in with: 'Because the best comedy, even more than music, lets you believe that living is about more than surviving.' "

"Not a bad attempt."

"He's getting near it, I think. There's also the fact that comedy is essentially communal—you laugh much louder when you laugh with other people—and fandom is a way of recognising that." He shook his head. "But you can't really explain it. The greatest philosophers of all the ages have tried and failed, I don't suppose I'll beat them at their own game."

"I suppose, doing the fanzine, you get to meet a lot of your heroes?"

"I don't know about heroes—I have met a great many comedians, and I'll tell you what, they're all the same: tight-fisted, paranoid, humourless."

"Really?"

"Well, all right, not all of them—but most of them. Harry Secombe, though, I met him a couple of times—interviewed him for the fanzine—he was a thoroughly nice bloke, and very funny. But the modern generation: they're just businessmen, frankly. Just suits with scripts."

"Sad," said Don.

"On the other hand, it doesn't make them bad comics—just bad company. Some of the funniest men in history have been absolute bastards. You two want another cup?"

"Wouldn't mind," said Don. "Very nice coffee."

On the way back to the kitchen, Frank noticed a framed photograph sitting on a shelf in a small alcove. It was an old photo, of a youngish woman. "Is that your first wife, Bernie?"

"What? Oh, the photo—yes, that's right."

"Lovely photo," said Don.

"Thanks. Took it myself—in fact, I do most of the photos for the fanzine . . ."

And they were off again, the suspect and the DI, gossiping about which comedy stars wore the most make-up, which ones could only be photographed from the left, and which ones would sue you if you snapped them without their teeth in. Frank waited for a break in the conversation, and when one didn't come he decided he'd have to make one himself.

"Did Bruce know her?"

Ponting turned a puzzled face to Frank. "Who, Hattie Jacques?"

"No, your wife."

"He met her a few times, I suppose, years ago."

His tone was dismissive. *Well, too bad*, thought Frank: *I have to ask my questions, even if you would rather be chatting about dead clowns.* "You were married twice, were you?"

"That's right," said Ponting and went back to his conversation with Don.

Haven't spotted a picture of the second wife, Frank noted; pain too fresh perhaps, or maybe it just wasn't a happy marriage.

Towards the end of the second cup of coffee, Don at last turned the conversation to the case in hand. "Bernie, you seem to have known Bruce better than just about anybody."

"I suppose I did, once upon a time."

"You had a falling out with him, years ago." Ponting was obviously keen to shrug this off, but Don pressed him. "I appreciate it was a trivial matter, but tell us about it anyway."

"In all honesty, Don, it was something so trivial to anyone not involved that I'm almost embarrassed to talk about it. All right: years ago, maybe twenty years ago, there was a split in a fan organization that we were both members of. This is something that happens quite commonly in comedy fandom—in any kind of fandom, I'm sure. In theory, you've all got the same aims in mind, the same interest, but you know—personalities clash, egos get swollen."

"And you and Bruce were two of the personalities who clashed?"

"No, not really—we just happened to end up on opposite sides when the dust settled."

"I see. But you made up eventually?"

"Like I say, it was something and nothing."

"And before this split came between you, you were good friends?"

Ponting thought before he answered. "I suppose you could say we were fairly close for a while, when we were younger."

"Was there any lingering ill feeling? On either side?"

For the first time, Ponting's patience seemed to be wearing thin. "Look, I don't know what else I can say—it was a minor misunderstanding, a lifetime ago, long forgotten. That's *it*."

"Right," said Don. "So you haven't had a fight with him lately?"

"A *fight*? Of course not! What are you talking about?"

"Evidence has emerged that Bruce had been involved in a fight recently."

Ponting shook his head. "I can't believe that. No way. Not Bruce's style. He wasn't a physical man, in that sense."

"You've never known him to have a confrontation with someone?"

"Look . . ." Ponting put his cup down, and folded his arms. "I'm not really comfortable talking about him like this."

"I don't suppose he's really comfortable being dead," said Don. "Sadly, neither of you has a choice in the matter."

"Even so . . ."

"Bernie, if you know something you have to tell us. OK?"

Reluctance screamed from every muscle in the builder's face. "The only person I've ever seen Bruce have a stand-up row with was Stella Wardle."

"What about?"

He shrugged. "No idea. I *saw* them, I didn't hear them."

"When?"

"Oh, I don't know—this was months ago."

"*When?*" Don repeated.

"Last Christmas. There was a bash, a do, you know. Every year, I have a bit of a drinks party around Christmas or the New Year—for the fanzine, I mean. A few fans, a few comedians. Sort of a thank you to the contributors. The *Cachinnation Times* doesn't pay its writers, you see."

"And Stella and Bruce were arguing? Here, at your place?"

"No, we hire a room above a pub. I saw them in the car park, when it was breaking up."

"But you don't know what it was about?"

"I'm sure it was nothing. Disagreement over some bit of comedy history that got out of hand, most likely."

"But you said Bruce wasn't an argumentative bloke—so it must have been something pretty big to have him ding-donging in public with a woman."

Ponting smoothed his hair. "It wasn't a *ding-dong*. Shit, I wish I hadn't mentioned it—I don't suppose it was anything, and if it was I don't know what it was."

Outside, Frank said: "Stand-up row? Do you suppose that was mean to be a gag?"

"What?"

"When he said it was a *stand-up* row, I wondered—"

"Frank," said Don, "not everyone finds murder as amusing as you do. We don't all have your advanced satirical instincts."

He put on a Derek and Clive tape. Frank was revolted—as, he had no doubt, he was supposed to be.

CHAPTER FOURTEEN

"She denies it," said Don, putting his phone away. They were sitting in the car, parked in a residential street a few blocks from Bernie Ponting's house.

"So . . ." Frank still wasn't sure he understood the strategy. Wouldn't it have been better to have visited Stella Wardle, to put the new evidence to her in person, rather than just calling her up and asking for a comment? The DI had said no, before he interviewed her again he wanted to have a bit more in his pocket than "fluff and conkers"—whatever that meant. "So we believe her, or what?"

"Doesn't matter whether we believe her or not."

"It doesn't?"

"Not for the moment. The important thing is—this story about Stella and Bruce having an argument is now officially significant."

Now Frank got it. "Right—because *one* of them is lying."

"Must be. It's not the sort of thing you'd imagine you saw, in his case, or forget taking part in, in hers."

"Unless she was drunk."

"You'd have to be very drunk, I'd think, to forget that. Besides, Bernie didn't say she was drunk, did he? And that's the sort of detail you'd expect him to mention."

"I suppose so."

"Especially when he was backtracking—trying to play it down. He could have said to us, 'Look, she'd had a bit too much to drink, that's all it was.' But he didn't."

"So either she's lying about not having had a row with Bruce—"

"Or Bernie's making up the whole thing. Either way, whoever's lying is doing so for a purpose. Of course, it might not be a purpose connected with the current investigation. But on the other hand . . ."

"It might be. Where to next, then?"

"If Stella and Bruce were fighting at the Christmas bash, the chances are it's because they were having it off together. Either at that time, or earlier."

"I suppose it's not unlikely."

Don smiled. "Ah, Frank—is that the sound of regret in your voice? You're beginning to get fond of old Brucie, are you? Don't like to think of him getting up to no good."

Honestly, the things the man came out with! "I've never met Bruce, how can I be fond of him?"

"Frank, I hope you don't mean that." He gave the DC a reproving look. "The victim is always central to any investigation of this kind."

"Well, yeah, obviously. But—"

"All that we do, it's all about getting to know the victim. Once we know him, we can see the suspects through his eyes. How well do you get on with your mother-in-law?"

"What?"

"If you were murdered, and you didn't see the killer, during your last few seconds of life would you know who had killed you? I bet you would."

"It wouldn't be my mother-in-law." Frank thought he ought to make that clear, at least.

Don tutted. "It doesn't matter who it is—"

"Of course it matters who it is! That's what we're here for, to find out who did it."

"My *point,* Frank, is that an ordinary person doesn't have many people in their lives who would be willing to kill them. If you were a clairvoyant, and you'd gone up to Bruce Lester a day before he died and told him he was going to get done in, I bet he'd have said to you 'Ah-ha! I know who that'll be.' "

"I bet he wouldn't."

"Why not?"

"He'd have said 'When? Where?' And then he would have made sure he was somewhere else."

Don rubbed his eyebrows with his knuckles. After a while he said: "Right, Frank. I want you to go and talk to Bruce's cousin."

"Ivan Lester?"

"That's the boyo."

"Talk to him about Bruce, you mean?"

"Bruce and Anna. And both together."

Frank understood. It wasn't his idea of a good time, but then nobody ever said work was supposed to be fun. Except his old careers teacher, and she was a notorious liar. "Right you are. Where will you be?"

"I shall be at Cowden Central Library."

"The library? Why?"

"To eat my lunch, what do you think?"

Cousin Ivan lived in a flat on the twelfth floor of a council block in the City, a short walk from some of the financial world's most resonant addresses. He opened the door to Frank with a tea towel in one hand, and a pair of rubber gloves tucked under his arm.

"Come in, mate, come in—excuse the mess."

"Not at all. Do you live on your own?"

"No, I live with my girlfriend. But we've got a bit behind with everything lately—you know, what with me spending half the time at poor Anna's."

"Of course. How is Mrs. Lester?"

"Well, she's holding up. I'll probably go back down there at the weekend. Do you fancy a cuppa? I was just about to have one."

"Yes, thanks." They walked through to the kitchen, which Frank couldn't help noticing was a lot bigger than his and Debbie's; big enough for a whole family to sit around the breakfast table. Built in the days before everyone had a telly, presumably. "Will your girlfriend go with you to Bristol?"

"No, I shouldn't think so."

Frank waited, but Lester didn't add to his statement. "She's not as close to Anna as you are, then?"

"No, it's not that, it's just that she often works weekends. She's a branch manager at a supermarket."

They took their tea through to the spacious living-room, which was when Frank noticed the view through the patio doors. As far as he was concerned, views were all very well in their place—which was from a hotel room, on holiday—but even then, it wasn't in his nature to ooh and aah over them the way some people did. They'd gone to Italy once with a colleague of Debbie's who'd spent half her time staring, trans-fixed, at distant valleys and looming mountains. Which was fine, except that it meant they rarely got to where they were going in time for a punctual meal.

Still, he did recognise the value of views as conversational gambits. "You can see it all from up here, Ivan."

"Not bad is it? In fact, why don't we sit out on the balcony? It'll be a bit cooler than indoors at this time of day."

At least it wasn't a mountain or an Italian valley. They were facing roughly west, and many of London's most famous sights were visible. More than that, though, he had to admit, seeing so much of the capital at one time, spread out before them like an unusually sharp computer graphic, sunshine reflecting from thousands of different points in all directions . . . it wasn't without its appeal.

"Was it the view that attracted you to the place?"

"Well, sort of! Actually, it's a hard-to-let. The rent's dirt cheap. Which is important—I'm a firefighter."

"Oh, right." Frank wasn't sure what he should say to that. The differential in pay between police officers and other emergency workers was a delicate subject. So was the fact that if Anna Lester *was* planning to run off with Cousin Ivan, she wouldn't be able to rely on his earnings to keep her in the style to which she was accustomed. "I'm surprised it's classified as hard-to-let. It's a fine place."

"Yeah, the flat's terrific. Great views, lots of space. But the lifts don't often work, and this isn't an especially nice area after dark, when the City workers have been evacuated back to the suburbs."

"I see."

"Still—it'll do while we're saving up." He laughed. "Another three hundred years or so, and we should have enough for a deposit on a dog kennel the other side of the M25."

"It's not easy," Frank agreed. "I wanted to ask you a bit about your cousin Bruce. You'll understand, there's a limit to how blunt we can be in our questions to a widow, at a time like this."

"Of course. Go ahead. I've got to say, though, there's not much to tell about old Bruce. Nice guy, hard worker, enjoyed his hobbies. That's about it."

"Were the two of you pretty close?"

"Fairly, I suppose. Given that he was a bit older than me, so we weren't childhood mates or anything. But, yeah, we kept in touch. He was the kind of bloke—like, he was someone you could always turn to, if you needed help or advice."

"People we've spoken to," said Frank, "they mostly say the same thing—nice guy. But maybe, if you'll forgive me saying so, a little dull?"

"I don't know—the kind of work you and I do, don't you sometimes think excitement is a bit overrated?"

"Aye, I know what you mean."

"Like, people talk about other people being dull, but how do you define it? It's not a term anyone applies to themselves, is it? No, I wouldn't call him dull. He was a bit more reserved, perhaps, than is fashionable these days. But I always enjoyed his company, that's all I can say."

Frank put his cup down on a wrought iron table. "I have to ask one or two questions which are—what I mean is, in an investigation of this nature—"

"Frank, I do know how coppers work. Yeah? Being in the fire service. So, you ask your questions and I promise not to take it personally."

"Thanks." Frank knew his relief showed, but he didn't care. It was a pleasant change to be interviewing someone who knew the score. "We're wondering about the state of Bruce and Anna's marriage."

Ivan Lester nodded. "Of course you are."

"Specifically, whether—as far as you know—there was anyone else."

"Bruce wasn't the sort. I know that's the sort of daft generalisation you hear all the time, but I'm sorry—it's the truth as I know it."

"That's fine. You mean that he wasn't the sort that would be tempted, or he wasn't the sort who'd have the nerve, or . . ."

"He had very strong views. He wasn't a man of strong

opinions, generally speaking—you know, politics or any-thing—but on this particular matter, I was never in any doubt where he stood. Bruce was always very protective towards women who he thought were being misled by men. He'd have had to be a *monstrous* hypocrite to be doing anything extracur-ricular, at the same time expressing the kind of views he did."

Frank wasn't precisely sure what Lester meant. *Misled by men*—he assumed the phrase was Bruce's, not his cousin's; it sounded old-fashioned. But what opportunities would a quiet-living accountant have to be protective towards such women? "Can you give me an example?"

"I can, as it goes. A couple or three weeks ago, we went for a pint, just me and Bruce, and he was telling me about someone he knew who was being harassed by a man who wouldn't take no for an answer."

"He didn't say who?"

"No, no, he was very discreet—he wasn't a gossip. Just someone he knew. Through work, maybe? But it was really bothering him. He pretty much had steam coming out of his ears. I mean, fair enough, no-one likes to see a woman being mistreated, but Bruce had a bit of a bee in his bonnet about it."

"OK. Thanks." Frank finished his notes. "I also have to ask you—"

"No." Lester shook his head. "Anna wasn't at it, either."

"You're quite sure about that?"

"I can see the way you're bound to think—investigating a murder and that, looking at a younger wife, you've been told Bruce was maybe a bit dull, she's a good-looking woman. Sure. But they were really very happy. She's always made it clear she wasn't interested in anyone else, and Bruce used to say he'd only been in love twice, and one of those turned out to be an infatuation. The other was Anna."

"Only in love twice," said Frank, wishing Don had sent him to the library instead—this was much more the DI's territory than it was his. "But some people have said that when he was younger, Bruce had quite a few girlfriends."

"I daresay he did, but that was years ago, when he was *much* younger. In the few years before he met Anna, he hardly had any girlfriends."

"Really?"

"Or if he did, I've never heard of them."

Frank quickly reviewed his notes. As far as he could see, he'd got nothing, except confirmation of things they already knew. But also as far as he could see, there was nothing more to be got. Lester had answered the one substantive question he'd asked and given the same answer several times in several different ways. What more could he do? "OK, thanks—I'll let you get back to your spring cleaning."

They shook hands at the door, and Lester asked: "Is this how you lot solve murders, then? You just wander around talking to people?"

"Oh aye," said Frank. "It's called Dialectical Profiling."

"Is it?"

Frank nodded. "Latest thing, it's all the rage in CID circles."

Following Stella Wardle's career in comedy was proving an easy matter for Don, at Cowden's newly opened reference library, thanks to that miracle of ancient technology—the book index. The only difficulty he was encountering, as he followed Stella's wanderings through one biography or volume of memoirs to another, was keeping his mind focussed on the task in hand; the temptation to browse and reminisce was powerful.

Any gaps in the record—or in the library's stock—were

plugged by internet searches. By the time Frank arrived, Don had whittled the lacunae down to just one. This one, however, was both stubborn and extensive.

"Right," said Don, checking through his scribbled chronology. "We've got her up to nineteen seventy-two, when she's working as PA to a light entertainment executive—she's mentioned in passing, in a book about John Cleese. Now, her boss gets the sack—or gets a sideways promotion, or whatever—and after that Stella is off-radar for more than three years."

"Couldn't that just be because nobody mentions her in their books?"

"It *could* be, yes, but the absence is a bit glaring. There's no other comparable period when she doesn't at least get a minor name check, somewhere or other. She was, evidently, a well-known character in the business."

"But then she reappears?"

"Let's have a look . . . yeah, here we are. In nineteen seventy-five, she turns up as secretary to a guy called Billy Besters."

Frank shook his head. "Don't think I've heard of him."

"Died years ago, completely forgotten now. He was quite a big comic in his time, but—interestingly—his time had long gone by nineteen seventy-five."

"I see . . . so she's taken a step down?"

Don smiled his approval. "Exactly. *Definitely*. Before the hiatus, all her jobs are impressive. You couldn't call it a career, exactly, in the sense of an ever-upward curve, but certainly she's up there amongst the stars. Afterwards, however, she's in decline—in terms of status, I mean. So: why?"

Frank did the sums in his head. "Can't be age—she was still in her thirties. Maybe she got married, wasn't looking for such demanding work?"

"I don't think she ever did marry, as far as I can tell. We'll have to check."

"Might have been a common-law marriage."

"Yes," said Don, thinking that Frank Mitchell must be the last person in the country who used the phrase "common-law marriage." "We'll check. But if not marriage, then what?"

"She's never been in prison. The computer would have known."

"Pregnancy?" Don suggested.

"Mental illness?" Frank offered.

"Bankruptcy?"

"Prostitution?"

"Pornography?"

"Fancy some lunch?"

They bought falafels in pita bread from a stand in the pedestrianised square outside the library. Frank peered at his, and ate it cautiously in small bites. Don wolfed his, and then bought another and wolfed that, too.

"What do you mean—pornography?"

"I'm just thinking," said Frank, "of things that might cause her to disappear for a few years, and which might damage her standing in the comedy community when she returned. Also, something that might be a source of shame."

"Shame?"

Frank folded his paper napkin and placed it in the receptacle provided. "Because if her missing years aren't something she's ashamed of, then they're of no interest from our point of view."

"Oh, bloody hell—a good point, cynically argued! I hope you're not turning into a policeman, Frank? I'm trying to make a detective out of you."

"It's got to be something, though, hasn't it? Something

she wouldn't want people to know. Otherwise we're wasting our time."

"I'm not arguing, Frank, you're quite right. If this business matters to us, then we have to assume that Bruce found out Stella's sordid secret, and she killed him because of what he knew."

Frank looked unconvinced, but then looking unconvinced, Don believed, was one of the lad's most valuable skills. DC Mitchell's sceptical frown could be worth its weight in gold during a formal interview—especially as it didn't show up on audio tape. "That would mean, though—or it would suggest—that Bruce Lester's wounds came from fighting with a woman. Is that likely, given what we know about him?"

"It is if she attacked him—even a gent will defend himself." Don winced. "Especially if she went for his goolies."

"Do we talk to her, then?"

"No, not yet. At the moment we're all theory and no evidence." He grunted. "Come to that, we're not over-endowed with decent theories."

The young, middle-class audience at the Cafe á Tee-Hee seemed to be enjoying Declan Donohue's act, but Don wasn't convinced. The thing with most of these young stand-ups, in his view, was that their material was just too easy. In a culture where everything's funny, where there are no significant taboos, laughing becomes as routine as breathing. *It shouldn't be,* Don thought: *it should mean more than that.*

"And women are much more competitive than men, that's simply a fact. Yeah? Everyone thinks men are more competitive, but you *know* that the most competitive thing most men do in their entire lives is watch sport on TV. OK? So men watch sport on TV, and women dream of killing each other."

Not that Don had ever been keen on alternative comedy, all those anti-sexist, anti-racist, self-admirers in the nineteen eighties. An alternative to comedy was just what they supplied, in his view.

"No, no, listen to me—you *know* this is true. If you doubt me, then try this experiment. All right? At your office, next time one of your female colleagues gets cancer, and after she's had the chemo, she comes back to work to visit the girls, because she needs them to be *supportive,* she needs her girlfriends to *be there for her,* right?"

But one thing you could say for alternative comedy—it was a reaction, albeit an unconscious one, to the whole direction of post-War British comedy. It had no-go areas. And the point about comic no-goes is that they make you work harder with what's left. Not just the comic; the audience, too.

"Sure enough, they all air kiss her and they all hug her and they all hold her. They tell her that they're there for her. And they cry. They don't cry so much their makeup runs, obviously, because you got to have a sense of priorities about these things, yeah? But they do cry—just like men cry when their team gets knocked out of the cup."

Warmth—that was what Don found lacking in most of the modern breed. All the old masters, right up to Tommy Cooper and Morecambe and Wise, even the first waves of graduate comics, some kind of heat radiated out from them. Something that made you think their material mattered to them.

"But then as soon as the cancer woman leaves the room— the very *second* that woman exits the door—one of the women will turn to another and say, 'Who chose that wig? Her guide dog?' " Donohue surfed the laugh, raising his voice and his body language just a little. "And you *know* that's true! Even at a funeral, it's—'You call that a coffin? I've seen classier cardboard boxes outside Sainsbury's with *tramps* sleeping in them.' "

As Donohue left the stage to enthusiastic applause, Don reminded himself to be fair: the best today were as good as the best ever. It was just the middle-rankers who'd declined.

They gave it five minutes—"For decency's sake," Don claimed—and then the two detectives entered the communal dressing room, just in time to see Donohue receiving a slap on the back from the Tee-Hee's manager. A slap on the back, and his fee, counted out in tenners and agreed by the Irish comic with a single nod of the head.

Don nudged Frank. "Paid in cash. What a surprise."

Donohue was less than delighted to see them, and even without the distraction of a giant TV screen he seemed disinclined to grant them his undivided attention. Nonetheless, sitting on a chair in the corner of the room with two cops standing in front of him, his avoidance strategies were limited—assuming he didn't resort to closing his eyes so that they couldn't see him.

"You told us the other day that Eddie Tarr 'had it in' for Bruce. What did you mean by that?"

"God, is that what's kept you out so late? Eddie wasn't keen when he heard I had Bruce in the side for the Comedians' match, went on about what a fat tosser he was, that's all."

"Why did he react like that?"

"Sure, how would I know? I've no idea, the man's a fast bowler. He takes it all desperately seriously. Probably didn't like the idea of having to mix on the field with non-cricketers, something like that."

"When was this?"

"When was what?"

Don was distracted by the sound of Frank sniffing. Did he

have a cold? *Ah, of course* . . . Don caught a whiff of what Frank's nostrils had been detecting. Yes, Frank, people smoke dope in comics' dressing rooms. Now, can we get back to work?

"When was it that Eddie made these remarks to you?"

"Night before the match, I rang him to check arrangements."

"Does he have a temper?"

"Eddie? On the field, sure. He's a quick, isn't he? You know what they're like."

"And off the field?"

Donohue looked uninterested—even by his high standards. "No idea. We don't exactly hang out together."

"What did Bruce and Stella fall out about, last Christmas?"

"I didn't know they did."

"You didn't attend the *Cachinnation Times* party?"

His only reply was a snort of astonishment at the very idea.

"So you know of no area of personal disagreement between those two?"

"Nope. There again, Stella's such a miserable cow nothing would surprise me."

"All right, Declan, that's about it for tonight. If you could just write down for me the name and contact details of your former accountant."

"My former . . . ?"

Don took a moment off, just to enjoy having finally raised a real emotional reaction from the supercilious comic. Donohue looked horrified. "Whoever was doing your accounts before you hired Bruce Lester."

"Why the hell should I—"

"Declan, think about it: we can get that information. It'll be a minor nuisance for us, but we'll get it eventually. Or you could just give it to us now, and avoid annoying us."

As they left the room, having secured details of Declan's accountancy history, Frank bestowed his best copper's stare on a group of semi-dressed gigglers sitting by the door; a stare, and an expressive sniff. Don allowed him that. Just as long as he didn't start arresting people for possession. They had quite enough paperwork to be going on with, thanks very much.

CHAPTER FIFTEEN

In the canteen at South Cowden police station—because
Don refused point blank to work in the CID office—a moment eventually arrived on Friday morning when both detectives put down their mobile phones at the same time.

"I wonder if it's true," said Don, "that these things fry
your brains."

"So they say."

Don rubbed at the right side of his face with a handkerchief. "They fry your bloody ears, that's for sure."

"If it is true," said Frank, finishing off the notes on his
latest phone call, "then this country's doomed."

"Country's doomed anyway," said Don, cheerfully.

"Must be at least three-quarters of the population have
mobiles, nowadays. In some parts of Europe it's ninety per
cent."

"Well, there you are—that's comforting. Knowing that
the Europeans will go mad before we do. As usual." Don
smiled. "There again—perhaps it's already happened.
That'd certainly explain a few things."

They ate their bacon rolls and drank their tea in silence for
a while, as each of them reviewed the information they'd
gathered so far during their marathon mobile session.

"What it comes down to," said Don, licking the last blobs
of brown sauce off his fingers, "is that no-one knows where
Eddie Tarr got his injury from."

"Looks like it. Nobody he plays cricket with, or trains with, can remember him getting injured in the last few weeks."

"Or complaining about an injury," Don added. "Which makes him a decent possible for the other participant in Bruce's mysterious punch-up."

"But if so, why?"

Don shook his head. "Don't know. And I don't want to ask him until we can at least guess at the answer."

"Right then," said Frank. "In that case, moving on, I got through to the liaison officer at Garda Headquarters in Dublin."

"Excellent—when will he get back to us?"

"No need," said Frank, trying to sound nonchalant rather than pleased with himself. He knew the DI wasn't very big on smugness. "He was able to transfer me to the relevant guy in their fraud section."

Don's face brightened. "So, there *is* something there! I knew it."

"There is indeed. Seems that Declan Donohue's previous accountant is no longer practicing in his profession, as he is currently helping the Gardai with their inquiries."

"He's bent," said Don.

"Well, they weren't quite that forthcoming—if we want more detail, it'll have to be done formally, at superintendent level."

"But . . . ?"

"But, I got the clear impression that the fraud guy was choosing his words with some precision—"

"Of course he was, Frank, he's Irish. They handle language with the care and respect a watchmaker accords his cogs."

"Quite. And he told me that if I wished to pursue inquiries

concerning the defrocking of a crooked accountant, I should do so with the relevant professional body."

"Defrocking, eh? Very nice." Don's voice was rich with professional respect. "It's a privilege to work with such people."

"I did thank the gentleman on your behalf."

"I'm pleased to hear it, Frank. They place a high premium on civility over there. Did he say how long ago this defrocking took place?"

"I gather that the accountant in question has not been able to pursue his trade for about the last four months."

"Now we know why he isn't answering his phones." Don cleared a space on the table in front of him, as if, as Frank had noted before, he needed a blank canvas on which to project his thoughts. "OK, so at last we have a rock solid motive for one of our suspects. Declan was using a dodgy accountant to cook his books. The accountant gets caught—over something else, presumably, not involving Declan—so now Declan needs a new accountant. He picks a comedy fan, assuming that his star status will so impress the acolyte that he'll do whatever he's told and keep his mouth shut."

"But he's picked the wrong fan—Bruce Lester is a man of high moral standards."

"Bruce confronts Declan with the discrepancies in his accounts—whereupon Declan bashes him over the head." Don paused, and sighed. "Bloody baseball bat—still no news on tracing the ownership of that, I suppose?"

Frank shook his head. "Nothing."

"Bloody thing's got to belong to someone. Unless it was just lying around in those bushes, waiting for a passing murderer to make use of it. In which case, we're totally buggered."

"One thing, though," said Frank. "If Declan Donohue is

the killer, then does that mean it was him who had the fight with Bruce?"

"Could be." He thought about it, staring at his area of clean table. "How about this? Bruce confronts Declan, they have a fight."

"When?"

"Whenever—a couple of days before the match. At the end of it, Declan says sorry to Bruce, of course he didn't mean him to do anything crooked, not to worry, he'll get it all sorted out."

"Meanwhile, he's planning to bump him off at the cricket match."

"Or as soon as a suitable opportunity arises. Works OK, doesn't it?"

"I suppose so. Are you going to tell the DCI that Donohue is now prime suspect, then?"

"No . . . No, not yet. I still think we've two good suspects—Donohue, and the widow. Maybe Eddie Tarr, too, if it was him that Bruce fought with. But without any meaningful forensic evidence, we're going to have to be as sure in our own minds as we possibly can be before we take it any further." Don lit a cigar. "We need to eliminate everyone else—keep looking for any possible motives, and then try and knock them down. For the moment, we'll forget the chief suspects, and have another proper look at the others. You sniff around about the Brummie cop."

"Will do. Who will you do?"

"Oh, I don't know—I'll pick one of the others. At random."

I'm sure she'll be delighted to see you, thought Frank.

As it happened, Frank knew a bloke in Kentish Town—a uniformed sergeant who he'd been on a course with—who had a sister-in-law, also a cop, who now worked in Glasgow, but who had previously been with the York police. With his mobile clamped to his ear, Frank followed a complex and at times frustrating chain of connections and introductions. It took him a couple of hours, and a good deal more matey chit-chat than was to his taste, but eventually Frank received a call from a York DC who had known Dick Kidney for seven years—which, in the peripatetic world of police assignments, was very nearly a lifetime.

"This is about your murder, yeah? At the cricket match?"

"That's right," said Frank. "How did you—"

"Spleen didn't do it, I can tell you that."

"Spleen?"

"Yeah—Kidney. Spleen. Right?"

"Oh right, I'm with you, yeah. Very good. So how do you know he didn't do it? Not that I'm suggesting that we think—"

The Yorkshireman's laugh rattled Frank's earpiece. "Because the daft bugger's been talking about nothing else all week! Not to management, like, he'd rather keep them out of it."

"Naturally."

"But with the lads, you know—to be honest, it's not often Knobby finds himself at the centre of attention in the pub."

Frank wasn't going to ask about "Knobby." He'd figure it out later if it proved to be of relevance. "No?"

"No, don't get me wrong, nice enough bloke, mate of mine, but you don't engage him in conversation unless you're really fascinated to know about all the famous comedians who've been born in Birmingham in the last hundred years."

"Right." Frank wondered if there were people in his own nick who would be as happy to discuss his shortcomings with a stranger. Probably.

"What I'm getting at is, if he was your doer, he wouldn't be blabbing it all over, would he?"

"I suppose not."

"Sure, OK, some teenage scrote who's hijacked a lorry load of tobacco—he'll brag to anyone who'll listen. But not a copper who's bashed his best mate's head in with a tyre lever."

And embellishment of a story wasn't a crime, after all; except when you were giving evidence under oath, obviously. There again, telling everyone the killing had been achieved with a tyre lever might be a way of establishing witnesses to his ignorance. "Does he seem very upset by what's happened?"

"Oh aye, don't take me the wrong way. He's well cut up. Seems him and this Bruce lad go back yonks. Pretty much grew up together from what I gather." The detective laughed again. "But, fair play, it is a bloody good story, isn't it? A copper getting caught up in a murder investigation. Bit better than 'I spent the weekend cataloguing my autograph collection,' any road."

"What sort of bloke is he, generally?" Frank hated asking questions like that. He was always afraid that the person he was interviewing would ask him what, exactly, he meant. And Frank had no idea how we would answer. "I mean, he gets on all right with people, and that?" *Shut up. You're making it worse.*

"Spleen? Yeah, he's all right. Does his share, you know."

Frank did know. Every relief, in every cop shop in the country, carried at least one passenger. Superstars were equally unpopular with their colleagues, but a cop who 'did his share' was unlikely to make too many enemies. "He's not coasting, then? With retirement coming up."

"No more than half of them are! Got a total phobia about paperwork, mind. He'll do anything to get out of it. I mean, *anything.*"

"Surely that causes some friction? It does round our way."

"No, see, the thing is, you write a report for him and he'll do something for you. It's not like he's skiving. For instance, last week, he got one of the uniforms to write something up for him, and in exchange he took her next job—which was doing a death knock."

"You're joking!" Frank really thought he might be; surely no-one hated paperwork so much that they would actually volunteer to deliver news of a relative's death to the bereaved.

Clearly delighted that his anecdote had achieved the hoped for effect, the Yorkshireman laughed louder than ever. "Unbelievable, isn't it? True though, hand on heart. But no, listen, don't let me send you away with the wrong impression. Spleen's all right—doesn't spend half his time in the canteen and the other half in the bogs, like some of the old guys. And old as he is, he's very rarely last out of the van when something kicks off."

"Really?" Frank made a note. So, Dick Kidney didn't mind the physical side of the job? He wondered what the DI would make of that.

"To be honest," said Louise Ogden, "I think he took it more seriously than I did."

"By he, you mean Bruce?"

She nodded. Don wished she wouldn't do that, because of the knock-on effect it had on her t-shirt. "Yeah, poor Bruce."

"How did he find out about you and Eddie?"

"I think . . . well, I must have told him."

"Yes?"

"I don't know how it came up, but Bruce was very easy to talk to, you know, he was very sympathetic."

"And his reaction, when you told him that Eddie had been making unwanted advances to you—"

"He was angry. He just kept going on about it, how disgusting men like that were, how it made his blood boil." She laughed. "It seemed very out of character, if you know what I mean. Quite un-Brucelike."

"Why didn't you mention this to us when we saw you the other day, Louise?"

She sighed. "Yeah, I know . . ."

"We are investigating a murder." *And you're still keeping something back, Gorgeous.*

"I *know.* I'm sorry. It's just—I find the whole thing a bit embarrassing, really."

Don wanted to tell her that embarrassment was one of the things sex pests relied on. But he wasn't her father, and he didn't work in the Domestic Violence Unit. "Louise, do you want to make a formal complaint against Eddie Tarr? Because if you do—"

"Oh no, really." She shook her head, causing further movements in her upper torso. Or, at least, Don assumed so—he couldn't actually see her, since she'd been unable to meet him at such short notice, and so they were speaking over the phone. But he could *imagine* her shaking her head, and that was distracting enough. "Really, I know how to deal with his sort."

So did Bruce, it seems, thought Don.

In answer to Frank's ring on his doorbell, Eddie Tarr stuck his head out of the front window of his second-floor flat in Camden Town. "Who is it?"

Don stepped back onto the pavement, so that Tarr could see him. "All right, Eddie? Mind if we come in? We want to talk to you about Louise."

They heard a muffled *Shit,* then a louder: "Wait there. I'll be down."

Opening the door a slit, Tarr slipped through it, and snicked it shut behind him. "Mind if we walk and talk? Only I'm a bit pushed."

Don nodded towards the front door. "Girlfriend at home, is she? No, don't worry, Eddie—we'll walk. This won't take long, anyway."

They set off in the direction of the tube station, Don slowing the pace for no better reason than that Tarr kept trying to quicken it. After a hundred yards or so, Don simply stopped walking, leaned against a wall, and lit a cigar.

"What?" said Tarr.

"We'll talk here, Eddie. It's a nice day to be outside."

Tarr looked at Frank, but the DC's face was studiously blank. "Shit, all right. But look, I'm in a hurry. Can we—"

"You had a fight with Bruce Lester," said Don. "When was that, exactly?"

Tarr licked his lips once, rubbed his nose with his knuckles twice, and looked at his watch once. But—and Don had to admit to himself that he was quite impressed by this—all these displacement activities put together only took about five seconds. Long enough, evidently, for Tarr to work out his strategy.

"Mate, I wouldn't call it a *fight*."

"When?"

"Thursday. The Thursday before the match."

"Where?"

He pointed back the way they'd come. "There's an alley down there, sort of a short cut. I was on my way to the bus stop, just minding my own business—that fucking maniac must've been waiting for me."

"He attacked you? That doesn't sound very likely, Eddie—fit young geezer like you, beaten up by a middle-aged accountant."

177

"Look, I didn't say I was beaten up!" Tarr looked genuinely outraged at the suggestion. "He got in a couple of lucky swings before I even knew what was happening."

"And did you get in a couple back?"

"No way, I'm not going to go around brawling in the street with some sad old fool. I just pushed him off—kept him at arm's length until he calmed down. Wasn't that hard, he was half dead with exhaustion from his first couple of punches."

It could even be true, Don thought. A man like Eddie Tarr— a man who took pride in his physicality—might well be too much of a body snob to fight someone like poor old Bruce. The marks found during the post mortem weren't defence wounds, after all; they didn't, in themselves, serve to confirm or deny Tarr's version. "Why did he attack you?"

"How—"

"And before you answer, remember what I said to you just now, when you poked your head out of the window."

They watched him remember. "Mate, he'd got some stupid idea about me and Louise."

"Had he? Right. Two days later, you're feeling humiliated at getting beaten up by a man old enough to be your father—"

"I didn't get—"

"And the rage has been bubbling away inside you, and at close of play on Saturday it all boils up and—"

"That's crap! Look, sure, I have a bit of a temper—on the cricket field. If someone drops a catch or a batsman gets away with one, doesn't walk when he knows he's out, whatever, I'll give it some verbal. But I am not violent—and you won't find anyone who's ever met me who'll say different. And I am not into holding grudges, or getting revenge." He laughed. "God, I work in *comedy*, for shit's sake! If you held a grudge against everyone who ever shafted you in that business, there'd be nobody left to work with."

"You just forgot and forgave? That's very grown-up of you, Eddie."

"I kept out of his way. I didn't speak to him the whole day. Seemed to me like that was the grown-up thing to do, yeah." Tarr folded his arms. He looked tired, suddenly. "What do you think I am, Inspector? I love cricket, I love writing gags, I love my girlfriend. And you've met me three times, and you think I'm someone who would kill a human being over a misunderstanding. I mean—Jeez!"

"A misunderstanding?"

"Look, mate, he'd got it all wrong about me and Louise. I'm not interested in her. She is most definitely not my type."

"You asked her out, Eddie." *It probably wouldn't be a good idea to hit him,* Don told himself. *It could have pension-related repercussions.*

"I was joking! Yeah? I was winding her up, because she's such a little ice maiden."

"You asked her in a manner which could be described as persistent. If not threatening."

Tarr walked a few paces away, and then back again, as if made restless by the frustration of having to listen to endless calumny. "See, this is the same crap Bruce was coming out with. Same source, too, I'll bet. She should be so lucky! Bruce was *crazy* with this stuff, red as a lobster, just about frothing at the mouth. Like some bloody evangelical preacher—as if it was any of his business!" He shook his head. "In the end, the fact is I was just *embarrassed* by the whole thing. Embarrassed on *his* behalf, I mean. He was making a fool of himself."

"Why," said Frank, "do you think he was so worked up?"

"Guess he fancied her himself." Tarr smiled at Frank, and pointedly didn't look at Don. "A lot of the older guys do, you know."

CHAPTER SIXTEEN

"A what?"

"A collector's mart," Frank repeated. "Saturday and Sunday, at the new convention centre."

"In Cowden?"

Frank sighed, but moved the phone away from his mouth first. Why did Don, in certain moods, only believe things if you said them to him three times? "In Cowden. At the new convention centre. The Cowden convention centre. It's new."

"And PC Kidney gave you the details?"

"I subsequently checked them in the *Cachinnation Times*, but yes—he rang me half an hour ago."

"Why would he do that?"

"To tell us that he'd be there if we wanted to ask him any more questions. Instead of, as he put it, 'interrogating my workmates.' He seems quite cross about that, in fact—threatening to take it up with his Fed rep."

"He can take it up with Tony Blair if he likes, I don't give a toss."

"Yes, sir. He also mentioned that several of the others would be there."

"A collector's *mart?*"

"It's another word for market. I looked it up." He'd had to look it up twice, in fact, because the first definition didn't seem to fit: a fattened ox, salted for winter use.

"All right," said Don, eventually. "Might be worth a sniff. You never know, maybe I can sell some of my bootlegs there."

On Saturday morning, they sat in the car park for a while, waiting for the mart to start; evidently, comedy collectors didn't keep quite such unsocial hours as CID men. Don had spent much of the night thinking about Louise Ogden, and it had not been as pleasant an experience as one might have expected.

"It's a motive of sorts, isn't it? Mistaken identity."

"I suppose," said Frank. "Certainly, you can imagine her wanting to take a baseball bat to Eddie Tarr. But they're not exactly similar physical types, are they—Eddie and Bruce?"

"Not really. But—from behind? Wearing fancy dress?" He could tell by Frank's frown that the DC was not so much unconvinced, as inconvincible. "All right, forget mistaken identity. How about this. She *was* planning to attack Eddie, or actually began to attack him, and Bruce intervened. The chivalrous peacemaker, caught in the middle. He gets the wallop that was meant for Eddie, and she figures—well, it was an accident, no point in ruining her life over it. Just keep dumb, trust that Eddie does the same."

"That is possible," Frank allowed.

"Or even, that she resented Bruce's interference. I mean, virtually fighting a duel over her—could be flattering or humiliating, depending on which way you take it."

At that moment, the doors opened and a queue of collectors began to snake into the convention centre. Don deputed Frank to organise their official queue-barging, and to get them a sight of the registrations.

"Jerry Marsh is here," Frank reported back. "Networking, I suppose."

"Do we have any reason to fancy him?"

"Not really."

"Apart from the fact that he's American, and so is baseball. But then, maybe that's what we're supposed to think . . . Frank? You're gazing into the distance. Are you having a fit?"

"The baseball bat," said Frank, quietly. "Maybe we're coming at that the wrong way round."

"How do you mean?"

"Well, we've been trying to figure out who brought it to the pavilion, right?"

"Obviously."

"But maybe nobody did."

Don shook his head. "What? Frank, do you need a cup of coffee? He was killed with a baseball bat! If nobody took it there, then how—oh shit, I see what you mean. Yes . . . not a bad idea."

"If it was already there . . ."

"Wait a minute." Don hated to discourage Frank, but they were both overlooking something here. "Didn't someone sort out a list of baseball clubs in London?"

"Oh yeah, that's true."

"As part of the effort to tie one of the suspects to the bat. So if there was a baseball club using the cricket pavilion, it would have shown up then." Don suppressed a shudder, at the thought of people putting a cricket ground to such perverted use. At the thought of anyone in Britain choosing to play baseball at all, in fact.

"So, do we want to talk to Jerry?"

Don thought about it. "Might as well, since he's here. There is one thing that slightly nags at me about him, as it happens. I don't find his enthusiasm for all things British entirely convincing."

"His wife's British."

"Rather proves my point. Let's have a wander around, see who we bump into."

The first room they entered turned out to be hosting a talk by an elderly gentleman who had apparently been one of the special effects engineers on several nineteen fifties radio shows. Before a rapt audience, consisting mostly of bearded men in their forties and fifties, he was reminiscing about some of his greatest moments. It was all a bit technical for Don, but when the question and answer session started things livened up. It soon became obvious that the FX wizard was significantly deaf.

"Is it true that Spike Milligan used real custard in a sock for one of his effects?" a man in thick spectacles asked from the floor.

"Mustard?"

"Custard. In a sock."

"A rock?"

"A sock. Custard. Spike Milligan?" The questioner was bright red by now, obviously regretting ever having troubled the old boy.

"Mike Mustard?"

"There you are," said Don, in Frank's ear. "All you have to do is mention Spike Milligan's name, and everything turns surreal. What powers, even from beyond the grave."

"Shall we have a look in the main hall?" whispered Frank.

They tiptoed out. Just as the door shut behind them, Don distinctly heard the distinguished guest insist: "Buzzard? No, no, we never used a buzzard in our effects. That would be against the law, surely?"

Jerry Marsh wasn't in the main hall, where the dealers in ephemera, records, books, and autographs had set out their stalls, but they ran into him soon enough, in the snack bar. Don began by asking him about his act.

"I'd like to see it some time. Have you got any gigs coming up in London?"

"Oh, you know, there's irons in the fire. It's matter of feeling your way, getting to know the circuit, and so on. I'm hoping to do something at Edinburgh next summer."

"But nothing specific in the diary at the moment?"

"Nothing—well, nothing actually specific I could mention right now, no."

"What sort of act is it? Most of you Americans seem to do observational comedy."

"I guess." Marsh seemed to relax, as the conversation turned from the specific to the general. "I started off over here doing a lot of stuff about America. You know—guns, stupid presidents, fat jokes, that kind of thing. I thought that was what people would want from a Yank."

"Didn't it go well?"

"It was OK, but my next gig, instead of doing anti-American stuff, I took some advice, and did anti-British stuff, instead."

"And that went over better?"

"Much better. Seems British audiences really enjoying having the piss taken out of them by foreigners." He looked bemused. "Kind of weird, but if that's what people want . . ."

"Well," said Don, "we did invent masochism, after all."

"Really? I thought that was another one of Al Gore's." Don and Frank looked at each other. "Sorry," said Marsh. "American joke. It obviously didn't travel."

"Speaking of things not travelling," said Don, "I've always wondered—why don't you Yanks play any proper sports?" He saw Frank's reaction out of the corner of his eye; good. If Frank was taken aback at his rudeness, with any luck young Jerry would feel the same. "I mean, world sports. You only play sports that are only played in one country."

"Well—"

"Oh no, sorry, my mistake—they play ice hockey in Canada as well, don't they?"

"Well, you know it's not true that Americans don't play international team sports." The little sod was smiling, Don couldn't help but notice. "Cricket, soccer, rugby, snooker, darts—you name it, there's a Team USA competing. Even though most Americans are unaware of the fact. But I take your point: why aren't any of Planet Earth's big sports big on Planet America?"

"And . . . ?"

"I think it's simply this: if you don't compete, you can't get beat—and not getting beaten is pretty much our national religion. You know, like refusing to take anything seriously is Britain's national religion." Don saw Frank nodding at that. Traitor! "But, Inspector, you should know that the American media has a much narrower social focus than the UK media. So the America you see on TV, movies, that's not the America that ninety per cent of Americans live in."

"You mean *Friends* isn't a documentary?"

"Seriously, I'd never been served mocha latte by a shaven-headed Nigerian lesbian in a Kurdish café, until I came to London."

"Not even in L.A.?"

"Oh—well, yeah, you know. I guess L.A.'s pretty cool."

I wonder, thought Don: *I wonder if he's ever even been to Los Angeles?*

"You had the makings of a comedy career back there in L.A., Jerry. You had family in the States, friends. Your wife must have liked it there, or she wouldn't have married you. So what really brought you to the UK? You have a rain fetish, perhaps?"

Marsh ran one of his hands over the other, in a gesture that seemed artificial—and vaguely familiar—to Don. "Truth is, I got fed up with living in the seventeenth century, so I came to Britain." He smiled. "Thought I'd see what the nineteenth century had to offer."

It was the timing that gave it away. "You use that in your act, do you?" *Of course!* That business with the hands—Jack Benny.

Marsh's response was half embarrassment, half delight. "You got me!"

"Not a bad line. I really must try and see your show. But tell me, Jerry, what is the worst thing about living in London?"

Nodding at Frank, Marsh said: "You know, your colleague asked me that once before."

"Ah, but you won't have wanted to hurt his feelings. To me, you can tell the truth."

"Well . . . the place is filthy. I mean, where I come from putting litter in a litterbin isn't considered, like, actual *proof* that you're a homosexual. You know? I'm not the fussiest guy on earth, but I don't know how people can live like this—wading ankle deep in garbage all day long. If my mother saw this place? She'd commit suicide, I think. Or send for an exorcist."

"I blame the IRA," said Don. "They kept putting bombs in litter bins."

"They did? When?"

"Oh, twenty-odd years ago."

"You know why you don't see more rats in London? I think it's because all the fast food that people chuck on the ground has poisoned them. Also, this is an amazingly unfriendly place."

Don and Frank exchanged puzzled looks. Don spoke for

both of them. "It's a *city*," he said.

"Yeah, a city with laws against eye contact."

We're going to get his whole act, thought Don. Poor bugger doesn't get much chance to try out his material; his wife must've heard it all a thousand times. "Listen, thanks for your help, Jerry. We'd best move on—we've got a whole list of people to annoy today."

They headed back to the main hall. "What do you think?" Frank asked.

"He's a charming lad. I like him." Don looked around to make sure he wasn't near a smoke alarm, and lit a cigar. "His timing's not at all bad, too. Tell you what, though: he's lying to us."

"Oh, I don't know," said Frank. "London is pretty dirty."

Don laughed. "Yeah, but how many mediaeval palaces have they got in Iowa fucking City?"

"Lying about why he came over here, you mean?"

"I'm sure of it. Well, maybe not lying—maybe just not telling the truth. Either way, if someone is untruthful during a murder investigation, we need to know why."

"Is it possible . . ." Frank began, and then dried up.

"Out with it, Frank." Don was irritated. When had he *ever* done other than encourage Frank to speak his mind?

"It's just—I got the impression that maybe Jerry's comedy career back home wasn't as far advanced as he'd like us to think."

"I suspect you suspect correctly. If it becomes necessary— and if we can blag the resources—I'd like to get that checked out."

"In which case," said Frank, "is it possible that Bruce found this out, and Jerry killed him—to prevent damage to his standing over here?"

"It's very possible. In fact, my mind has been drifting in

the same direction. So, I'm going see if I can interview his wife, on her own. Meanwhile, you talk to Anna Lester's neighbours. The Bristol cops claim to have done it, but it's not their case. I want someone I trust doing it."

Man-management, Don thought, watching Frank and his beam of pride hurry off towards the car park. *There's nothing to it. I should write a book.*

Frank enjoyed the drive down to Bristol this time. He didn't stop—except for a pee and a takeaway tea, when he was only a few minutes away from his destination—and he made good time. Besides, he preferred driving alone; he was a confident enough driver, but still it was an act he'd rather not perform before an audience.

During the rest of the afternoon, he spoke to people in thirteen houses in Bruce and Anna Lester's street. In eight cases the interviewees said they'd never met the Lesters, although a sub-set of this group had at least heard of them, since the name of the road had been mentioned in local press reports of the murder.

Occupants in all of the remaining five residences were unanimous: Bruce and Anna had, as far as anyone could tell, a sound marriage. They seemed to get on well, to spend time together, to be perfectly happy. No-one was at all encouraging of the idea that either party might have been having an affair. "They're just not the type," Frank was told, over and over.

One man, in particular—a Mr. J. Hardwick, of The Elms—was insistent that Anna most certainly would never engage in extra-marital adventures, and he should know if anyone did.

"Because I offered, that's how I know. I tell you that frankly—and in confidence, of course."

"Of course."

"One of the neighbours had a garden party last summer—well, they called it a garden party, it was a wine and cheese do, actually, all standing around on the patio getting cramp trying to hold onto a glass, a paper plate, and a cigarette in two hands—and I made it clear to Anna then that I was available, if she was interested. No pressure you understand, just a friendly invitation."

"Quite."

"And she said no. Perfectly polite about it, but no thanks, not interested. So there you are, young man, I think I speak with some authority on the matter."

Amazing, thought Frank. This dreary, pink-faced, middle-aged banker with protrusive nasal hair honestly believes that because Anna Lester turned *him* down that must means she isn't in the market. Ah, well; at least he didn't say she was a lesbian.

"What about Bruce? You never heard anything to suggest that he was—"

"Bruce?" Mr. Hardwick guffawed. "Chance would be a fine thing—let's be honest, he was hardly God's gift, was he? Never been in a gym in his life, that one."

He patted his stomach, from which Frank deduced that the man's large gut was muscle rather than fat. Frank couldn't see that it made much difference; a firm potbelly was still a potbelly. "Doesn't necessarily stop a man trying though, does it?"

"True, true." The banker nodded wisely, apparently unaware of any irony. "But old Bruce was very stern about that sort of thing. Very old-fashioned. There was a bloke we both knew, for instance—ran off with a young nurse he met when he was in a hospital having his haemorrhoids fixed. Bruce was *most* disapproving—said one mistake like that could haunt the rest of your life."

"Was he speaking from experience?"

"Well, obviously not—as I say, he was happily married to the lovely Anna."

"You never heard Bruce talk about any woman in particular? Someone he met through business, or through his hobby, perhaps, that he seemed more than usually interested in?"

Hardwick hooked his fingers into his braces—possibly to give his muscular gut a breather—and thought for a moment. "Now you mention it, there was a girl he was talking about recently; he knew her through all that comedy nonsense, I think."

"Did he mention a name?"

"I don't think so; if he did, I've forgotten it. She came up in conversation, in fact, when we were discussing that guy I mentioned earlier—the one with the piles and the pretty little nurse. Bruce was . . . what can I say? Very *interested* in her welfare."

Frank interpreted Hardwick's unpleasant smile. "Fancied her, you mean?"

"Well, I can't think what else it would be, can you? I don't suppose he wanted to give her advice on long term savings plans."

Louise, thought Frank. Perhaps Eddie Tarr had been right, after all—maybe Bruce did fancy Louise himself. And if he did, and he tried to do something about it . . . how might Louise have reacted?

CHAPTER SEVENTEEN

Remembering the old Cowden General, Don had to admit—Cowden's newly opened hospital was impressive to behold. He couldn't remember ever having been in a brand new hospital before; one that still smelt of paint and plastic, instead of blood and vomit. The millions of pounds spent on the place were evident in the shining surfaces, the bright signage, the uncluttered corridors and—most contrasting of all with the state-of-the-art Victorian pile it had replaced—the general sense that the whole facility had been planned by someone who had an idea of what went on in a twenty-first century infirmary.

Reception told him that Nurse Marsh was on a break, so he tried the nurses' common room. There he found just two people, neither of whom admitted to being married to Jerry Marsh—denials he was inclined to accept at face value, since both deniers were male. After an unintended, but instructive, solo sightseeing tour, he was finally advised to try the rear doors—the ones that led to the car park.

Outside the main building he found, as promised, the answer to the common room's emptiness: the new hospital was, of course, a strictly tobacco-free building. Beneath the stairs of a fire escape made of orange tubular steel, seven young people in medical outfits were speed-smoking filter-tips and roll-ups, before or after, he assumed, heading to the cafeteria to drink mineral water and eat low-fat sandwiches.

"Excuse me, is one of you Sarah Marsh?"

"That's me. Are you here about the assault?"

Don wasn't surprised that she'd guessed his profession; he'd have been more surprised at a nurse who failed to do so. He explained his true purpose—well, perhaps not his *true* purpose, but near enough to avoid lying—and the young nurse detached herself from her colleagues. They found a perch a few yards away, on a low retaining wall surrounding a well-stocked, if somewhat dry, ornamental bed.

"I must say, this place doesn't look much like a hospital. And I intend that as a compliment to the architect."

"It's certainly an improvement on some of the places I've worked in, here and abroad." Sarah Marsh had a pleasant voice, quiet but distinct, with a touch of East Anglia in the vowels. She was maybe a couple of years older than her husband, with long, dyed hair, large ears, and an expression on her face which Don could only describe to himself as a friendly frown.

"I thought the NHS was supposed to be collapsing—at least according to what you read in the papers."

"Sure," she said, stubbing out her cigarette on the wall, then burying the stub amid the flowers. "But who owns the papers? Same people who own the private healthcare companies. If they can convince everyone that the National Health is on its last legs, not worth saving, then they can get their tame politicians to push through privatisation, and make a killing."

"You could be right."

"The truth is, overall, services and facilities are better than they've ever been. Nye Bevan wouldn't *believe* what we can do for people now."

"I know," said Don. "I saw the mini shopping mall in the lobby."

Nurse Marsh, however, was not to be deflected. "The trouble is these days, maybe because of TV, or because nobody trusts politicians, people believe what they hear in the media much more strongly than they believe their own experience—the evidence of their own senses. Even if *their* local NHS services are first rate, they think that's just chance—and that everywhere else the whole system's crumbling."

"But you do have staff shortages," said Don. "That's not made up by corrupt journalists."

She took out a packet of cigarettes, offered Don one, and when he declined she put the packet away again. "There are always staff shortages! Every democratic country in the world has staff shortages. They're endemic, chronic. For some strange reason, kids today would rather go to university and doss about for three years, then get a well-paid job in the media with a big car and an expense account, rather than wipe old people's arses and hold children's hands while they die. Inexplicable isn't it?"

"Utterly," Don agreed. He saw that her right hand was restless in her tunic pocket, and took pity on her: he lit himself a small cigar, and held the light for her.

"Ta. I hate smoking on my own."

"Quite right too. So, what's the answer, then?"

"To . . . ?"

"To people not wanting to go into medicine. To the chronic overproduction of Business Studies graduates and media whores?"

"Asking me? National Service."

Don was astonished. He wouldn't have had her down as an old-fashioned authoritarian. On the other hand, she was a nurse, and nurses wouldn't be much use to the sexual fantasy industry if they didn't have a starchy streak in them. "Conscription, you mean?"

She shook her head, the cigarette held tightly between her lips. "No, no. Not military service. But people who want the taxpayer to pay for their education should be required, on graduation, to put in a few years in something socially useful. Medicine, teaching, local government, whatever—*then* they can go out and make their fortunes in advertising."

Don smiled. "You mean, when they're too old to enjoy it?"

Her friendly frown crinkled. "Exactly! That'd wipe the smiles off their Porsches."

He hoped, at that moment, hoped very much that he would soon be able to arrest her husband for murder—because then she'd be single, and he was in love with her. Her sound ideas, her friendly frown. Her starched uniform. "It's not only money, though, is it? I mean, a busy plumber can earn seventy thousand a year—and yet there's a national shortage of plumbers." Don's own theory on the matter, which he decided not to share with his beloved at this early point in their relationship, was that trades like plumbing were seen as being not only manual work, but *male* work—and thus twice damned in the eyes of fashion conscious young people, and especially in the eyes of their mothers.

They finished smoking, and then Don decided, not without reluctance, that he ought to move on. "Did you ever meet Bruce Lester?"

"I don't think so. Jerry described him to me, after he was killed, but I don't remember him."

"And you weren't at the match last weekend?"

"I was working." She paused, then added: "Besides—cricket. If I want to watch paint dry, I can do that in this place."

"You're not a fan?"

"I don't mind football, but no—I'm not keen on cricket."

Don fell out of love. He should have known; the ones who seemed too good to be true always had some deep, underlying, psychological flaw lurking beneath the surface. "So Jerry's interest in the game wasn't one of the things that attracted you to him?"

"Hardly. Though, I don't know—at least it made him a bit different."

"Where did he acquire such an unusual interest, do you know?"

"I think it was some friend of his at high school, who lived in New Zealand for a year. To be honest, I think him and a few of his friends just enjoyed being a bit eccentric. You know what lads are like."

Not in L.A., then. "Whereabouts did you live in the States? One of the big cities?"

"They called it a city—over here it'd be a large village! It was a nice place, though. A little, rural town in Iowa. Bit dull, but very friendly."

"What made you leave?"

"Oh, I don't know." She took out her cigarettes again, looked at the packet, then put it away. "I was finding it difficult to get nursing jobs where we were, and Jerry wanted to make a serious go of the comedy. He's very good, he really is."

"I can believe it. He has that air about him."

"Yeah! I honestly believe—anyway, London seemed like a better bet than Iowa for that. Well, for both of us."

"Jerry must miss home, though."

"He does, in many ways, but . . . well, there are advantages over here, too."

He'd got what he wanted, Don reflected; Jerry was lying about Los Angeles, lying about his American comedy career. He wasn't a natural liar, clearly; otherwise, he'd have thought

195

to get his story straight with his wife's. Sadly, that didn't mean he wasn't a killer.

"Well, thanks for your time, Sarah. I'll let you get back to your arse-wiping. Do you want me to explain to your supervisor why you're—"

"No, don't worry." She stood up, and brushed ash off her lap. "They're pretty cool here."

"You were lucky to find such a congenial post," he said, as they strolled back towards the doors. "Your first job back in the country."

"Yes, it's not bad, can't complain. And it's convenient, of course, because this is where Jerry . . ."

She wouldn't catch his eye, and was obviously never going to finish her sentence voluntarily, so Don stooped walking. "Where Jerry what?"

She took a couple more paces forward, then turned to him, a look of resignation replacing her customary expression. "Look, I'm sure this isn't relevant."

"You're a nurse, Sarah. You mix with coppers all the time. You know the answer to that."

"Yeah . . . It's nothing, really. It's just that Jerry has a chronic health problem. An incurable stomach condition. Nothing life threatening, or anything like that, but it does require quite a lot of ongoing treatment."

"Which he receives here?"

She nodded. "The thing is, he doesn't like to talk about it. Or for me to talk about it, either."

"Why not?"

"He just doesn't, that's all."

They continued their walk, their pace slightly faster now. "That's a pity," said Don. He didn't specify what was a pity—Jerry's illness, or his reluctance to have it known about. He hoped she'd realise, under the circumstances, that he meant both.

The coffee wasn't very good at the convention centre, but it was better than the tea.

"What's the opposite of flaky pastry?"

"I don't know," said Frank. "Why?"

"I was just wondering what they made these Danish pastries out of."

"They are a bit hard. Sunday morning, I suppose."

Don gave up on his cake, took a swig of coffee to rinse his mouth, and then gave up on that too. "What sort of excuse is that, Frank? Sunday morning! It's a bloody convention centre. They've got a convention on today. If they can't provide the catering, they shouldn't take the bookings."

"Look on the bright side," said Frank. "We didn't pay to get in."

"I'll bet you don't get rock hard Danish pastries and piss-flavoured coffee in bloody Iowa, Sunday or any other day. They may be crap at sport, the Americans, but they know a thing or two about breakfast."

Frank, who had already had his breakfast—at breakfast time, funnily enough, not at ten in the morning—made no further contribution to the Danish debate. The mart attendees were beginning to arrive in numbers, and he wanted to know what he and Don were supposed to be doing today. "Do we really need to talk to Jerry Marsh again? You seem pretty sure he's not the one. Despite the fact that we now know for certain he's been lying to us."

Don shook his head. "He's not the murderer, Frank."

"Why? Because he's got a nice wife?"

"Because I think I know what this is all about. The lies, I mean."

"Here he is," said Frank, waving at the American who'd just entered the café.

Now that he knew Marsh was chronically ill—subject, perhaps, to periods of pain—Frank wasn't surprised to see him wearing the look of a hangover victim. Besides, when he got home last night, his wife would have told him about her conversation with Don. He couldn't be looking forward to this encounter. He was hiding it well enough, though, with a big smile.

"I *love* Sunday mornings in this country! Where I come from, everyone goes to church on Sundays. I mean *everyone*. You have no idea how naughty I feel spending the whole of Sunday morning in bed, then going down the pub for a game of darts. Or even going to a comedy mart, come to that. It's liberating."

"What would your parents say?" Don asked.

"Oh, they'd say good luck. They don't go to church because they want to, they go to church because that's the kind of neighbourhood they live in. You know how many people go to church in Britain?"

"Of course I don't," said Don. "Why would anybody know that?"

"Well, I do. I Googled the stats."

"Absolutely," said Don. "I'm sure you did."

"Eight per cent," said Marsh, as if he were announcing that his kid brother had been awarded a degree with honours by Harvard.

"I'm surprised it's so many," said Frank, who didn't know any churchgoers. His second cousin Mary didn't count, because the staff at the home took her. They said it made a nice outing.

"That's in Britain," Marsh explained. "The figure for England is even lower. You know, in England more people worship at mosques than they do in Church of England churches."

"Ah well," said Don, "you're making the common mistake of imagining that the C of E is a religious organisation."

"Of course, you're all going to burn in hell, but in the meantime—*shit!* What do they put in this coffee?"

"See?" said Frank. "Beware the Church of Iowa, it has a long reach."

"Coffee doesn't aggravate your condition, Jerry?" Don spoke quietly, in a voice which mixed sympathy with accusation.

Marsh put his cup down, and sat back in his chair with a long sigh. "It doesn't do it a lot of good. But then, nothing that's worth eating or drinking does, I find."

"A stomach complaint, your wife said?"

"You know stomach ulcers? It's similar to that."

"And it was that," said Don, "rather than an appetite for cultural diversity, which brought you to the UK."

"Partly." He nodded. "Well, yeah, pretty much. Do you know much about the medical system in the United Sates?"

"I know you don't have a national health service."

"Friend of mine," said Frank, "was knocked down by a cab in New York once. He said the ambulancemen checked his credit cards before they checked his pulse."

"It works by insurance," Marsh began, then he stopped. "Listen, do I really have to talk about all this?"

"Just tidy it up for us, Jerry. Then we'll move on."

"All right. The brief version: my condition was diagnosed when I was twenty-one. At that time, I didn't have any medical insurance of my own. I didn't have, like, a career, you know—I was doing minimum wage type of jobs, pizza delivery and all that, because most of the time I was working on an act. For stand-up? That's all I was interested in. So anyway, I wasn't in any corporate insurance scheme. And of course, now I couldn't *get* any insurance."

199

Frank got it. "Pre-existing condition." He'd had the same trouble with a car once. Don nodded at him, in confirmation.

"Despite what your friend with the New York cab story might have told you, you wouldn't actually be left to die on the street. But . . ." Marsh's voice faltered.

"But you had a British girlfriend," said Don.

"We were talking about getting married anyway. I've always wanted to visit this country. But that's not the point. The point is, by moving to Britain I can get all the medical care I'll ever need, and I'll never have to pay a penny for it." He looked as if he was about to burst into tears. "So there you go, guys—I'm a scrounger. I'm an economic migrant."

"Bollocks," said Don.

"Thanks, Inspector, but—"

"*Total* bollocks." Don lit a cigar, let a lungful of smoke trickle out of his nostrils, and continued. "First of all, all the most successful countries in world history—Britain, the US, Ancient Rome, you name it—were built by economic migrants. It's not a term of abuse. Or it shouldn't be. Where do you think the English came from? Not from these islands, that's for sure. Secondly, how can you be a scrounger; you work, don't you? You pay taxes?"

"In the unlikely event I earn enough to be liable for any taxes, yeah."

"You pay taxes every time you go shopping, mate, and at a proportionately higher rate than the Duke of Westminster. Well there you are then, you're a taxpayer, you're using the service you help pay for, no problem. Whatever gave you the idea that people would think you were a scrounger?"

Marsh didn't look convinced, but at least he was smiling again. "Inspector, have you ever read a British newspaper . . . ?"

"Oh yeah." Don laughed. "Fair point. Did Bruce know about all this?"

"I don't think so. And yes, I do understand the implications of your question. Believe me, even if he had found out, I wouldn't have killed him over it. I admit, it's not something I'm proud of, it's not something I shout about, but that's my problem. I mean, you think about it, whoever caved poor Bruce's head in, that's got to be someone who loved him or hated him, surely? Or both."

Don smoked his cigar for a moment, studying Marsh quite unmercifully as he did so. "All right," he said at last. "Remember what I said, Jerry. And give us a buzz when you've got a show on. Frank'll probably bring the family along, book the whole front row. Isn't that right, Frank?"

"If you're paying, sir, I'll bring the neighbours as well."

Don shook hands with Marsh, quite solemnly, Frank thought. Then, just when the young comic thought it was over, Don said: "There is one more thing."

"Yes . . . ?"

"Do Americans keep hedgehogs as pets?"

"I . . . Yes, I believe so. Some Americans, you understand, not all. You going to arrest me for that?"

Go on, thought Frank; *ask him about the potato skins, I dare you.*

"Do they keep them indoors?"

"I'm afraid I have no idea, Inspector. I've never actually *known* anyone who kept a hedgehog, it's just something I've read in magazines."

"Hmm," said Don, stubbing out his cigar. "Now I come to think of it, I haven't seen a hedgehog in London in ages."

"Well, that's something else to blame the Yanks for, I guess." Marsh, Frank noted, was thoroughly back in character now—the cheeky young comic, relying on his timing and his charm. "Global warming, World War Three, and now the great London hedgehog shortage."

"We did see a dead one on the road, sir," Frank pointed out. "Coming back from Bristol the other day."

Jerry Marsh widened his eyes, and held his hands up above his shoulders. "Oh, now, that wasn't me. I have an alibi."

CHAPTER EIGHTEEN

"Was he the obsessive type, would you say?"

"Who?"

Frank waited for the DI to finish flicking through the hardback of Bob Hope's *I Owe Russia $1200*, which he'd just bought for £4-50 from a stall in the convention centre. No point trying to talk to him when his attention was so obviously elsewhere. They were sitting in Frank's car, having found privacy elusive within the centre. Both the driver's and passenger's doors were wide open, as a form of energy-conscious air-conditioning.

"Sorry, Frank—is who an obsessive?"

"Bruce Lester. I was wondering if you thought he might be an obsessive type. After all, a man who can spend that amount of time on a hobby—"

Don snapped his book shut. "Just because we live in a world where watching soap operas and going shopping are considered healthy recreational sports, and taking an interest in anything outside your own tiny life is considered embarrassing and nerdish, doesn't mean that anyone with a hobby is a psycho, Frank."

"No, of course not. All I'm thinking is, it could be a motive for Louise Ogden. Supposing Bruce did become obsessed with her—not just fancied her, I mean, but got spooky about it."

"A stalker?"

"You can imagine a strong, capable woman like her dealing with a situation like that in a direct way."

"Yes . . ." Don absentmindedly riffled Bob Hope's pages. Frank could never remember; was he the one who sang "White Christmas," or was that the little black guy with one eye? "Yes, you're right, it is a possibility. Bruce certainly seems to have been—well, yeah, *obsessed* with her, doesn't he? At least a little bit."

"From what people tell us."

"We will have to talk to her again, but let's save up that treat—first of all, I want to tick Dick Kidney off the list."

"Just tick him off? You've no hopes of him as our man?"

"Christ, I hope not! I'm buggered if I'm going to court to give evidence in a case where the accused has a funnier name than the judge. It's just not on."

"He's still got a motive, though. Looks like Bruce was actually going to write the book which Dick never would write."

"Yes," said Don, lighting a cigar. "Doesn't quite fit with the Brucie we've come to know, does it? Bit insensitive, if not downright brutal."

They caught up with PC Kidney in the main hall, queuing to get an armful of books autographed by the convention's guest of honour, a TV comic-turned-novelist. He wasn't eager to lose his place in the queue.

"Don't worry," Don told him. "You can always use your warrant card to barge back in."

"Just for the record," said Kidney, as they escorted him to the café. "I don't appreciate you lot talking to my colleagues behind my back. I suppose I shouldn't expect anything better from the Met, but where I come from that kind of thing is basically considered underhand."

"Just for the record," said Don, "shut up and stop whining."

They found an empty table in a corner of the café. Don and Frank sat down; Kidney did not. "As long as we're here," he said, "I might as well get myself a cup of—"

"Sit down," Don said, sitting back himself, and nodding at Frank.

With Kidney reluctantly seated, Frank said: "Here's why we're worried about you, Dick. Everybody who knows you, knows that you're supposed to be writing the definitive book about Bob Wilton."

"*Robb,*" said Kidney.

"About Wilton. But what *we* now know is that writing things is not exactly your strong suit. Meanwhile, as *you* well know, your old friend Bruce Lester was writing a book about the same subject."

"*Was* writing a book," Don emphasised. "Not just shooting his mouth off."

To Don's considerable displeasure, Kidney laughed, shook his head, and gave every impression of being entirely relaxed. "Is that it? Is that what you lost me my place in the queue for? Is that what you came harassing me about, on my day off?"

"It seems to us—" Frank began.

"All right, Geordie—lick your pencil and get this down." Kidney took a deep breath and let it out slowly. Not looking at either of the Met officers, he spoke in a steady, dead voice, as if giving uncontested evidence in court. "I've never written a word, you're quite right. Never could. Never will, most likely. Writing has never been my thing, as you so kindly pointed out. Horses for courses, isn't it? Some cops are good at paperwork—some are good at nicking villains, protecting the public, and defending the Queen's peace. Each to his own, eh?"

"But when you found out that Bruce was—"

Mat Coward

"I didn't find out. It was basically me that asked him to do it. I've done years of research about Wilton; I know as much about him as anyone alive today, I reckon. I know more about him than he knew about himself. So: it was a joint enterprise. I do the research, Bruce does the writing—not that he was that good, but he was better than me—and the book comes out under both our names. That was the plan. He did it as a favour to me. Right? As an old friend."

"But this wasn't public knowledge?"

Now Kidney looked at Frank. "No. Why? because I was *embarrassed,* that's why. Do you understand? I don't suppose you Met tossers ever get embarrassed, do you? It wouldn't go with the hard-man image."

And he did look embarrassed, Don thought; or ashamed, even. Don wondered just how deep the constable's problems with writing ran. Surely it wouldn't be possible for a semi-literate man to survive in the job these days? But Don had encountered stranger things in his career. And out of it.

"Doesn't matter now, though, does it?" said Kidney. "Won't be any book, now."

"Perhaps you'll find someone else to collaborate with," Frank suggested.

"Oh yeah! What—put a small ad in the paper?"

Don half-listened to Frank's well-meaning attempts to mitigate Kidney's gloom. With the greater part of his mind he was wondering what further use the Brummie cop might be to the investigation now, if any. They were still left, he was sure, with two probable motives for the murder: sex or money. Of the two, he reckoned money looked favourite, given the evidence piling up for Bruce and Anna's happy marriage. Still . . .

"Dick, a couple of people have mentioned to us that Bruce

was in love once before, years ago. Before he got married."

"He was, yeah."

"But nobody knows who with?"

"Well, I certainly don't. Can I go now?"

"Could it have been a married woman? Might that be why her identity is unknown even to his old friends?" Because if he'd done it before—albeit years ago—it made it more believable that he'd been doing it recently.

"Could be, I suppose." Kidney thought about it, and the idea seemed to afford him some grim satisfaction. "That'd be a turn up! Yeah, I suppose it could be—he was certainly very secretive about the whole thing, which was a bit out of character."

"When was this?"

Kidney shrugged. "Twenty years ago? Tell you what, you want to ask Bernie. Or maybe Stella. Bruce might be more likely to confide in a woman, you never know. He got on well with women." He made it sound like a character flaw.

Quietly, Don said: "Were you married back then, Dick?"

"Me?" Kidney laughed. "Forget it, Inspector—my darling wife was long gone by then. I was married young, and divorced not much older. Anyway, I can't see *her* taking a lover. Not really one of her great interests, sex."

Stella had never married, Don remembered. So it couldn't have been her, if there ever was a married woman in Bruce's youth. "You knew Bernie and his wife? First wife, I mean."

Kidney frowned. "I knew her the first time round, if that's what you mean."

"First time round?"

"Ah!" Kidney's sudden smile was large and unlovable. "Didn't know that, did you? Bernie married the same woman twice. They split up, I don't know why, he never said—usual,

I imagine—then they got back together again, couple of years ago."

Why do people do that? Don wondered. It almost seemed to be a fashion, people getting divorced and then remarrying each other. Don didn't really approve of marriage, and one reason why he didn't, was that he didn't approve of divorce much, either. But surely adults should learn to make their bloody minds up? "What was her name?" he asked.

"Tonia. Nice girl. Pretty girl, too."

"You say you knew her the first time? Not the second time?"

Kidney shook his head. "They basically kept themselves to themselves, second time."

"You weren't invited to the wedding?"

"None of us were. From fandom, I mean."

"Bit odd, isn't it?"

"Not really—she was already dying when he married her."

Ah well, thought Don. *That's different; fair enough.*

"It was a reconciliation, I suppose you'd call it," Kidney continued. "Of course, we were all very pleased for him—for both of them. Bruce organised a whip-round and bought them something as a wedding present. He was delighted; he liked a happy ending."

"Had he known her the first time round?"

"Not particularly, I don't think so. Probably met her, but I got the impression he hadn't really known her. If you think about it, he was a youngster back then—he wouldn't have wanted to hang around with a boring married couple, would he? I felt much the same about my own marriage, God knows."

"People's lives, eh, Frank?" Don commented when they were on their own. "You never know, do you?"

"No, I suppose not."

Don smiled. *Too young. Life and death were still abstracts for him.* "I think it's time for Stella," he said.

"The missing years?"

"It can't be anything to do with Bruce, can it? The dates are wrong. But that doesn't mean he hadn't found out something about her—or that they weren't lovers some time in the past, and one of them wanted to rekindle the old flame."

"Like you said," Frank said, "people's lives."

At first, bearded in her untidy, paper-stuffed, obviously long-inhabited flat in Hendon, Stella Wardle reacted with studied sangfroid to Don's questioning.

"Hardly worth disturbing my Sunday, Inspector—or yours. There's no mystery."

"No?"

"No. Truth is, I took a rest from the bloody comedy business—I needed a few laughs, frankly—so I went abroad for a couple of years."

"Where abroad?"

"Europe."

"Where in Europe?"

"Here and there. It was a very freewheeling time, the early seventies."

"Doing what?"

"Just bumming around, doing bar jobs, that kind of thing. Grape-picking, lying on beaches, seducing French boys, the usual sort of continental adventure." She turned a nasty smile on Frank. "I'm sorry, Constable—is it too hot for you in here? I'll open a window."

Right, thought Don. *No-one was allowed to deliberately embarrass his DC. Well—no-one else.* "And then, a few years later, you seduced Bruce Lester?"

"What?"

"That's the information we've received since we last spoke to you. In fact, Stella, it's only fair to tell you that you are currently at the top of our suspects list."

She sat down, not bothering first to remove a pile of padded envelopes from the sofa. The envelopes squirted out from beneath her and took refuge under the coffee table. "Look—for God's sake! I was *never* involved with Bruce Lester. You *must* realise how . . . I mean, for God's sake!"

She'd gone pale, and her hands were shaking slightly. Don had seen it before; smart people, finding themselves on the periphery of a criminal investigation for the first and probably only time in their lives, treating it all as a rather amusing diversion. And then, suddenly, realising that it wasn't—that it could, conceivably, involve them.

"You want to convince us, Stella? You could start by telling the truth about your 'Continental adventure.' "

She put her hands between her knees to steady them. "You have a revolting job, Mr. Packham. I'm glad I'm not—"

"Yes, yes." Don made get-a-move-on motions with both hands. "Etcetera, etcetera."

"I was a mistress. To a rich man." She gave him a defiant look; or the nearest to it that she could currently manage.

"Hardly the first woman to undertake such an assignment. Why the secrecy?"

"He was—the man I was with was an accountant."

"A showbiz accountant?"

"*Showbiz,*" she mimicked. "Quite. And to put the thing bluntly—which I'm sure is how you prefer it, Inspector—he had ripped off a number of his clients, and gone walkabout on the proceeds. I didn't know this when I agreed to go with him, of course. But when I came back—if people in the comedy business had known of my involvement with the horrible little shit, I would have been despised. For sleeping with the enemy. More to the point, I'd have been unemployable."

"Bruce was an accountant," said Frank.

"So what?"

"What the DC means, Stella, is that Bruce might well have found out about your secret, him being in the same trade as your friend. Is that what you were rowing about, at Bernie's Christmas party? Bruce found out and was threatening you, blackmailing you?"

"God no!" Her reaction was so loud—and so physical, as she recoiled against the cushions as if shot—that both men took an involuntary half step backwards. As Don picked himself up, having tripped over a pile of video cassettes, Wardle recovered her voice. "Oh, shit! You're serious about this crap, aren't you? Listen—we were arguing about Declan."

"Declan?"

"His . . . OK, I don't owe him any loyalty, God knows. His accounts."

Ah-ha! It was all Don could do not to rub his hands together, or dance a jig. "Oh yes, we know about Declan's bent books."

"You do?" She puffed out her cheeks in a long, relieved exhalation. "I only didn't say anything before because if Declan goes down for tax fiddling, bang goes my job. And at my age . . . the youngsters in the business have never heard of me. Why would they hire me? All my references are in Golders Green cemetery."

"You could retire," said Don, softly. "Or get a job outside the comedy business."

Looking at the ground, she said: "I couldn't leave the business. It's been my whole life."

Don shifted some papers, and sat down next to her. "Look, Stella—I'm not supposed to say this, but you would be within your rights to refuse to speak to us again without the presence of your lawyer."

"Lawyer?" she said. Then: "Speak to me again? But I've told you everything, now!"

"Maybe, maybe. But see it from our point of view. You've just given yourself two terrific motives for murder. Bruce was threatening to reveal your old secret, earning you the undying contempt of your peers; or Bruce was threatening to shop Declan, thus making you jobless."

Her tears came as suddenly and violently as a burst water pipe in winter. "You *fucker!* You *shitty* little man!"

"Stella, listen—it was Bernie Ponting put us onto you. He told us about the row." Don was almost whispering in her ear. "Your best chance is to do what he did—point the finger at someone else. Play pass the parcel."

She shook her head, droplets of eye makeup flicking in all directions. "That's another of your tricks. I don't believe Bernie would do that—he's too soft. Look at how he took his wife back, when she was dying, devoted himself to her, even though the break-up had been her fault."

She was trying to convince herself, not him, Don knew; for all her front, she needed the respect, even the affection, of the other inhabitants of her small world. "He was under some pressure at the time, Stella. You understand that. But right now, we're down to the shortlist: Declan, Anna, or you."

She swallowed with difficulty. "It must be Anna, then," she said. "Assuming you're right, which seems unlikely. Bet she was having it off with someone else, and anyway she inherits all the money, doesn't she?"

But her face gave it away: she thought it was Declan.

I'm with you, girl, thought Don.

CHAPTER NINETEEN

Lunch consisted of a hurried sandwich in a pub that was about to close for the afternoon, as many suburban pubs still did on Sundays.

"It's got to be Declan," said Don, not the for the first time that afternoon. "He was fiddling his accounts, expected Bruce to go along with it because he's a fan, but he wouldn't. Bruce threatened to expose him, so Declan killed him."

"Definitely money, then? Not sex."

"I'm going off sex," Don said. "For the purposes of this investigation, I mean. Even if there was adultery on either side, they don't seem the sort to get divorced over it, let alone resort to murder."

"Have we got a case against Declan?" Frank finished his watery fruit juice. Mango, possibly? He wasn't sure what mangoes tasted like, so it could be mango.

"A circumstantial case, admittedly. We can have his books seized and analysed but even if we prove motive, there's no actual proof of murder. Maybe we can bluff him into telling us that he killed Bruce by accident, and take it from there."

But Declan Donohue—when they'd tracked him down to a pub in Kent, where he was due to perform that night—seemed in no mood to confess, even to an accident. In the pub manager's cramped, first floor office he shook his head in anger at the idea that he had been promoted to chief suspect.

"This is all down to Stella Wardle, isn't it?"

213

"Our sources are confidential," said Don.

"That old witch. I only hired her because she works for next to nothing. Well, that's the last time I try to do anyone a favour."

"Nonetheless—"

"Wait." Donohue took out his mobile phone, staring levelly at Don while he waited for his call to go through. "Stella? It's Declan. Yeah . . . yeah, I know . . . yeah. That's not why I'm ringing. I'm ringing to tell you're sacked, you gossipy old cow." He folded his mobile, and put it back in his pocket.

"Right, Mr. Donohue," said Don, and Frank could tell from the tightness of his jaw and the formality of his tone that he was cold with fury. "For that little display of cruelty, I am going to have you. You're going down for this murder. I no longer care whether you did it, you are now guilty, as far as I'm concerned."

Something in Don's tone must have got through to the comic, Frank reckoned, because his expression rapidly changed from one of hostile insouciance to one of real concern. *That's right,* thought Frank: *this is serious, mate. You are, seriously, being suspected of murdering your accountant.*

"Perhaps you'd like to try and persuade us otherwise, Mr. Donohue," he said. "I'm sure your lawyer would advise you to—"

"I don't need a lawyer. I haven't done anything."

Too tight to pay for one, you mean. "You must see that, from our point of view, your motive is very—"

"Look, get a grip, will you? Just supposing Bruce did find something dodgy in my accounts. Which, if he did, I know nothing about—but I can tell you, in confidence, that my previous accountant turned out to be less than scrupulous in his methods—but even if he did, I'd just sack him, wouldn't I? Get myself a new one. London's full of accountants."

"Not if he was going to blow the whistle on you," said Frank, glancing sideways at Don; the DI was silent and still, only his gaze—which bored into Donohue's skull like a power drill—proving that he was awake.

"It'd be his word against mine. And mine would be—any questions concerning irregularities should be directed to my previous accountant."

"Sounds like you've already spoken to your solicitor on this matter, Mr. Donohue. Already rehearsed your answers."

Donohue ignored that. "Even if I got done for tax evasion, half the comedians in the country have been done for that—doesn't do their careers any harm in the long run. Compared to *murder*, for God's sake! Now that *would* be a downer on the career!"

"We're not necessarily convinced that it was murder," said Frank, hoping this was the right moment to raise this, and unable to tell from Don's lack of reaction whether or not it was. "It could have been an argument that got out of hand, even an accident. Perhaps you only intended to have a—"

Donohue bounced in his seat and clapped his hands together. "Well there you are—now you're contradicting yourself!"

Oh, shit, thought Frank. *Wake up, Don!*

"You're saying I killed him to prevent him reporting me for fiddling my taxes, right? Which is a premeditated crime. It could hardly be anything else. Now, if that were the case, I'd have done a neater job of it, don't you think? Taken my time, chosen my place. I wouldn't have whacked him over the head with a blunt instrument, yards away from a couple of dozen potential witnesses!"

"As I say, we're considering the possibility that this was a spur of the moment act by a desperate man."

"In which case, your motive for me is no good, is it? Of

course it was a crime of the moment! Violent, sudden, full of hate."

"Not necessarily," said Frank, who couldn't think of anything else to say. He knew he'd lost ground to Donohue, and not only couldn't he think how to get back on course, he couldn't quite figure out what course he was supposed to be on. "There are indications in both directions."

"Oh, are there?" Donohue tilted his chair back, and crossed his arms. He was enjoying himself now. "All right then, Detective Constable, let's see if I can help you further. If it *was* a planned crime, then you're looking at a money motive, surely? In which case, you check the poor man's will. Surely, whoever inherits has the best motive?"

"Thank you, Mr. Donohue," said Don, getting to his feet. "We won't detain you any longer at the moment."

Donohue smiled and spread his arms wide. "Not at all, not at all—I'm in no hurry. Let's chat some more."

"I must ask you to inform us if you plan to leave the country," said Frank, rather hurriedly, as Don had already left the room.

As soon as they were in the car, Don said: "He's right about the will."

Frank couldn't keep up. Which hare was the man chasing now? "So we're back to the widow?"

"Putting the widow to one side for a moment—what else is in the will?"

Frank ran it through in his mind. "Nothing worth bothering about, is there? A couple of grand here and there, one or two charities, that bottle of wine for Bernie Ponting."

"Bottle of wine." Don nodded. "The only anomaly, the only odd thing in the will. A bottle of wine? He specified which bottle, didn't he? Get on your mobile, Frank, find out how much it's worth."

As far as Frank knew, the Metropolitan Police did not retain a specialist Wine Squad—and even if it did exist, you could be sure it wouldn't be in the office on a Sunday—but directory enquiries were able to furnish him with the numbers for several up-market wine merchants, one of whom was open for business, and willing to cooperate.

"Around six hundred pounds."

"Well," said Don. "A very special bottle. And the will says it's an apology, right?"

"For not being a better friend, something like that."

Don drummed his fingers on the dashboard. "Got to be apologising for more than some petty fandom dispute, which by all accounts was forgotten years ago. Hasn't it? We've been told that relationships between Bernie and Bruce were not noticeably rancorous, though not exactly friendly, either."

"Right," said Frank, not quite sure where this was going.

"But a six-hundred-quid bottle of grape juice in the last will and testament, Frank—that surely suggests that there *was* ill-feeling, on one side at least, which Bruce hoped to settle posthumously, in the event that he predeceased his former pal. When was the will drawn up?"

Frank checked his notes. "September, two thousand."

"I'll bet that fits. We'll check, anyway." Don turned to look at Frank. "Bruce was having an affair."

Frank shook his head. It didn't clear. "So Anna killed him? I thought we were on Bernie Ponting, now?"

"He had an affair with Tonia. Bernie's wife."

"Tonia? But she was desperately ill—dying. Bedridden. She was—"

Don smiled. "Not when Bruce was screwing her, she wasn't."

They had to get the dates of Bernie and Tonia Ponting's

two weddings via the police, rather than directly from the usual channels, because on Sundays the usual channels were at home watching football on TV. It took a little longer. Don walked around the car, smoking and muttering to himself. Frank, sitting in the car trying to think it through, assumed Don was muttering to himself—if the mutters were aimed at him, he'd have to speak up.

The call came. "Married nineteen seventy-five, divorced nineteen eighty-one. Remarried August two thousand."

"So Bruce's last will was made after the remarriage."

"That's right." Frank's phone chirped again. "That was the—"

"I know who it was, Frank—have they found someone?"

They had. Tonia's closest surviving relative was an older brother, Charles Knight, who lived in a retirement home in Tunbridge Wells.

"Bit of luck," said Don. "At last. How long will it take us to get there?"

"Half an hour," said Frank, once he'd checked the road atlas. "I'll drive if you ring ahead."

"Good idea. Might as well check he's still alive."

Charlie Knight was alive, and had all his faculties, and was perfectly happy to chat with a couple of London detectives, while taking tea on a beautifully-kept lawn under the shade of an enormous horse chestnut tree. Indeed, from the point of view of the two officers, he was too happy to chat. They weren't really here to chat, for all that it was a nice day, and a Sunday, and a fine tea.

"That must have been a proud day for you, Charlie," said Don, bringing one of the old man's anecdotes to what—judging from the gentleman's disappointed reaction—was a premature conclusion. "A proud day, indeed. Wonderful woman, the Queen Mum."

Funny, thought Frank: last week she was a "poisonous old dwarf."

"But we really wanted to ask you something about your late sister, Tonia—and her husband, Bernie Ponting."

"Ah, sad story," said Mr. Knight, and moistened his lips in preparation for its telling.

"Yes," Don said. "Happy ending, though, with them getting back together."

"Oh. Oh, you know about that, do you?"

"We do, but—"

"Oh. I was just about to tell you about that."

"Quite, but the bit we're more interested in is when they split up, after they were married the first time."

"Oh, you don't want to hear about that. All water under the bridge, that is."

"Of course it is, Charlie, long gone, but do you remember why they got divorced?"

Knight studied his liver spots for a full three minutes, before speaking again. "You have good reasons to ask me this, do you? Even if you can't tell me what they are. Because it's not a matter I would willingly—"

"Charlie, I promise you. I only bring this unpleasant business up because I absolutely have to."

The old man exhaled noisily through his nostrils, then nodded. "All right. My sister . . . had sexual relations with another man."

"Thank you, Charlie. I'm sorry we have to ask. One more thing, do you happen to know—"

"No. No, she never mentioned a name—just said it was a friend of Bernie's, that's why Bernie took it so hard— and she also said that Bernie blamed her for it entirely." He cleared his throat, and wiped his lips with a handkerchief. "Which I don't think is entirely fair. The girl always gets the blame, doesn't she?"

"Seems so, Charlie. But eventually they got back together?"

"She was dying, you probably know. I phoned Bernie to tell him, I thought he ought to know. I suppose he just took pity on her. Just because you hate someone, doesn't mean the fact you were once in love vanishes, does it? And all the feelings that go with it."

"Have you seen Bernie lately?"

"He's been to see me a few times since Tonia died." Charlie Knight put his hand on Don's wrist. "If you see him, young man, I wish you'd tell him that he shouldn't go on tormenting himself. He did what he could."

"He feels guilty," said Don, as they walked back up the lawn towards the car.

"Charlie?"

"Bernie. Either that, or he only got back together with Tonia so he could spend her last few months punishing her for having an affair."

"Or both," said Frank, to which Don just nodded.

CHAPTER TWENTY

"First thing Monday morning," Don had said on Sunday evening. "I don't want to start interviewing him tonight, and then have to break for him to sleep. Have him brought in by two uniforms, tell them not to arrest him unless he refuses to come."

"How early? Breakfast time?"

"Get him out of bed, if possible."

Now, at just before eight in the morning, Don and Frank sat on a bench in the custody suite, awaiting Bernie Ponting's arrival. Don was wearing a dark suit and tie, and his hair was freshly cut. Frank wondered where he'd found a barber so early in the morning—or so late the previous evening; surely the cut was too neat for him to have done it himself with a pair of scissors and a mirror?

"You're sure it's him?" He was loath to risk irritating the DI with such a question, and at such a time, but it was not entirely unknown for Don Packham to let his enthusiasms run away with him. "What I mean is, we haven't exactly got a complete case against him, have we?"

"Not enough for an arrest, no. Enough for a search warrant—you sorted that, Frank?"

Frank reassured him. "They're standing by, don't worry. If he happens to have a receipt from a sports shop for one baseball bat, medium size, they'll find it."

"They won't, of course." Frank wasn't sure if Don was depressed, or just nervous. He wasn't jolly, that was for sure.

"You think he'll confess?"

Don nodded. "I think he might. He's not a criminal after all, just a man of passion. With any luck, he'll be desperate to spill it all, first chance he gets. He's lost his wife—again—he's killed an old friend, his psyche can't be in the best of shape."

"And if he doesn't?" Frank asked. "And if the search of his house doesn't—"

"House!" said Don. "Shit—I almost forgot."

"Almost forgot what?" Was this the vital clue that would seal the whole case? Had the word *house* unlocked some overlooked piece of evidence, obvious with hindsight?

"Frank, can you help me move house next week?"

Oh. "Sure, no problem." *Wait a minute* . . . "You're moving again?"

"Here he is." Don stood, his hands wrestling each other behind his back, as Bernie entered through the back door, preceded and followed by uniformed constables.

"Officers present are Detective Inspector Don Packham of Cowden CID and Detective Constable Frank Mitchell of Cowden CID. Mr. Bernard Ponting is attending voluntarily, and has not been arrested. He has been advised of his rights, and has declined for the moment legal representation. He understands that he may leave at any time, and that he may change his mind about a lawyer at any time. Is that accurate, Bernie? You know why you're here, you know what's happening, and you don't want a lawyer just yet?"

"That's right." Ponting looked tense, but no more so, Frank thought, than any man unaccustomed to such proceedings might be expected to look.

"OK, Bernie. Now, you were divorced in nineteen eighty-one, is that right?"

"Correct."

"So you actually separated from your wife some time earlier?"

"Yes."

"When was that?"

"Early in nineteen eighty."

"Right. And it was at about the same time, I think, that you and Bruce Lester became—what shall we say—estranged, yes?"

"About then. I don't remember exactly."

"You don't remember?"

"I don't remember exactly."

"Why did your marriage fail, Bernie?"

Ponting shrugged. "Marriages fail. You're a copper, you must know that."

"Of course they do," said Don. "But there's always a reason, isn't there? It doesn't just happen, it happens for a cause."

"I suppose so."

"So what was the cause in your case?"

Frank thought he could see the cogs turning in Ponting's brain. "It's all in the divorce papers. It's not a secret."

"If it's not a secret, Bernie, you can tell us, can't you?"

"Adultery." Ponting coughed, and wiped some dust off his jeans. "Adultery occurred."

"I see," said Don. "On which side?"

"On my wife's side."

"Your wife, Tonia, committed adultery, and as a result you divorced her."

"That's right. Not unusual, is it? Happens all the time."

"Sure," said Don. "Very sad though, isn't it? Whenever it happens. Two people in love, making a life together, and then . . . who knows? Something happens, something goes wrong, and suddenly it's all over. It's a sad business, Bernie."

Ponting tried to wait out the pause, but couldn't quite manage it. "Yeah, I suppose so."

"You must have been well cut up. It's not as if you and Tonia were a pair of daft kids, who got married on a whim and it just didn't work out. Right, Bernie? I mean, you married comparatively late in life, didn't you? Not old, I'm not saying you were old, but you were . . ." Don smiled. "You were in your late youth, I think that'd be fair to say?"

Another pause. Ponting fidgeted, and then said: "Is that a question?"

"Observation, more like. Neither of you had been married before?"

"No."

"So you must have been very sure of each other. Very sure of the basis of your marriage." Ponting said nothing. "Treat that as if it was a question, Bernie."

"I don't know what you want me to say. Yes, we were in love. We got married. Then it went wrong, and—"

"Did it go wrong before Tonia started tarting around?"

"She wasn't."

"Wasn't what, Bernie?"

Ponting knew what the DI was doing—Frank could see that he knew—but it was having an effect, even so. The builder's lips were narrowing, his jaw was clenching, his voice was tightening. Just because you know what's being done to you, doesn't mean you can stop it happening. "She wasn't tarting around. Tonia wasn't like that at all."

Don put on a puzzled frown. "So what are you saying, Bernie? Her sleeping with another man was out of character? She wasn't the type?"

"She made a mistake," said Ponting. "Something you've never done, I'm sure."

"She just made a mistake? It wasn't in character, there was

224

nothing fundamentally wrong with your marriage, neither of you were sleeping around like sailors. But your wife made a mistake, you're telling me that's all it was?"

"Yeah."

"OK, Bernie." Don sat back in his chair. "So why did you divorce her?"

Ponting searched the table, and then the ceiling, for an answer. He eventually settled on a single word. "Adultery."

"Those were the *grounds*, Bernie, the legal grounds. Sure. But what I'm after is why you used those grounds. You see the difference? If there's nothing wrong with your marriage, you've got a good marriage, and your wife makes a *mistake*, why throw it all away?"

No reply.

"Perhaps you have very traditional views on such matters, Bernie. Some people do. Twenty years ago, more people did. Maybe—I don't know—maybe you were brought up religious, were you? You thought she'd committed a sin, is that it? Even though you loved her, even though you believed that it was just a *mistake*, her shagging someone else, you didn't feel it was your place to forgive her, because she'd committed a sin. Is that it?"

No reply.

"You don't feel moved to comment on this, Bernie?"

"I don't feel I have anything to add which might be helpful to you in your inquiries."

"No?"

"No."

The two men looked at each other for a while, both sitting back with their arms crossed, in a parody of relaxation. It was Don who blinked first, or appeared to. Frank had seen him use this technique before.

The DI leant forward, his face beseeching, and said:

"Come on, Bernie! You know where I'm going with this. Don't pretend you're an idiot, because you're not. You know what I'm saying—that there was a particular reason why you couldn't forgive Tonia for her one mistake. Who was she screwing, Bernie? Tell me that. Who betrayed you?"

Ponting let out a breath, and shifted in his seat. "I killed Bruce Lester because he had sex with my wife."

A brittle silence filled the room, until Don said: "Should I treat that as a question, Bernie?"

Ponting smiled for the first time. "That's your theory, is it? Twenty-odd years ago, Bruce broke up my marriage, so I wait until now to kill him."

"Bruce was a pal of yours back then, wasn't he? A real friend. God, that must have hurt! OK, so it's a classic set-up—the wife and the husband's best friend—but just because it's a cliché doesn't mean it doesn't hurt. That's why you divorced her, isn't it? Not because of what she did so much as who she did it with."

"Twenty-odd years ago." Ponting shook his head, slowly. "Crimes of passion happen overnight, don't they? They don't simmer for twenty years like that. No, Inspector—even if you managed to pick a jury made up entirely of your close relatives, you'd never get a conviction on that. Whatever happened between me and Bruce, it happened when this one—" he gestured at Frank—"was in short trousers. It was finished with long ago."

Don wrote something on his pad, and drew Frank's attention to it: *Bat.*

"Do you own a baseball bat?" Frank asked.

"A baseball bat?" Ponting's expression said that he couldn't begin to imagine what this new line in questioning had to do with anything. "No, I don't."

"Have you ever owned a baseball bat?"

"Why would I own a baseball bat?"

"I don't know. For self-defence, maybe. That's why taxi drivers carry them."

"I've never been a taxi driver. I'm a builder."

"You've got a nice house. Maybe you wanted it to protect yourself against burglars, or . . ." Frank trailed off, as the whole thing entered his head at once. He turned to Don, and immediately saw from his stunned smile that he'd got it, too. "Well, bugger my cat," said Frank, softly.

Laughing, Don leant towards the microphone. "For the benefit of the tape, DC Mitchell invites suspect to bugger his cat. Suspect declines. Interview suspended . . ."

"We've been thinking of the baseball bat being used *as* a baseball bat, or else selected deliberately as a murder weapon," said Frank, in the corridor outside the interview room, while Don drew deeply on a small cigar and bounced back and forth on his toes and heels. "But why do most people who have baseball bats have baseball bats?"

"Self-defence," Don agreed. "Taxi drivers, shopkeepers, prostitutes."

"Because a cricket bat not only makes an inferior *offensive* weapon, it's also no good for defending yourself."

"Perfectly legitimate thing to have around, even though you've never seen a game of baseball in your life. Right, Frank—good stuff. Call that caretaker at the cricket ground—what's his name?"

"Groundsman, you mean. Curtis."

"Right, call him up."

Frank phoned the cricket pavilion, and got no reply. He rang Cowden Council, got the self-styled groundsman's mobile number, and rang that. "Not answering," said Frank. "Shall I leave a message?" Don nodded, urgently, and Frank dictated his and Don's mobile numbers into the phone. "It's very urgent," he added. "Please call back as soon as you get this message."

"Right," said Don. "We'll see. Now we'll see."

"What do we do meantime? Carry on?"

"No." Don snared a passing PC. "Can you get a cup of tea for Mr. Ponting in interview room one, please? And then sit in with him. DC Mitchell and myself have other inquiries to pursue."

The uniformed officer knew when he'd been nabbed, and made no more than a token attempt to escape CID's clutches.

"Oh, and mate?" Don added. "If he wants to admit to killing those twenty-three professional wrestlers with his bare hands, you can take the statement. All right? Be a nice little collar for you."

They waited in the corridor until the PC returned with a half-spilled cup of milky tea, and then went off to pursue their other inquiries.

"Bacon, baked beans, chips," said Don.

The waitress in the market traders' café nodded, and then turned to Frank. "And for you, love?"

"Hold on!" Don cried. "I haven't finished yet. Mushrooms, two slices of bread and butter, and some fried onion rings. Ta."

The waitress waited a moment, just to make doubly sure that he really had finished this time, and then redirected her order book to his companion.

Frank was still scrutinising the menu on the wall. "Ah . . . do you do muesli?"

"Please, Frank!" Don slapped the table, making the salt and pepper jump. "You mustn't use language like that in front of ladies. I do apologise, madam—my friend will have the same as me."

Will I, buggery, thought Frank. "Plain omelette, please."

She paused in her scribbling, and looked at Frank with a mixture of disgust and deep respect. "An omelette on top of that lot?"

Frank felt sick at the thought. "God, no! *Instead,* please."

"He's just had a baby, love," Don explained. "He's trying to get his figure back. And two teas, please. Oh, and a sausage."

Still feeling a little shaky at his narrow escape—he didn't know where Don Packham put it all, but wherever it was it had to be a cavity which hadn't evolved on other humans, because the DI was far from overweight—Frank said: "So, do you reckon we're—"

"You're definitely all right for helping me move? Maybe Thursday afternoon, if we can get away. No later than Friday night, anyway."

"Sure. Be glad to help."

"Good man, Frank. Much appreciated. Tell you what—after we're done, I'll buy you a curry to say thanks."

He wasn't sure if he could even face the omelette now. "No, really, no need. It's a pleasure to be of assistance." Did he dare ask? He'd have to; he wasn't a man given to tormenting curiosity, but even so. "So, you're moving again? I thought you'd only just moved."

"What? Oh, that—no, it didn't work out, that's all."

"Ah. Sorry. Because of the plumbing?"

"Plumbing? No, Frank, it didn't work out for the people I'm house-sitting for. In Barbados. So they're coming back early."

"Right," said Frank. He could think of other questions—seven of them, in fact, without trying—but he decided he'd spent his ration of curiosity for the day.

The teas arrived at the same moment that Frank's mobile rang. He checked the incoming number, and stood up. "I'll take this outside," he said. He didn't really want to receive potentially crucial evidence in a murder investigation to a background of chomping, slurping, and clattering.

"What I need to know, Mr. Curtis, is simply this: you said you'd had some trouble with youths at the ground—vandalism and so on. Do you keep a baseball bat in the pavilion?" Guessing the cause of the hesitation at the other end of the line, he added: "There's no law against it, Mr. Curtis."

"No? I thought maybe there was." The caretaker sounded as if he half-suspected a trick, even now.

"If you were to use it, there might well be legal complications. But just having it there, that's not an offence. I give you my word."

"Well . . . yeah, I think there might be one, you know. I mean, I don't know who put it there, or—"

"Is it still there, do you know?"

"I suppose so, yeah. Unless someone's . . . Oh Christ!" Frank heard Curtis gasp, as the reason for the questions suddenly struck him.

"That's all right, don't worry about that. This is just routine inquiries. What I want you to do, is take the phone with you now and go and check if the bat's still there. OK?"

"Yeah. OK. Right."

"Right—before you do that, where's it kept? Where do you keep the bat?"

"It's in an old kitbag, in the supplies cupboard. At least, you know, I *think* it is, I don't really—"

"That's fine—but *do not* touch it. You understand? Do not touch the kitbag, if you have to touch it to see inside it, just use a handkerchief, touch it as little as possible, you understand?"

"Well, yeah, only—I haven't got a hankie."

Use your bloody imagination, you halfbake! "Use your shirt, or your cuff, or anything. OK? Doesn't have to be a handkerchief. Just don't use your fingers."

Two minutes later, Curtis informed DC Mitchell that the bat was missing.

"Right—now you stay there, stand right by that bag, do not touch anything, and an officer will be with you shortly. One more thing—do you happen to know a chap called Bernie, he was playing in that match where the guy was killed. Bernie Ponting."

"No, I don't think so. Why?"

"OK, nothing, just I was trying to get in touch with him, and his mobile's not working. Doesn't matter."

"Like I told you before, I only knew a couple of that lot. Bernie what was it?"

"Doesn't matter, forget it. It's on a different matter, anyway."

Frank broke the connection, and immediately dialled another number. When he'd finished speaking, he went back to face his omelette. His appetite had returned.

"A forensic team is now checking the bat's hiding place for fingerprints and other traces, Bernie," said Don. "Now, the only prints we expect to find there are those of the caretaker, Glenn Curtis. His—and the killer's. I can't think of any legitimate reason why your prints would be there, can you?"

"Unless you wiped your prints off?" said Frank. "But hiding prints from modern technology is nowhere near as easy as people think, you know."

"We'll find out how you knew the bat was there," Don continued. "Maybe you'll tell us. No? Never mind, we'll clear that up soon enough, I'm sure. Now we know what we're looking for, Bernie . . ." How he knew about the bat was a loose end that could wait. What mattered now was making him see there was no way out.

Bernie Ponting said that he thought he might as well see a lawyer now, and the interview was suspended.

CHAPTER TWENTY-ONE

When they restarted, the lawyer told DI Packham that his client wished at this point to make a full statement.

"Bruce Lester and my wife did have—well, not an affair. A one-night stand. Bruce was staying with us one weekend—there was a Peter Sellers season on at the Everyman cinema, he and I were going along to it, and I invited him to kip in our spare room for the night. Make an early start."

"Where were you when the sexual act occurred?"

"Got called out. In those days, I was doing all sorts—plumbing, electrics, the lot. Anything that came along, we were saving for a new house. If you do emergency call-out work, you can make a lot of money at that. If you're willing to put in the hours."

"What was the call-out?"

Ponting seemed irritated at the interruption. "I don't know, I don't remember."

"Of course you do, Bernie," said Don. "You remember every detail of that weekend. If I asked you what colour toothbrush you used that morning, you could tell me."

"Drains. Some old dear, her downstairs lav was flooded."

"So Bruce and Tonia didn't know what time you'd get back?"

Ponting looked Don in the eye, as if to show he wasn't afraid of what he was saying. Nearest thing he's got to dignity at this stage, Don thought.

"I walked in on them. I was being quiet, you know, because the lights were out, I thought they'd be asleep. Didn't want to wake them."

"They were in your bed?"

"Yeah." He ran his hands slowly down the back of his head, the fingers twined. "Which should have told me something, really. But it didn't."

Don had no idea what he meant by that, but he wasn't worried; people tell their own stories in their own way—people in Bernie Ponting's position—and as long as it made sense to them, that was all that mattered. "You caught them in the act?"

"More or less. They'd finished, I think."

"But there was no doubt what had been happening?"

"Not really, Inspector, no. They were both naked. She was lying with her head on his chest. He was stroking her—he had, like, his hand—"

Every detail, thought Don. Etched. "What did you do?"

"I told them to get out. Both of them. Get dressed, and get the fuck out. Those were my exact words."

Don watched the spools of tape spin round. No need to torture the man; there was plenty here. "All right, move forward a few hours." *Skip the weeping and the pleading.* "When did you next hear from them? Each of them, I mean."

"Early in the morning. I mean, later the same morning, you know, but breakfast time. Bruce rang me from a call box. Kept feeding ten pence pieces in. He must have changed every pound and penny he had into tens."

Now, that *was* a slight surprise. "You were on the phone for a while, then?"

Ponting asked for a glass of water, and took a long time to drink a very small amount of it. *The crux,* thought Don; *here it comes.*

"I wouldn't have thought you'd have much to say to Bruce," he said, when the tape was again spinning.

"He told me—well, his side of it, I suppose you'd say."

"Must've been a convincing story, keep you listening through all those ten pences."

Ponting shook his head. "That's just it, really. It was because he wasn't convincing—I mean, he wasn't a good liar, or a fluent one, he wasn't that sort of bloke—that's precisely why what he said *was* so convincing."

"And what was his side?"

"That she'd led him on. She'd initiated it. The older woman, you know, the seductress, the temptress. A young man, normal young man—he knew he'd done a terrible thing, but he just couldn't resist her. He didn't know how to say no. Our friendship was so important to him, he knew what he'd done was unforgivable, but blame his hormones, not him, blame his naivety. Maybe, one day, I could forgive him, not now, he knew it wouldn't be now, but maybe one day . . . ."

"She'd come to him, that was the gist of it?"

"Yeah. So why weren't they in *his* bed? I should have spotted that, but I didn't."

Ah. Now he got it. "And you believed him."

"Yes! Shit! Yes! I got to spell it out?"

"When did you hear from Tonia?"

"Hour later, hour and a half. She was at her brother's. Full of remorse, she'd been drunk, it'd never happen again."

"But by then it was too late. You'd decided who you believed."

"Too late," Ponting echoed. "Much too late."

At last, his tears came freely, and the solicitor called a break.

"I suppose we'll never know," said Frank, in the corridor,

"which was telling the truth."

"The young stud or the mature temptress? No. In my experience, however, the chances are they were both lying."

"Oh. Wouldn't that mean they were also both telling the truth?"

Don chuckled, and took a drag on his cigar. "No, I'm afraid it wouldn't, Frank."

Twenty minutes later, back in the interview room, Ponting continued. "We split up, got divorced."

"Over one *mistake?*" asked Don.

"What Bruce said—well, if that was true then it wasn't a mistake, was it? It was more of a . . . I don't know, a character trait. How long would it be before it happened again?"

Balls, thought Don. Takes more than that to break up a marriage—more than the word of a frightened, ashamed kid. They were already on the rocks, even if Bernie didn't know it. Or couldn't admit it. But at the time, and over the years afterwards, he'd convinced himself otherwise.

"How did you come to remarry her?"

"Charlie rang me. That's her brother. Said she was ill— dying. Said it would mean a lot to her if she could make it up with me before she, you know. Went. Said she hadn't remarried, hadn't lived with anyone. Always hoped I'd . . . Well, I don't know. Charlie always was a bit of a bullshitter. Don't know how much was true, how much was his imagination."

"But you went to see her."

"I didn't hate her any more, did I? It fades, that kind of thing. That kind of emotion. I'd even begun to think, maybe I'd overreacted. But anyway, whatever, it was all in the past, you know. Someone's dying and they ask to see you—what you going to do?"

It was Don's turn to take a sip of water, slowly. He didn't get any pleasure from sliding the swords into the wounded

bull—even when the bull was a sadistic conman, or an unre-
pentant mugger; let alone when it was just a screwed-up murderer like poor old Bernie Ponting. "When did you realise,
Bernie?"

Ponting didn't pretend not to know what Don meant.
They were beyond that now, the two of them. "Soon as I saw
her, Don. Soon as I saw her. The second I was through her
front door, we were in each other's arms. Crying, squeezing.
Both apologising, you know? To ourselves as much as to each
other."

"And you knew then that Bruce Lester had lied to you."
All those years, Don thought, when Bernie couldn't allow
himself to even suspect for a second that Bruce's version
wasn't the whole truth. Because if he did, then what had he
done with his life? Built a business, and run a hobby.
Nothing, in other words.

"Yeah, I knew. Couldn't understand how I'd ever not
known, really."

"You got married again as soon as you could."

"She swore blind that she felt no bitterness to me at all,
and I couldn't detect any in her." He snorted a brief laugh.
"Not that my track record on such matters was all that good.
Maybe she just wanted someone to look after her, who
knows? Anyway, we had a bit of time together, at the end.
Went on a couple of holidays. Did a bit of gardening. You
know."

"Marriage stuff," said Don. He hoped they'd been happy.

"Yeah. Marriage stuff."

"And then she died, and you killed Bruce Lester with a
baseball bat."

The lawyer gave his client a warning glance, but retreated
when he saw the look his client returned him. The lawyer held
out his hands, palm upwards, cocked his head to one side,

and turned down the corners of his mouth: *Up to you. As long as you know what you're doing.*

"All those years," said Bernie, and it was again as if only he and Don were in the room; two friendly acquaintances in a quiet weekday pub, ruing life's ways. "All those wasted years, all the years of marriage I missed. We missed, I mean."

It didn't matter what the truth was, because Bernie had been taking revenge on himself as much as on Bruce. He knew he was an idiot all those years ago, and he'd just never allowed himself to think it through until she died. "And all those years," said Don, "you remained friends with Bruce, the liar. Sort-of friends, anyway. A little polite, perhaps, a little cool, but friends of a sort."

"Yeah. Wasted years twice over, you see?"

"I do see," said Don. "So once Tonia was dead, you began to think about taking revenge."

Ponting shook his head. "Not quite. Wasn't as . . . cold blooded as that. Not at first."

"What happened to change things?"

"After Tonia died, I stuck with the fanzine, you know—fandom and all that. It had been a part of my life for most of my life, it was a way of keeping going."

"So you were still seeing Bruce quite a bit? Did you ever have it out with him?"

"No. Not until—it was that business with Louise Ogden."

Don looked at Frank. Frank gave a minute shake of the head.

"Louise?" said Don. "I'm not sure I'm with you."

"She was getting a bit of bother—well, more than a bit actually—off that ersatz Aussie. Eddie Tarr, yeah?"

"Yes, we know about that."

"All right. Well, at one point it was getting quite serious. I mean, he was virtually stalking her, I think she was getting quite scared."

I knew she wasn't telling us everything. "She confided in you?"

"Yeah, well that's how bad it was—she's a tough girl. Not the scream-and-faint type, you know. So I was just beginning to think that maybe I should have a word with him—Eddie. Nothing heavy you know, just 'I think you're wasting your time there mate,' sort of thing. But I wasn't sure how to handle it."

"I see," said Don; and then: "Oh. I *see.*"

"Yeah." Ponting nodded. "Before I could figure out what to do for the best, there was bloody Bruce Lester—steaming in uninvited, like some gallant knight."

"The last straw."

"Bloody right it was. I mean, come on—what a hypocrite! I told him, I said, 'Bruce you can't make up for what you did twenty years ago by suddenly going all chivalrous now, mate! It's *too late!*' "

Don waited for the echoes to fade, and then said: "When did you tell him that, Bernie?"

And Bernie Ponting looked at Don, at Frank, and at his lawyer, and then said: "While I was killing him."

"Tell us that bit now, Bernie. Might as well."

"When Bruce came in from batting, I intercepted him just as he was about to get in the shower. Could he come outside for a private chat? I wanted to clear the air. Bruce didn't take much persuading; he was delighted, he'd wanted to scrub his conscience clean for years." He smiled. "Well, I did for that him all right."

It was at that point that the preliminary forensic evidence from the pavilion supplies cupboard arrived.

"Are they . . ." Don had been going to say "Are they sure?"

but of course they were sure. Forensics didn't *guess* at people's fingerprints. They didn't have a quick shufty at the whorls and go, *Yeah, looks about right*. If they said the fingerprints on the metal locker and the kitbag which had held the baseball bat were Louise Ogden's then that's whose they were.

"Are they *sure?*" he said.

"They've got the best part of a full set. Looks like she wiped the bat, but she didn't think to wipe where she got the bat from."

"Maybe she wasn't planning to kill him when she took the bat. Maybe she wasn't planning to do anything to *him*."

"Yeah." Frank shook his head, as if he had a bubble in his ear that wouldn't shift. "I suppose we're back to thinking she was going after Eddie Tarr, and Bruce got in the way. Or something."

"Something like that." Don was still trying to persuade his brain to do a hundred-and-eighty-degree turn, away from Bernie and towards Louise. Wipe all the pictures in his mind and start again. "How did she know where to find the bat?"

"Curtis, probably. He fancied her, he probably told her about it. 'Young lady like you, you should know how to protect yourself.' He'll never admit it, though."

"Surrounded by chivalrous men, wasn't she?"

"Anyway, we'll find out soon enough, with any luck. Uniform are out looking for her now."

"No," said Don, pacing the corridor, shortways. "She's not a confessor, like our Bernie. Not in her nature. We'll be lucky to get anything out of her, unless the search warrant turns up something. Which I doubt." This one was going to get away, Don knew it for sure. Not the first in his career, wouldn't be the last, but this one seemed particularly cruel.

Then again—wasn't the first false confession he'd ever received, either.

"Why did Bernie confess?" Frank asked, and the way he asked it—as if he honestly thought Don might know—made Don feel even worse than he already did. Which was pretty bad.

"I don't know, Frank. It happens."

"He doesn't seem like a loony, though. Attention-seeker, or whatever. What made him do it?"

"I don't *know,* Frank. Maybe he *did* do it. Maybe Louise's prints are just a coincidence. Maybe she plays baseball, or . . . I don't know. Doesn't matter. Prosecution Service won't proceed in a case like this, on an unsubstantiated confession, not when we've got another perfectly good suspect loitering in the wings, forensically linked to the murder weapon."

"Or maybe they were both in it together."

"Not very likely. But if so, we have to hope she'll incriminate him."

Frank wouldn't let it go. "It's an amazingly convincing confession though, isn't it? I mean—"

"Come on, Frank—it's what the man *fantasised* about doing. I'll bet you every word of it is true up until the bit where he asks Brucie outside and bashes him on the bonce. The rest of it's what he wishes he'd done, what part of him thinks he *ought* to have done."

"I suppose so. Or maybe he'll just take any opportunity to talk about his wife, and how Bruce ruined their lives."

"Or maybe he's had a breakdown," said Don. "Or maybe he just did it to stuff me up." After all, Don added to himself, every last atom in the universe seemed chiefly concerned with causing Don Packham misery; why should Bernie Ponting be any different?

"What are we going to do next?"

Crawl under the bed. Hide in a cave. Get inside a cricket coffin and put it in the attic of an abandoned house. "We'll have to take him back to his cell for now. Explain to his lawyer. We can't just let Bernie wander off, not after this. Get the duty shrink to look at him."

"The lawyer's going to enjoy himself," said Frank.

"Lawyers always enjoy themselves. That's how you know there's no God. Depending on what the shrink says, we'll bail him. Anyway, that's the least of our problems. We've got to start thinking of a strategy against Louise."

Ponting was plainly baffled when Don told him that the interview was being terminated, but that they wouldn't be charging him "at this time." More baffled than his lawyer, who fancied he could smell the lovely fragrance of a procedural balls-up.

In fact, Don thought—as they stood at the custody desk waiting for the sergeant on duty to finish dealing with another customer before tucking Ponting back in his cot—Bernie looked disappointed, as if unfairly robbed of the chance to conclude his gripping narrative. *Tough luck. None of us are having a particularly splendid day today. Except the lawyer.*

"Right, gents. Sorry to keep you waiting." The custody sergeant cleared his screen, and smiled at Don, Frank, and their guest. "Medium Margarita to go, extra Brussels sprouts—is that right?"

"Bed and breakfast for one, Sarge," said Frank.

"Oh my God," said Ponting.

"Don't worry, Mr. Ponting," Frank assured him. "We'll have the doctor give you a quick once-over, then you'll be on your way home."

"Oh, God." Ponting gripped Don's elbow. "I think you'd better take me back into the interview room."

"Why's that then, Bernie? Forgotten to tell us what position they were doing it in?"

"I've just realised what's happening here. You found Louise's prints didn't you? Where the bat was stashed."

"We didn't find yours, mate, that's all you need to know."

"No, you wouldn't find mine. Of course you wouldn't."

"Yes, I think we've all worked that out by now, Bernie, thanks very much."

"I wasn't thinking straight. When you started going on about the caretaker and the bat, I just thought I'd been careless. It didn't occur to me, *she* might have left her prints all over the bloody place."

"Hold on, Sarge." Don led Bernie a few steps away from the desk, and gestured for Frank to follow. "You knew Louise was the killer?" This was a nightmare! As well as a possibly loony false confessor, he now had a possibly loony prosecution eyewitness, and a possibly loony former chief suspect, and it was all the same man.

"She's *not* the killer, Don—that's my point! I am."

"No, listen Bernie—"

"I feel no remorse for Bruce, no regret. But I can't let Louise get arrested for this. She didn't actually *do* anything in the end, did she?"

"In the end?"

"I saw her earlier that afternoon. Out the back—you know, where I killed Bruce."

"Doing what?"

"Hiding a baseball bat under a loose plank at the back of the pavilion. I think she was—well, you know, she wasn't really going to *hurt* anyone, she just meant to . . . have a word, I think. Tell him to lay off."

"She was going to beat up Eddie Tarr." Don looked across at Frank, and hoped that his own mouth wasn't hanging slackly open the way the DC's was.

"No, no, no," said Ponting. He looked genuinely affronted on Louise's behalf. "I'm quite sure it wasn't anything like that. Maybe she was going to *threaten* him a bit, that's all."

"Or kill him," said Frank.

"Well anyway, it doesn't matter now, does it? Because I took the bat off her. Talked her out of it. Calmed her down." He put a finger to his lips, as if he was telling them a naughty secret. "Shared a joint with her—only a little one. She was grateful. After all, she could have got into terrible trouble. Off she went, a lot happier than she was when I found her. So at least that's one good deed I've done in my life, eh?"

"And what did you do with the bat?"

"Shoved it back behind the plank. For later."

"So, she can confirm having given you the bat."

"Yes. And will do when you bring her in, I'm quite sure."

"Which is why you're telling us all this now."

Ponting ignored the insinuation. "I told her the next day that I'd dumped the bat in the shower room without anyone seeing me, and I promised not to mention it to anyone. Her little moment of madness."

If we'd given out the nature of the weapon to the press, thought Don, *she might have come forward straight away. Saved us all a week of our lives.*

Bernie Ponting was eventually returned to his cell. Don still didn't charge him—he wasn't taking any chances at all until the psychiatrist had examined his prisoner. And until he'd spoken to Louise Ogden.

"So why did he confess?" said Frank, over a cup of tea in the canteen.

"Because he did it. Try and keep up."

"No, I mean why did he confess in the face of the fingerprint evidence, when he must have known there *was* no fingerprint evidence. Not of him, at any rate."

Don had been thinking about that. "I think perhaps we didn't make ourselves very clear. We said 'The place where the bat was hidden.' He must have thought we meant the place *he* hid it—not the place where the caretaker kept it."

"Bloody hell." Frank's mouth was hanging open again.

"I know." Don laughed. "Precision is a much overrated quality in police work, I've always said so."

"*Bloody* hell," said Frank.

"At least we can grass Declan up to the taxman."

"True."

Don drank some tea, and looked around to see if the canteen manager was watching. She wasn't, so he lit a cigar. "You know in the café this morning, while you were outside phoning Curtis? I called Cowden Animal Rescue."

"About Bernie?"

"No, about Doberman's neighbour."

"Who?"

"The three-legged cat with the ugly face."

"Oh, yeah. Why?"

"I thought I might adopt the poor misshapen bastard."

"Really?"

"Close your mouth, Frank, I can see your fillings."

"Sorry. So—are you going to, then?"

"No. Stupid thing died peacefully in its sleep last night."

"I'm sorry to hear it. Still, I'm sure there's plenty of other animals that—"

"What do I need a bloody cat for?" Don demanded. "Living in a third-floor flat? Honestly, Frank, you do have some daft ideas."

"Sorry sir."

Don looked out at the car park. No sign of Louise Ogden yet. He wasn't looking forward to his interview with her. And she wouldn't be looking forward to it, either. Poor woman. Poor Bruce; poor Bernie. Poor Frank, having to hear all this stuff. He's a detective, but he's only a kid.

"Frank, has Joe got a cricket set? One of those little ones with the plastic stumps."

"Well, he's a bit young for—"

"Bet he's got a bloody football, though, hasn't he?" He swilled the rest of his tea down, and stood up. "Come on, then."

"Where are we going?"

"Regent Street. We're going to buy your lad a cricket set, before it's too late." He didn't feel up to it—he wanted to go home to bed—but he felt he had to do this. He could summon up enough energy just to do this, couldn't he? He could endure another hour on his feet, for the sake of little Joe's immortal soul. "Then you can take it home and play in the garden with him." *And I can go and find a bottle of dark red wine.*

"Sir, I don't think we can disappear just now. What about Louise?"

"She'll wait."

"But—we've got about a mountain and a half of paperwork to do, before we can charge Bernie."

Don shook his head, in despair and also to keep despair at bay. "I worry about you sometimes, Frank. Honestly I do. You want to learn some priorities, mate."

ABOUT THE AUTHOR

Mat Coward is a British writer in many genres, whose short stories have been nominated for the Edgar and the Dagger, broadcast on BBC Radio, and published in numerous anthologies, magazines and e-zines in the UK, US, Japan and Europe. His first collection, *Do the World a Favour and Other Stories*, was published by Five Star Publishing in 2003. *Over and Under* is the third novel in his mystery series featuring Detective Inspector Don Packham and Detective Constable Frank Mitchell. The first two books in the series, *Up and Down* and *In and Out* were also published by Five Star. Amongst his recent books in the UK is a short history of British radio comedy, in the "Pocket Essentials" series.